The Africa Run

The Africa Run

LUCILLA ANDREWS

HEINEMANN : LONDON

First published in Great Britain 1993
by William Heinemann Ltd
an imprint of Reed Consumer Books Ltd
Michelin House, 81 Fulham Road, London SW3 6RB
and Auckland, Melbourne, Singapore and Toronto

A CIP catalogue record for this book
is available at the British Library

ISBN 0 434 02133 4

Phototypeset by Intype, London
Printed in Great Britain
by Clays Ltd, St. Ives PLC

ONE
June 1955

Paddy Brown was pretending to be asleep in the extended deckchair in the particular place on the boat-deck that for the past ten days at sea had become 'Dr Brown's corner'. The polished mahogany and brass rail was too hot to lean upon, and he knew that if he stood supported only by his stick for more than a few minutes in the heat of that June morning in 1955, it would probably write off his going ashore in the afternoon and the young ship's doctor's heavy date ashore that night. Paddy Brown had had over two years practice in dealing with his physical limitations, but still, when possible, he salvaged his pride by taking refuge in pretence. And behind the dark glasses and brim of his panama, he registered with ambivalent gratitude that his fellow passengers lining the rail had left a gap in front of his chair, and all the women were much younger than himself.

The passengers had come to watch their ship, the MV *Rose of Africa* enter Port Said and in British, Rhodesian and South African voices were congratulating themselves on being bound for ports from Mombasa to the Cape, and that by this afternoon the last of the mere trippers would have disembarked and the ship be left to the real travellers. The pink or reddened faces of the first-timers-out and golden to teak-tanned of the old-Africa-hands, wore the same smug smiles. 'The Med.,' said the latter, 'was all right for cruise ships, but the old *Rose* was a passenger liner on her regular run round Africa. Regular as a milk run. Seven weeks from London to Cape Town – give or take the odd day or two's delay by monsoons down the east coast – then two weeks back to London. And who minded the extra day at sea when living this life of Riley, eh?'

The first-timers-out agreed happily. Though the *Rose of Africa* was one of the oldest and smallest vessels in the Africa Flower Line, for these past ten days they had enjoyed a standard of luxury and super-abundance of delicious food they had either long forgotten or never known in the UK, where food rationing, far more stringent than in wartime, only ended last year and post-war austerity had still properly to release its iron grip.

The harbour was crowded with ships of all sizes waiting to go down the Suez Canal in the midday convoy. The *Rose of Africa* edged in, escorted by a small armada of little boats laden with leather goods, carpets, camel stools, beaten silverware, fake jewellery, straw hats and vendors yelling the superiority of their cargoes and cheapness of their prices to the passengers lining the three upper decks. Paddy Brown watched without altering his position until directly into his line of vision there loomed up on the waterfront the great, full-length statue of Ferdinand de Lesseps, the architect of the canal, standing with his right arm outstretched towards the man-made waterway. The decades of exposure to sand, salt, sun and wind had pock-marked the stonework and in the heat haze rising from the harbour water and white stone land it had a greenish tinge, but nothing detracted from the impressive solidity of the Victorian figure. Paddy sat forward, abandoning pretence, in the bemused wonder he had first experienced six days ago when seeing on the southern horizon the mountains of North Africa, black and sharp-sided as Bedouin tents. And, as on that former occasion, he crossed himself involuntarily.

George Ashden, standing at the rail about a yard away, noticed the gesture and frowned to himself. He had forgotten old Paddy's superstitious streak – though how a chap with his brains could swallow – scrub that! Too hot, he thought, mopping his heavy, red face. Dr Ashden was a tallish, sturdy Englishman with fading flaxen hair and vivid blue eyes that still retained a hint of the wary vulnerability that had been so apparent when he and Paddy Brown entered the medical school of St Martha's Hospital, London, from separate universities, in the autumn of 1938. They had qualified at the end of 1940 and worked their first six months as junior housemen in their parent hospital. In July 1941, George Ashden had been called up into the Royal Army Medical Corps. Paddy Brown had remained in Martha's for the rest of the war, and there they next met, briefly, in April 1945, then not again until three days ago when George boarded at Genoa and they discovered they were fellow first-class passengers on the *Rose of Africa*. During the ten year interval their occasional news of each other had come from mutual friends and announcements of appointments, engagements, marriages and deaths in the St Martha's *Gazette*, an in-house publication circulated annually to all old Martha's men who remembered to pay their subscriptions. Three days ago in Genoa, as in London in 1945, both had outwardly reacted to the reunion as if parted five minutes. They were now thirty-seven, but for differing reasons, looked older. That neither had yet mentioned those reasons to the other was a measure of their friendship that properly dated from their working as final-year students through the first, long London blitz and surviving physically unscratched with their youthful conviction that 'it can't happen to me' still intact.

Solid as the British Empire when that was put up, thought Paddy, glancing from the statue to the Red Ensign hanging limply from the stern mast-head. 'The Old Red Duster' the innumerable merchant seamen in Martha's during the war had called it, and, without exception once strong enough to talk, demanded, 'Wouldn't you be Irish, doctor? . . . Dublin, eh? No offence sir, but seeing as Ireland's neutral – and many's the good shipmate I lost from Ireland not letting us use her ports – what the hell you doing here?'

'No offence taken, old chap. I'm here – because I'm here. Well now, let's get you a bit higher whilst I listen to your chest . . .'

A nice bunch and good patients, he reflected, but only momentarily, having trained himself to avoid professional nostalgia. He hitched down his glasses and narrowed his eyes against the glare to look down at the bright green harbour water. This was his first long sea voyage and the constantly changing colour of the sea was one of the many aspects of life he now regarded as an unexpected, undeserved bonus. Amongst the others

4

was his ability to walk with a severe limp and just one stick.

Yesterday he left lunch early to watch from the then empty boat-deck the great swirls of mud from the invisible Nile Delta turn the Mediterranean yellow. The young Fourth Officer leisurely patrolling the upper promenade deck immediately below saw the tall, thin figure leaning bare-headed on the starboard rail and paused uncertainly. Obviously the chap had forgotten his hat and since getting up and down companionways were one hell of a sweat for him – should he nip up top and offer to get it? Dodgy, mused the Fourth. Medics could be damned tricky when on the receiving end of that kind of tip and a chap couldn't be too careful when dealing with a chum of the Owners. All the same . . . ah! Panic over! Mate on watch. The Fourth sauntered on to exchange 'Afternoon's' with George Ashden strolling by suitably hatted and carrying the panama Paddy left in the smoking room when they went down to lunch.

'Bung it on, Paddy. If the sun poleaxes you Morgan'll spring a premature coronary and being the only other qualified man on board I'll have to volunteer as locum and scupper a bloody good bridge foursome.'

Paddy laughed and slammed on the hat. 'Thanks, George and you're right. For that decent boy's sake I've got to stay healthy if it kills me.'

George grunted amicably. He wondered if he should suggest that even when hatted prolonged exposure to the early afternoon sun just one day out of Egypt in the hot season was poor therapy for a convalescent only previously accustomed to the northern sun, then decided against it. Old Paddy didn't need the advice. Far too highly qualified – and even although he,

George, had known equally brilliant chaps act like bloody fools with their own health, that Paddy had to an art just how far he could push himself was plain from his medical history. Last night young Morgan had told him privately that this time last year the poor chap had been in a wheelchair with the odds stacked against his walking again. Yet here he was swanning round Africa on his own and if one wing was badly clipped, the other was visibly functioning better daily. Still – bloody tough turn-up that the brightest and wildest chap in their year should have been poleaxed by polio a few months after he had made the step up to the teaching staff. Always liked him . . . used to envy him like hell . . . so bloody amusing and always with a blonde in tow . . . bloody bad show . . . but as that was how the cards had been dealt, as well he'd had the nous to stay single, reflected George, and beneath the khaki jungle hat his once very good-looking face tightened in self-reproach.

A year ago the nine years of his childless, mutually unhappy marriage had been ended when his wife, driving alone, skidded at speed into a brick wall and was killed outright. He had never understood why the marriage had failed. He was convinced he had loved his wife when he married her and that she had loved him. She had said she did, on their honeymoon. Sometimes he had wondered if she missed having children as much as he, but as they had never discussed this, he had never known the answer. And as his wife had only been eighteen when they married in November 1945 he had always felt guiltily responsible for the outcome, but never analysed this either, as his was not an analytical mind.

It had been the burden of that guilt that had

6

persuaded him to take his father's advice and accept an astonishingly well-paid two-year trial appointment as a junior partner in a general practice in Salisbury, Rhodesia. The principal was a Martha's man ten years his senior who had become one of his great friends during the last of the three wartime years he had spent as a prisoner, first in Italy and then Germany. The principal had emigrated to Rhodesia in 1947. 'You don't know how glad I am to have got clear before Aneurin Bevan shackled me into his National Health Service,' he wrote. 'This is a good country with a great future. Why not come out and give it a try . . .'

'The change and sun will do you good, my boy,' said George's long-widowered father, a retired zoologist. 'And unlike the Union of South Africa, Rhodesia is not withdrawing from the Commonwealth and turning republic later this year. Alas, indeed, for the old British Empire.'

'How to lose an Empire, Dad. Win a world war.'

'*Tout casse, tout passe*, George. The desire for national independence is as natural as breathing. But . . . er . . . if I were you . . . er . . . I would not be in too much of a hurry to relinquish your present personal independence.'

He was so moved by this first hint that his father had known of his marital unhappiness that he retorted abruptly, 'I'll be all right, Dad. Will you?'

'If you are, my dear boy – of course.'

George stared out over the yellow sea thinking of his father and of the mother he could barely remember, but not his dead wife. He needed a glass in his hand for that last and it was another four hours to sunset. A few minutes later he and Paddy left the boat-deck, George holding the stick whilst Paddy swung down the steep companionway using his hands on the rails and stronger right leg.

'Thanks, George. Back to the bridge table?'

'After the short kip. You?'

'Long kip after coffee with Mrs Mellor.'

George nodded and shot Paddy a sideways glance of mute incomprehension. He had disliked at sight the current doyenne of the first-class, an elderly thrice-widowed, naturalised US citizen of English birth, without realising this was because she vaguely reminded him of the long-dead maternal grandmother he had detested in childhood.

On the first evening of the voyage Dr Morgan, the ship's doctor, introduced Paddy to Mrs Mellor who had the next cabin to his on the port side of the lower promenade deck that accommodated the only six passenger cabins with private bathrooms. After a short spell of pleasantries the two had exchanged no more than bows until three days later when the ship called at Gibraltar. She anchored outside the harbour and a tender ferried to and fro the few disembarking and embarking passengers and crowds going ashore for the day. Paddy stayed on board partially to spare his fellow-passengers the embarrassment – and guilty impatience – his slow progress caused in queues, partially his own pride, and partially on doctor's orders.

'No bouncing in and out of bloody launches till you've got your sea legs, Paddy,' cautioned Mr Hoadley East, Martha's senior orthopaedic consultant, at his last follow-up before sailing. 'We poor bloody orthopods have our pride and when we discharge a chap in one piece we don't like having him back in plaster.'

At tea-time he looked into the lounge and was

promptly beckoned by the only passenger present, Mrs Mellor.

'Do please join me for tea, Dr Brown.' She waved him to an armchair with one beringed hand and with the other summoned the hovering steward and ordered tea with a look in her sharp eyes that silenced in time the 'Just give you a hand into that chair, sir.' She turned back to Paddy. 'Everyone rushes ashore at Gib. as if we've been at sea for weeks. Such a disappointment. Home from home. Red mail boxes, bobbies in blue helmets, Union Jacks and people talking English – but it does provide the first opportunity for getting away from rashly embraced new friends.' She looked at him sternly. 'When sailing to Africa, India or Australia, one should never start making shipboard friends before Gib., Dr Brown.'

He smiled, 'Is that a fact?'

'Most certainly. The first few days are essential for sorting out the bores always present in enclosed communities. They can be so trying when the temperature rises and on a ship there is no escape. Useless to try jumping overboard. The crew will have a lifeboat down before one comes up twice and the Captain far from pleased at having to stop his ship.' Their tea arrived. 'Milk and sugar? And do smoke whilst you drink and eat if you wish – all my husbands did and so do my children and grandchildren . . . No, thank you, I don't. Cucumber sandwich? . . . take a handful – one will go in a mouthful.'

He was growing amused. He liked women and though he had been educated in England since he was twelve, having no Anglo-Saxon blood he had no inhibitions about exhibiting his preference for feminine companionship. 'I imagine you've travelled greatly.'

9

Mrs Mellor inclined her elegantly dressed white head. She was in her mid-seventies, well-corseted, well-gowned, straight-backed and her still attractive but never pretty face was lined with intelligence, humour, a certain degree of self-indulgence, but no self-pity. She went on in her soft, well-bred, faintly American voice, 'I love travelling on passenger liners and visiting my grandchildren in London and Cape Town. This is my third trip from New York since the war and second in the *Rose*. I always break the outward journey with one month in London, another at the Cape, then have another two weeks in London on the return. Passenger liners,' she added, covertly appraising him, 'are infinitely more interesting than cruise ships. On cruises either everyone is my age or on honeymoon. Such a mistake that.' She raised one finger. 'Never spend your honeymoon on a cruise, Dr Brown. Even in paradise one does need a little time to oneself.'

He grinned. 'I'll bear that one in mind, Mrs Mellor.'

Mrs Mellor's nod concealed her pleasure in this opportunity of a quiet chat with the sadly frail and devastatingly attractive man about whom the first class had begun speculating before the ship was out of the English Channel. She enjoyed gossip – without believing one word until she had proved its veracity. That any attractive man – and particularly a doctor – sailing alone round Africa in one of the most expensive cabins, brooded over like an anxious sheepdog puppy by the ship's doctor, and seen off at Tilbury – according to gossip – by the Chairman of the Line, should attract gossip, was as inevitable as night following day, thought Mrs Mellor, without interrupting her discourse on who, in the first-class, was who and currently doing what with whom.

Paddy, hugely diverted, asked ' "Tiger" Blake? Now which one is he?'

'Red face, white military moustache, booming voice, purser's table.'

'I have him! Ex-Indian Army, moved from India to Kenya in '47.'

'That's him. Like Colonel Hastings – General Montgomery's double at the First Officer's table on the left of that beautiful South African child, Belinda Van der Mann travelling with her grandmother – lorgnette on her right. You'll have noticed Belinda?'

He spread both hands. 'What man on this ship hasn't?'

She liked that. She distrusted men of all ages who either pretended not to, or failed to notice a pretty girl. And as she continued detailing the other occupants of the tables in the first-class dining saloon, she thought it a pity all the single girls were so young and young women of an age to interest him, married. Her experienced eyes recognised he was too intelligent not to be bored by the inane chatter of schoolgirls or to risk his professional future with an illicit liaison. Nevertheless, she thought, he's a man who needs women as much as my dearest Frank (her second and most beloved husband).

She said briskly, 'Dr Brown, may I ask a personal question?'

He bowed his assent and braced himself for the inevitable probing into his health.

'Since you have different surnames – are you the nephew or godson of the Chairman of this Line?'

He laughed in relief. 'No relation at all. I've never met the man.'

'Oh dear. What a shame.' She smiled disarmingly. 'I was hoping to bask in your reflected glory.'

Paddy hesitated, then as it would neither break a promise nor infringe medical ethics, said, 'Any help if I admit one of the Owners is an old friend?'

'My dear young man, of course! Always helps to have friends in court. No doubt that was who saw you off at Tilbury?' She read the expression that flickered through his dark eyes. 'Naturally that got round. Everything gets round in seconds on a ship . . . very like in a teaching hospital so my eldest grandson Gerald says. He's a surgical registrar in St Benedict's Hospital – qualified a few years ahead of our nice young Dr Morgan. Where did you qualify?'

'St Martha's, London. Have you many grand-children?'

She picked up that cue with more understanding than he appreciated. On her first post-war return to London she had been appalled by the widespread war devastation and when calling upon Gerald had seen across the Thames the battered remnants of the once great stone buildings of St Martha's rising from a sea of flattened ruins. No, she thought, he won't wish to speak of that either. 'Just five from my son and daughter of my first marriage. Three girls, two boys, all but Gerald now married . . .' and she gave brief accounts of all, then returned to shipboard gossip for the remainder of their shared tea.

Six weeks before that occasion when Paddy had been in the final month of his stay in an orthopaedic convalescent home near London and still undecided about his future upon discharge, he had been surprised to receive an invitation to lunch from an ex-patient with business connections in shipping, who had been one of the governors of Martha's until the advent of the National Health Service in July, 1948, transformed it from a 'voluntary' to state-subsidised teaching hospital.

'St Martha's was such a well-endowed, reluctant bride, that the event might be termed a shotgun-wedding,' said his host, Sir John Foster-Green, when leading up to his offered gift of a voyage round Africa. After making it, he went on, 'I am reliably informed you would be well-advised not to contemplate returning to your profession before the end of this or early next year and that a restful spell in warmer climates and sea air should benefit your general health. Well, well. What do you say?'

Briefly, and uncharacteristically, Paddy was speechless. He knew that Sir John was a wealthy widower whose only child, an unmarried son, had been killed in the war, but his unexpected and staggering generosity, literally, left him breathless. He said at last, 'Sir – what can I say?'

'Those, as I recall, were my precise words to you and Sister Luke upon my discharge from her ward in December, 1943.' Sir John's jutting white eyebrows met over his small, shrewd eyes that could be cold as marble but were now softened by more than reminiscence. He had been warned of the poor fellow's condition and relieved to learn of the strong probability of his eventual return to medicine, albeit to an appointment that necessitated little standing or walking for long periods. But he was finding it more distressing than he had anticipated to contrast the lively, black-haired youngster of yesteryear with this prematurely greyed, pale, crippled fellow for whom he, at sixty-eight, had had to slow his pace when escorting him into the dining room of his club. 'I also recall I then added that no man can ever properly thank those to whom he owes his life . . . Nonsense, m'boy! Plain truth. Been on my mind for more than a few years . . . You'll oblige me by accepting like a good fellow and leaving all arrangements to me. We'll keep the business side to ourselves, but only courteous to inform the Captain of the *Rose of Africa* of our friendship – no doubt he'll offer you a place at his table . . . You'd prefer a less formal placing eh? Just so. I suggest the doctor's. The young fellow on the *Rose of Africa* is about to embark upon his second voyage in her since completing his National Service in the Navy. A pleasant, competent youngster, I'm told – only prudent to acquaint him with your medical history. I'll attend to it . . . Well, well, now that's settled – brandy?'

Dr Morgan was twenty-six, slight, dark-haired, very conscientious and a poor actor. His custom of anxiously watching Paddy at meals and hovering on the boat . . . deck 'Just up top for a breath of air, sir!' amused Paddy, but visibly perturbed his fellow-passengers. By the end of the first week when the ship called at Genoa it seemed to Paddy that if he didn't somehow get Morgan to ease off, his fellow passengers would be bracing themselves to attend his burial at sea . . . Would the *Rose* have an Irish flag to drape his body? . . . Sir John would have attended to it . . . The real problem was handling Morgan without hurting his professional pride. He was a very decent chap, remarkably lacking in the usual young doctor's conceit, and the type of intelligent, reliable, junior for whom he had prayed when Senior Medical Officer of Martha's. Needs more thought, he decided, and pro tem let it ride and suffer the older passengers', 'How are you today, Dr Brown?

I do hope a little stronger . . .' and the younger's, 'Hi, Doc! How goes it? Anything I can do for you? Anything at all. Only got to ask . . .'

Akin to being a diabetic in a chocolate factory, thought Paddy, courteously rejecting all offers from the teenage girls returning with older relatives from 'home leave' or 'holidays overseas' to British Colonial Africa or the Union, and young married women either still childless, or with small children, going to join their British husbands working in the former. The majority were blondes and varied from plain to the exquisitely pretty, seventeen-year-old Belinda Van der Mann. But as Mrs Mellor had recognised, whilst they appealed to his sexuality, he was too mature to be interested in girls young enough to imagine there was anything romantic about physical weakness, or to ignore – even in the unreality of shipboard life – the fact that for a doctor, adultery could, and often did, result in professional ruin.

The ship docked at Genoa in the morning and that afternoon he went ashore on his own. He limped slowly through the docks, round a street market, brilliant with flower stalls and vibrant with exchanges between vendors and purchasers that at one moment sounded as if murder would be done and the next exploded into laughter and slaps on the back. He enjoyed the rapid Italian voices, the vital sexuality of the women, and his own unaccustomed anonymity after the dragging years, first as dangerously ill, and always a prized, indulged patient.

'OUR Dr Brown . . . aren't we proud of you! . . . Gently, Doctor, leave it to us – mustn't try and run before you can walk . . . Dear Dr Brown, and how are we today? . . . My goodness, Doctor, aren't we doing well! Almost standing alone! . . .'

Mother of God, but they meant well and they did well, but save me from seeing any of them but Hoadley again. No soft soap nor soft talk from him, he thought, limping on, then stopping to lean against a wall.

'Stop bloody messing about, Paddy. Do as I say unless you want to be crippled for life.'

'Still on the cards, Hoadley?'

'What do you think I am? Bloody soothsayer?'

'Bloody good orthopod. Stick your neck out. Won't be the first time.'

'Right. On present form I'd say you'll be on your feet by '55.'

Two weeks ago at the last follow-up, 'Taking off round Africa, eh? Good God, some sods are born lucky.'

'Having been your patient, I'll go along with that. My regards to Prue and young Hoadley and thanks, again.'

The wall he leant against was on the corner at the foot of a narrow, cobbled street festooned with washing strung across from high, old, cramped apartment blocks. There were great patches of mould on the stone-work, the paint was peeling and wood splintering on the shutters and doors, but the flat roofs and rickety balconies were laden with flowering pot plants, women with babies in their arms shouting happily to neigh-bours from open windows and a group of sturdy, ragged, barefoot children played in the sunshine on the cobbles. Slums, he thought, but slums in the sun and sea air unlike the damp greyness of the dreadful slums round Martha's that had first horrified him when doing his three weeks as a district midwifery clerk in early 1939.

'You'll get used to the smell, Mr Brown,' his escorting District Midwife said cheerfully, 'but do remember always to have handy a small bowl of unsterile cold water. Only way to kill the bugs and fleas is to drown 'em.'

Hitler had done a major job of slum clearance in London but enough had survived for covered buckets filled with disinfectant and large brown paper bags for infected clothing to remain statutory items of equipment in Casualty, the present SMO of Martha's had told him when they met for a drink after his last follow-up.

'But at least now tubercle's been hit on the head, we're only seeing a fraction of the numbers in your time.'

'How about polio?'

'Still seeing more than the odd case. The Yanks seems to be on to something there, but whatever it is, we haven't got it yet. But kids with rickets are old history. When did that stop, sir?'

'Well into the war. Endemic amongst London's slum kids when I qualified. It took a good few years of free orange juice and cod liver oil to begin straightening out the legs of all British children.'

'How did they get hold of the orange juice in the war?' The SMO had qualified in 1947 shortly after Paddy's appointment to his present job. 'I've often wondered.'

'From the Yanks under Lease-Lend.'

'Ah, yes, Lease-Lend,' said the SMO, as if referring to an event in the Crimean War.

None of the barefoot children had rickets nor had he

seen one case this afternoon. The Marshall Plan and the sun have done that job, he thought. Too bad no Marshall Plan for the UK, and that Lease-Lend ended within days of the Labour Government's taking over in 1945. To the victors the spoils? Not this time round. The ten years since the war ended had been tired, shabby years in London. Tired, shabby people had crowded the benches in Casualty, and the trains, buses and trams – until the last went to the scrapheap and the tramlines were torn up to make way for the brave new Britain promised by the Labour Party before the '45 election. He had then been a medical registrar and had not voted, having not had time to discover if he were eligible to do so and in the event forgotten it was General Election day until the first results began coming in as he was finishing his night round. On returning to the Doctors' House, he joined the group of junior housemen listening to the common-room wireless and discussing Aneurin Bevan with more venom than he had heard any English voice direct at Hitler throughout the war with Germany.

'. . . this means the swine'll be Minister of Health and push in his bloody National Health Service.'

'Not to worry, chaps,' he said. 'Your side still hasn't finished off the Japs. On past form that won't happen overnight and this time next year you lot'll be toting your stethoscopes round the Far East and the C3s (men unfit for military service) and I'll be toting ours round the ruins of poor bloody Martha's.'

Not overnight, he thought. In just over one week of that August. Two atom bombs. Two new names, Hiroshima and Nagasaki, etched into world history when the second world war finally ended on 14th

18

August, 1945, with the words still echoing round Martha's, 'But what the hell *is* an atom bomb?'

The pain in his left leg dragged him back to the present. He limped back to a main street and flagged down what he hoped was a cruising taxi even though it was doing around fifty. The brakes screamed and horns blared as it skidded to a stop. The middle-aged driver leapt out pushing a faded US Navy baseball cap to the back of his head and vehemently protesting his incomprehension of Paddy's phrase-book Italian request to be taken back to the ship. The driver looked him up and down, broke off in mid-spate, flinging up his arms in triumph. 'Ah, ha!' He all but lifted Paddy on to the back seat, slammed the door, jumped into his own seat and shouted over his shoulder as he catapulted the cab into the racing traffic, 'OK, Signore, I take to buddies!'

'Thanks very much,' shouted Paddy, clinging with both hands to the back of the front passenger seat to avoid being pitched through the windscreen. A few minutes later, after taking every corner on two wheels, to another cacophany of horns, the cab screamed and skidded to a halt half way up a hill. The driver leapt out, hauled open the near-side back door and, with one hand, waved his cap at a large notice behind his head and with the other, crossed himself. 'Is here buddies, Signore Inglese!'

Paddy glanced at the beautifully lettered notice in English and for the only time in his life did not deny English nationality. It also prevented him from explaining this was the wrong destination. He climbed out, helped by the man, then held open his wallet in the certainty – later proved right by the purser – that only a fair charge would be taken. He was curiously touched by the driver's insistence on shaking his hand before leaping back into the cab and driving off as if out of the pits at Silverstone. He glanced after the cab then for several seconds at the notice before slowly climbing the stone steps up to the British War Cemetery.

There were red roses in bloom in the beds between the neat white graves lying in rows up an olive-green hillside that faced the Gulf of Lyons and was backed by higher, olive-green hills. The cloudless sky and smooth, shining sea were the same bright blue and the clean warm air was scented by the roses that looked as English as the wording on the headstones. On most were the British names, services, ranks and ages of the dead; but on others, AN UNKNOWN BRITISH SOLDIER KNOWN ONLY TO GOD. All the named had been men of his immediate generation, but few had lived to his present age and the youthful deaths of the majority, tightened his throat and blurred his vision. Instinctively he took off his hat and went slowly along the lowest line, pausing to read the names and for even longer by the UNKNOWN. He stood, leaning on his stick, looking down and seeing in memory the faces of so many school and Martha's friends, whose bodies, if ever found, had lain somewhere in unmarked graves for ten or more years.

He had taken off his dark glasses to dry his eyes and been looking down for some time before he was conscious of the sensation of being watched. He replaced the glasses to look around. The only people in sight were an elderly woman in shabby black kneeling by one of the graves in the next line above and, from her walk and short black hair, what looked like a young Italian woman going towards the steps he had come up. She was smallish and slenderly shapely and wore a tight-waisted full-skirted tan cotton dress and small natural-straw boater but he recognised neither her legs, seductively swaying hips, nor outfit as belonging to any woman he had seen on the ship. He turned back to the hillside and his own troubled thoughts. He did not see the retreating young woman pause on the top step and first glance, then take a longer look back, before going down even more quickly. She had vanished from the steps and his mind when he went down a little later, cursing his lack of foresight in not asking the cab driver to come back. He began limping wearily down the hill but had barely gone thirty yards before a blaring horn and screaming brakes made him turn joyfully. About ten minutes later, waved off by the baseball cap, he went slowly up the gangplank and as he handed back his shore-chit to the Fourth at the head, a man's voice just behind him said, 'Soon as they open I'll buy you the one I owe you, Paddy.'

Mother of God, no! he thought, recognising the voice and dreading what must follow. That he could not bear the shocked pity old friends tried to keep out of their eyes when seeing him again had continuously made him reject his married siblings' offers to convalesce with them. He had not been back to Ireland since he took his then fiancée to meet his family in the summer of 1952 and only returned to Martha's for follow-ups, and each time, writhed inwardly.

He turned slowly, smiling. 'You took your time, George. What kept you?'

George Ashden smiled stiffly. He was relieved to have had a few minutes breather to get over the shock of seeing the poor chap being helped out of the taxi and the past hour to handle his reaction to recognising his name on the first-class passenger list. He had checked with an assistant purser in the blind hope that it was some other Dr P. M. Brown and the chap's reply had hit him like a kick under the belt. Bloody turn-up, he thought. When a chap folded his tent and slipped away, last thing he wanted was to have the bloody tent re-opened from Genoa to Beira – and yet, good type, Paddy Brown – bad form not to close ranks.

He said, 'Had one or two things to do, old chap,' and they laughed and went into the first-class accommodation.

Two decks below Paddy's cabin the temporary sole occupant of a four-berthed tourist-class cabin on the starboard side, flung her straw boater and dark glasses on to her upper berth, unlocked and opened the porthole, breathing as if running. Then she washed her hands in the handbasin and in the mirror rivetted to the bulkhead above, her slightly slanting brown eyes looked black as her brows and her pretty, normally vitally-expressive face was immobile and pale as alabaster. Her name was Elinor Mackenzie, and for the first time since boarding at Tilbury, she was deeply thankful she had booked too late to get either a single, or double first-class cabin for her sole use to Cape Town, and for the strictly observed segregation of the two classes that had previously only amused her.

She stared at the mirror but did not see her reflection. She saw the long, limp, stooping figure in the cemetry and the sun exposing every new line in the thin, haggard face and the iron-grey hair that had been black as her own. And at their last meeting, black, lifeless, soaked in sweat, with only the greyish, glistening, high forehead, and fever-glazed eyes visible above the green, rubber oxygen mask, she recalled, and winced. No, she thought, oh no. Paddy won't want to see me again yet – if ever. Medically he's done wonderfully, but until I'm over the shock of seeing what it's cost him, he must not see me. He's too bright and we've known each other too long for either of us to kid the other. He won't forget I saw him in the pit of hell. Seeing me will pitch him straight back into that pit – like me, just now, coming up the gangplank.

Momentarily, she closed her eyes, but she could not close out the new mental picture of the heavy-faced, fading flaxen-haired man she had just seen leaning over the rail a couple of yards from the head of the gangplank. He had been scanning the docks and had not noticed her, but she doubted he would have remembered her had he done so. She had recognised him at once – because once, and at their only meeting, his uncanny resemblance to her husband had given her the immediate impression of seeing his ghost, even though, she recalled guardedly, she had not then heard officially that Alastair was dead. All over long ago and I had to take it at twenty-three – but I can't take it again.

She opened her eyes to look at her platinum wedding ring, and, as if of its own volition, her left forefinger stiffened and left arm assumed the position of being in a sling. Suddenly her recall was so total that she smelt the stuffy, steamy heat of a ward kitchen in wartime Martha's, felt the throbbing in her left forefinger, and the old, nagging ache for a husband she had not seen since their honeymoon and his seven day embarkation leave ended simultaneously in February, 1941.

April, she thought, yes, it was April '45 that I had this nail off and I was back in Luke on dry-duty when Paddy brought him to the ward and Sister Luke told me to make him tea.

'Captain Ashden will drink it in here whilst I take Dr Brown round, Nurse Mackenzie . . .' He had just got back to England after getting out of the bag and it was a Wednesday afternoon . . .

TWO
London
April 1945

The afternoon sun silvered the bulky grey sides of the barrage balloons and the east wind sang their swan-song through their long cables. It was just over three weeks since the Allied Armies had crossed the Rhine and the last V1 flying-bomb and V2 long-range rocket had been launched on London. But on the riverside terrace of St Martha's Hospital the wind still smelt of war-dust and destruction laced with tar, salt, and the soaking timbers of the three tarpaulined barges that had been anchored in front of the hospital for longer than the staff remembered – on the rare occasions when they saw them.

In September 1939 eight widely-spaced, massive, five-storey, stone ward blocks all lined that terrace. In the autumn of 1940 all the ground and first floor windows in the usable parts of the hospital had been bricked-in and the three upper floors emptied of patients and equipment. On that April afternoon in 1945 the three surviving blocks were flanked by burnt-out roofless shells, great mounds of rubble and flattened bombsites; the windows in the three upper floors gaped glasslessly; the bricks in the lower were blackened by smoke and grime, and embedded with glass and shrapnel splinters; and in the long, wide, thirty-six-bedded ground and first floor wards artificial lighting in daytime had become so unexceptional that only new patients noticed it and always with relief.

'Don't take more than a jiff to get used to lights by day, Nurse, and give me the bricks and keep the view. Nasty stuff, flying glass,' said Mr Banks, a middle-aged railwayman in Bed fourteen, Luke Ward, to Elinor Mackenzie as she gave him his afternoon tea. He was recovering from his second coronary thrombosis and though off the Dangerously and on the less grave Seriously Ill List, was not yet allowed to feed himself.

'I couldn't agree more, Mr Banks. How about another sandwich? Or more tea?'

Mr Banks accepted a second thin, crustless margarine and apricot jam sandwich mainly to spin-out this nice little natter with 'his' Nurse Mackenzie. Nursed him lovely, she had, when he'd been a D.I.L., and he'd missed her cruel – same as the others – the four days she'd been off sick with her poorly finger. 'I'll not say as I mind having the four floors and roof up top,' he reflected between slow chews. 'Papers and wireless keep on as war'll be over sharpish but our lads not fetched up Berlin yet and if old Hitler's got hisself a V3 I reckon he'll be bunging it over more than sharpish.'

She smiled into his sharp, pinched face. 'You could be right, Mr Banks. Let's hope you're not. More tea?'

'I'd not say no, ta, Nurse.' Lovely smile, she had –

and that wasn't all she had. Like old Taffy in Thirteen said, no surprise to none her bloke must've hitched her out the schoolroom seeing she still weren't more than a slip of a girl and her poor bloke been nicked by the Japs after Singapore packed it in, back in February '42. Shame, when you thought about it, but like old Taffy said, best not to think, wartime.

Elinor rose from his locker-seat to hold the spout of the china feeding cup to his mouth. She dried his lips with the napkin she had tucked under his chin. 'Manage another cup? Or perhaps a half?'

'Half'll do nicely, ta.' He watched her deft one-handed movements. 'Getting proper nippy in that sling nurse. Nelson best watch hisself or they'll be fetching him down and bunging you up Trafalgar Square.'

'Mr Banks, please! Spare me those pigeons.'

His breathless chuckle made Sister Luke glance up from her form-filling at the mid-ward desk and tighten her thin lips. She was pleased to see Mr Banks enjoying his tea – as was to be expected when a senior third year was performing a junior's task – but how careless of Nurse Mackenzie to let herself develop a septic finger! A good nurse should never forget that to take care of her hands and maintain her general health was a duty she owed to her patients and ward. When the whole hospital, indeed, the whole country was desperately short of young trained nurses, such thoughtlessness in a senior student – and, it had to be admitted, normally efficient nurse – demonstrated the weakness of her dedication to her work. But – as she had so often observed in Sisters' meetings since Matron had allowed married, childless, gels to enter the Nurse Training School – it was obvious that any gel who had already promised her life to some young man must lack the essential total dedication demanded by nursing. However, these things were sent to try us – and Mr Banks had finished his tea.

Sister Luke's eyebrows summoned Elinor to the large mahogany table that was the desk. Elinor came quickly and stood balancing a small papier mâché tea tray on the palm of her right hand.

'Yes, Sister?'

'Weigh the diabetic's supper bread next, please, Nurse. I've had to take the junior from her kitchen routine to help Staff Nurse Cotton with the D.I.L.s.' Sister Luke turned her piercing glance on the two screened beds on either side of the ward entrance as if – which none of her nurses doubted – she could see through the thick, red, cotton sides. 'Then prepare and witness the next penicillin round. And if at five I'm escorting Dr Brown on his belated afternoon round,' added Sister in the softer tone she reserved for mentioning or addressing the medical registrar, 'you may report off to Nurse Cotton.' She paused to tighten her lips. 'Aren't you the lucky one to be on dry-duty.'

'Yes, Sister,' said Elinor, honestly. With the entire nursing staff she regarded dry-duty as a sinecure since it forbade getting both hands wet and so, automatically, scrubbing up, giving injections, changing dressings, blanket-bathing and bedmaking and meant only working from nine a.m. to five p.m. in the six-day week. Normal day staff hours were from seven thirty a.m. to nine p.m. with three daily hours off between, that had to include a meal and, often, a lecture. 'Sister, I'm so sorry my finger's taking so long to – '

'These things are sent to try us, Nurse.' Sister Luke's eyes X-rayed Elinor's face. 'You look a little peaky.

Make sure you get a little fresh air before early supper and to bed by nine.'

'Yes, Sister. Thank you, Sister.'

'Thank you, Nurse.' The lace frills on Sister's cap fluttered in dismissal.

The ward kitchen lay at the far right end of the short, wide, inner corridor that opened into the main ground floor corridor that, pre-war, had connected the eight blocks and been half a mile long. It was now one-third shorter and had both ends blocked by temporary wooden walls. The bricks blocking the kitchen window and the simmering hot water urn had the stuffy little room so steamy that Elinor turned off the gas under the urn before adding Mr Bank's crockery to the stack the junior had left on the right draining board in the order insisted upon by Agnes, the ward maid, who was due back on at five and threatened to ask for her cards if addressed as Aggie. The muffled chimes of Big Ben striking the half-hour echoed over the river as she washed her right hand at the sink. Thank God, only another half hour, she thought, and that Paddy's late. He'll have to do his round before five when the official evening starts, and he turns Sister into an angel of sweetness and light for a good ten minutes. She may even forget I'm a blot on the entire British nursing profession – but I wish my damned finger would stop throbbing.

Seven days ago the nail of her left forefinger had been removed by the Senior Surgical Officer under gas in Casualty. She had spent four days off sick in the care of the Home Sister in her own room in the only one of the four Nursing Staff and Ward Maids' Homes to survive the months and weeks of the three major blitzes, the nine months of the V1 and six months of the V2 attacks. This was her third day back on duty and she felt tired as a night nurse. She took that day's Diet Sheet – a handwritten list on the back of an old temperature chart dog-clipped to a billboard – from its hook on the back of the door, and sat, illicitly, on the lid of the large, galvanised iron bread-bin that was the only seat in the kitchen. It was a strict hospital rule that nurses could only sit down on duty when feeding or special nursing patients, mending rubber gloves or ward linen, making stock (dressings), or writing, giving and receiving reports.

The names of the six diabetics blurred and her head fell forward. Oh, God, no! Not again! Not even Paddy could save me this time round, she thought, leaping up, smiling reminiscently. Very quickly she re-hung the Diet Sheet and set on the small scrubbed deal kitchen table the scales, weights, six side plates and saucers and the covered plate of bread the junior had sliced thinly before being called away. She weighed and apportioned the bread, still smiling at a long-forgotten incident in her first night as Luke night junior in October 1943. At half past three in the morning she had sat on the bread-bin to ease her aching feet before taking out and cutting the three long loaves for the patients' breakfast bread. A few minutes later she had been urgently shaken awake by a strange, black-haired, blue-chinned, gangling young man in a houseman's short white coat with a bit of pyjama collar sticking up over the neck of a dark sweater. He said he had just been called up by Alex (Alexandra Ward) and come in to scrounge a glass of milk as Alex had run short. She remembered seeing him do a night round in Luke earlier, but not his name. Her then junior second-year set had been moved to London for the first time on the previous day, and started their first three-month night-duty that night. (No Martha's first-years worked on nights, nor, since September 1940, did they work in London.)

'Brown by name and browned-off by nature – and who wouldn't be in this racket? Second time I've been hauled up tonight. There'll be a third. Always the way of it and if I'm not in Cas on the stroke of nine this morning, Sister Cas –' he sliced a thumbnail across his throat. 'A dog's life, no less, Nurse –' he noticed her wedding ring, 'Mrs –?'

'Mackenzie. And thanks awfully, Mr Brown. If Night Sister had come in –' she copied his gesture.

'Mother of God, but ours is a dangerous life, Mrs Mackenzie – and maybe more so than you'll know being just up from The Hut. (The inter-Martha's name for Martha's main evacuated base.) The grapevine up here beats radar. If I were you I'd not even tell your set you kipped down here on the bread-bin. Keep it twixt thee and me. OK?'

'Yes. And thanks most awfully, Mr Brown.'

'You'd do the same for me. See you around, Mrs Mackenzie,' he had said and vanished without the milk, or telling her he was the Senior House Physician.

I never realised till now, she thought, uncapping her fountain pen with her teeth to write the patient's name and bed number on the upturned back of a covering saucer, that it was Paddy's urge for the milk he forgot that turned us into buddies. And certainly saved me from being reported to Matron and, though as by then we were so short of nurses I probably would not have been chucked out, the major black on my record would have haunted me long as I'm in Martha's . . . that'll be three years this June . . . and it's over four since I last saw Alistair and as he's never answered my letters I don't even know – no! I WON'T think that – I WILL NOT!

She began quickly clearing the table and had just finished when Sister Luke swept open the door.

'Make a small pot of tea, please,' she said from the doorway, 'and Captain Ashden will drink it in here whilst I take Dr Brown round, Nurse Mackenzie. Mrs Somers (the wife of one of the D.I.L.s) is resting in the duty room.' Sister turned smiling graciously at someone in the corridor. 'Nurse will look after you, Captain Ashden and I must repeat, welcome, indeed, back to St Martha's. Now then, Dr Brown . . .' she moved away and a flaxen-haired young man in an obviously new and outsize battledress came uncertainly into the kitchen and closed the door.

The polite smile froze on Elinor's face. Alistair's dead and this is his ghost, flashed into her mind for the agonising two or three seconds before common sense and her wartime training whiplashed back – if he were dead, Matron would have opened the telegram as she always does, then sent for me and told Sister why before Sister handed on her summons in the voice she always uses when telling relatives patients have died. But though her intelligence accepted this, the boyishly good-looking, blue-eyed, thin young face so uncannily resembled Alistair that it took the final reassurance of the entwined snake insignia of the RAMC in the blouse lapels to produce her voice.

'Good afternoon, Captain Ashden.' She had to look away. She gestured to the bread-bin. 'Tea'll take a couple of minutes as the urn's off-boil. Do sit down. I'm sure Sister won't mind and I expect you've sat on one before.'

'Er – actually, yes, but – er – fine where I am, thanks, Nurse – er – '

'Mackenzie.' She moved to turn up the gas under the urn and kept her back to him.

George Ashden mumbled incoherently and backed against the closed door. Everything he had on was new, this morning he had had two baths, and before being flown back to England last night he had spent the previous twenty-four hours in a de-lousing unit in Germany, but he still felt alive. He was terrified of some ultra-resistant louse brushing off him on to her. She looked so pretty and young and so gloriously clean. He had forgotten how clean Martha's nurses had always looked and how to talk to one or any girl, as it was nearly three years since he had been alone with one. He was certain from the way she had just looked at him that she thought him a hideous bind and probably a heel for being swept into the bag. He had met quite a bit of that during these last few days in Germany. The Yanks had been rather decent, but not all our chaps. 'Just out of the bag, eh? Oh, well, nice work if you can get it. We poor bloody sods had to keep sweating it out.'

She moved to the dresser to set a tea tray and the movements of her smallish, slenderly curvacious, seemingly boneless figure, mesmerised his wary, vulnerable eyes. He was almost glad she despised him too much to face him. He needed the breather to get under cover the effect her entrancing, slightly slanting brown eyes, exquisite complexion and soft generous lips had on him. He did not know what to say to her. He recalled miserably how he never had known what to say to girls and had envied chaps like Paddy who made first base with their opening gambit.

'Er – why the sling, Nurse?'

She explained briefly, keeping her eyes downcast and fighting the resurgence of the old, nagging ache for Alistair. The long years of waiting for news and the letters that had never arrived, the non-stop hard work and the strain of living in a city that from last June to three weeks ago had been under continuous air-attack, had hammered numb that ache along with so many other emotions. But that dreadful intuitive 'Alistair's dead . . .' had stripped off the numbed area and exposed the raw nerve-endings beneath.

'Bloody monstrous – oh, sorry – monstrous, you're having to work! You should be off till that sling's off.'

The genuine indignation in his voice touched and shamed her. Not his fault and dirty trick to take it out on him, she thought, looking up and forcing a polite little smile.

'Quite honestly, I don't mind. I expect I would if I didn't know we're so short-staffed that one hand's better than none. Like the Army when there's a flap on. "All walking-wounded that can walk and carry a rifle, get fell in." ' She was further shamed by her belated recognition of why he was back. For the past week or two she had heard that British POWs from Germany were beginning to trickle home, and that most were pale, walking skeletons in outsize new uniforms – and hungry. She glanced at the battledress flapping like a tent on his tallish, strong-boned, too-thin figure, and added four biscuits to the side plate. She made and poured his tea and put in three teaspoonfuls of sugar without asking if he took it. She had never met the serviceman who did not.

'All yours, Captain Ashden.'

'I say, thanks – but can you spare all this? And what about you?'

She smiled naturally. 'Positive. Ward rations come in Mondays, this is Wednesday, Sister always draws full rations for every man in Luke and right now we've six sugar-free diabetics. And much as I'd love a cuppa, Sister would blow me through the roof if I had one with you.' Her eyes danced. 'Jerry may've knocked Martha's about a bit, but Martha's hasn't changed. Only staff nurses or night seniors may share a cuppa with a Martha's man when on duty. When did you leave?'

Her smiling face made him so light-headed he forgot to smile back. 'July, '41. I was in Paddy Brown's year. He's the only one of us left. Bit of a turn-up seeing him in a long white coat.'

'I expect so,' she said kindly. She had heard the undercurrent of self-reproach in his voice. He couldn't help being in and he can't help being out, she thought, and he had to sweat out the barbed wire as MOs couldn't escape and leave our lot without one of their own MOs on the inside. 'When did you get back on leave?'

His good-looking, gaunt, young face suddenly looked younger. She didn't despise him – she hadn't spotted – probably just shy – the chaps in the camps said lots of girls – always the nice types – handed out the frozen mitt at first only because they were shy. 'Flew back to somewhere in the midlands last night. They told me to make for London this morning as that's my best bet for getting north. I'm booked on tonight's 2000 hours from King's Cross.'

'Good show. Where north?'

'York. We live fifteen miles out. I managed to get a

trunk-call through to my father just before lunch. He's picking me up on his aged Norton in the small hours.'

'How lovely for you both!' She packed the warmth into her voice. This was the day he had dreamed of for months or years and if – WHEN – that day came for Alistair she would want to kill anyone who shadowed it. She opened the refrigerator and began laying rows of little bottles of penicillin crystals and of distilled, sterile water on her end of the table. 'Your father good on two wheels?'

He laughed. 'Menace. But he's always been hooked on motor bikes. Loathes cars. Much easier on petrol and he said he'd scrounge enough for tonight.'

She laughed. 'He sounds fun. He must've been bucked by your call.'

George flushed faintly. 'Actually – he was rather. He didn't know I was – er – back in England.' And to cover his own joy at the happiness in his father's voice, he held one of the little bottles of yellow crystals up to the overhead light. 'Like hell just our propaganda.'

'Propaganda?'

'That's the line Jerry's been shooting – ' He hesitated, realising what he had nearly given away. 'At least, that's's the gen. How long have civvy hospitals had it here?'

The sympathy in her eyes was unforced. He can't bear to admit being in the bag, she thought. Not yet. He's still in the shock of getting out. 'We've been using it here since – oh – around April last year.' And knowing he wanted more, but daren't expose his ignorance by asking, 'Works wonders on sepsis and chests, but a bit of a bind for the patients as it turns them into human pin-cushions. It can only be injected intra-muscularly usually every four, but sometimes six hours, on a five day course. Bit of a bind for staff as it has to be made up freshly before each injection – hence the distilled sterile water – and kept in the fridge. We use it in powder form on open wounds – it's a hideous yellow but works marvellously when it works, and it does on most people. I expect the same applies with the troops.'

He hedged, 'Damn useful stuff.' He couldn't lie to her. She was being so sweet and had a sweet voice and was so miraculously the type he had always dreamed of meeting, but she was no fantasy – she was real – here! And he was with her here, in poor old battered bloody Martha's and Luke's kitchen with the bricks still *in situ* and the old reek of steam and gas and the damp tea-leaves in the bucket under the sink the ward maid saved to use when sweeping the ward three times a day. But she was leaving!

'Sorry, but I've got to get this lot into the ward then gather up the patients' bedtickets (notes) and write their names in the Penicillin Book. We use the same form for penicillin as for Dangerous Drugs. We've eight on four-hourly, pro-tem. Do help yourself to another cuppa and don't stint the sugar.'

'Yes. Thanks. Thanks a lot. Sorry to be such a bind when you're so pushed.'

She smiled up at him as she had at Mr Banks. 'You're no bind, Captain Ashden. You're a shot in the arm for us all. We love welcoming Martha's men back to the old firm. If I don't see you before you go, have a glorious leave and all the best for what comes after.'

He blushed with happiness. 'Same to you, Nurse Mackenzie and – er – thanks for everything.' He opened then closed the door after her, wishing he had dared add, 'I hope we meet again,' then glad he hadn't. It would give him the excuse to write and suggest it. Of course, she might give him the brush-off – but perhaps she wouldn't, as, though he couldn't kid himself she had just given him the old green light, she hadn't shot him down and she had been so bloody sweet.

He poured more tea, drank thirstily, and looked around the kitchen in an awed wonder. This was reality and not a dream from which he would wake, shaking with cold, in another filthy, unheated barn, surrounded by roughly two hundred other chaps in filthy, ragged, infested British uniforms and boots falling apart. All their uniforms and boots had been clean, and more or less serviceable, when the Germans marched them out of their several prison camps in January. But for three months the Germans had marched them one thousand miles from east to west in their determination to keep them ahead of the Russian advance from the east, and later use as hostages. The Allied advance from the west had written off that second intention, but by their second month on the march, all the POWs had been alive with lice. At night they had been herded into filthy, unheated barns, or cattle byres or pigsties, or any shelter they could find in the open, always without sanitation and with only the heavy snow shrouding the countryside for washing and shaving. They had had to take their own wounded along with them from the start; many more had fallen sick on the march; many had died, if not as many as might have been, had they not known they were marching towards their own side – and home.

He blinked rapidly at Sister Luke's sudden return. 'Enjoyed your tea, Captain Ashden – good! I'm afraid Dr Brown has been called back to Alexandra Ward. He asked me to suggest you wait for him in the residents' common room – still over the road in the Doctors'

House as you'll remember . . . Not at all! Great pleasure! Do come and see us again when you are next passing through London.'

Safe bet, I will! thought George, thanking her so warmly that Sister Luke later confided to Nurse Cotton that there was nothing like active service for turning an awkward boy into a nice young man.

George left Luke Ward in an euphoric trance that lasted until just after opening time when Paddy joined him in the 'hospital' pub that was about forty yards from and on the same side of the road, as the Doctors' House. Paddy had exchanged the white coat for an aged tweed, leather-patched jacket, and when he raced in George was having a 'welcome back on the house' pint with the landlord.

The latter set down his glass. 'Here he is, Mr Ashden. Wings on his feet same as always.'

'And needed, Ernie. Same again for Mr Ashden and a half for me, please. Sorry to keep you hanging about, George, and may heaven and the holy angels bless my boss. He's let me off the hook for an hour, providing – say no more! Never know who's listening. Thanks Ernie. Cheers.' Paddy flicked the forelock out of his right eye and smiled over his glass. 'Sorry to ditch you in Luke. How'd it go?'

George tried to be casual. He didn't succeed. 'Not at all bad, thanks. A rather smashing popsie in a sling fed me tea and sympathy. Nurse Mack-something I think she said her name was.

Mother of God, no wonder the poor chap now looks like he's won the war single-handed! He always fell hard for Ellie's type and panted over them from a distance – and who in hell am I to hold that against him? thought Paddy, momentarily staring into his glass, as if at an insoluble problem that his head had long accepted as such, but never – wholly – his heart.

He looked up smiling. 'Mackenzie. Elinor Mackenzie. Yes, she's a bit of all right and damned nice with it.' He needed a sip of beer before handing out the blow in the teeth. He detested giving bad news and whenever possible left this to others, but he recognised he had no way out and that the knock-out was the kindest. 'She's bright as hell, too. If her old man doesn't make it out of the bag I'd lay good money on her as a future Sister Alex or Sister Luke. Japs have had the poor sod since Singapore.'

George, mentally deafened by the explosion of a new-found dream, muttered, 'Poor sod.' He slapped himself mechanically for cigarettes though his packet of US Army issue was on the counter by his glass.

Paddy offered a crumpled blue-paper-wrapped packet of ten Players. Not just lost the war but finally catching on that there are no fairies at the bottom of the garden, he registered empathetically. He began reeling off the war histories of the men in their year, plugging the good news, censoring the bad.

He was still talking and George staring dumbly at a point in mid-air when the landlord answered the telephone at the back of the bar, laid down the ear-piece and joined them, sighing heavily.

'You'll know what I've got for you, Dr Brown.'

Paddy groaned. 'Wouldn't you know it. Alex or Cas, Ernie?'

'Cas, sir. The Senior Medical Officer's compliments and apologies but he's tied up in Alex and you're needed in Cas, sharpish.'

'Thanks, Ernie. Will you say I'm on my way. Finish

this for me, George and if I can't get back before you've to push off for King's Cross—'

'The next one's on me, Paddy.'

In September, 1945, three weeks after the Second World War ended, Elinor heard from the War Office that her husband had died of dysentery in a Japanese prison camp in Malaya in August, 1944.

THREE
Suez Canal
June 1955

The three-quarter moon rose slowly and hung low and the petrified white ocean of sand that lapped both banks of the canal, glowed like mother-of-pearl. The midnight convoy, in single-file, crept quietly through the oily, black water, and to Paddy, sitting alone in an upright chair at the boat-deck rail, the clean, dry, chilly night air was a necessary anodyne after the few hours in Port Said this afternoon. And as his eyes devoured the beauty and lungs inhaled the cleanliness of the desert, his mind was haunted by the dust and flies, the hordes of ragged ill-fed, importunate beggars, small boys pedalling obscenities, abject women shuffling along in dusty shrouding black, crippled beggar-children with sad adult eyes, babies with fly-encrusted faces and the appalling numbers of untreated cases of opthalmia, glaucoma, bilharzia, rickets and other diseases of malnutrition he had spotted in those few hours. His republican sympathies were wholly with Egypt's new republic; but the contrast between the grandiose houses and large, meringue-coloured American cars of the rich, and the dreadful, degrading poverty of the masses of the poor, had resulted in his spending most of his time ashore in a tight-lipped, raging temper. In comparison, he fumed mentally, those barefoot kids in Genoa live in paradise.

To the young Egyptian driver of the gharri he and George hired for a wider tour, paradise had arrived. At every new building and road under construction he waved his whip, ecstatically, 'Now we have Nasser – all this is for the people! Now ALL is for the people! Not like when we had Farouk!' And each time he mentioned the deposed king, he spat into the road.

Tonight at dinner and later in the lounge, the old-Africa-hands grudgingly allowed that for real filth and flies he should have seen Port Said when fat Farouk was on the throne. 'Got to hand it to that so-and-so Nasser. He is trying to clean-up Egypt – in more ways than one, no doubt.'

'But isn't Nasser reputed to be incorruptible?'

'My dear doctor – so they say. But with every respect, old chap, the day has yet to dawn when I'll believe that of any dictator. All cut from the same jib. You take Hitler and Mussolini. Got to admit Hitler got decent roads built and Musso got his trains running on time. Here's Nasser throwing up new buildings left, right and centre. Trust any tyrant to know the best way of putting the kybosh on counter-revolutions is to keep his chaps busy.'

Mrs Mellor put in, 'Can one really compare Gamal Abdal Nasser with those two criminals? After all, when he deposed Farouk in '52 there were no mass-arrests and executions and he allowed the king and his family to leave Egypt in dignity in the royal yacht. Would you say that to show clemency to those they defeated was a quality for which either Hitler or Mussolini were renowned?'

The old-Africa-hands smiled with the indulgence they regarded as due her sex and age and drifted away to the smoking-room bar, the bridge tables, the veranda café, and the games room where an impromptu table-tennis tournament for the younger set was about to begin.

Belinda Van der Mann, golden-haired and golden-skinned, lingered to flap her mascaraed eyelashes. 'Do come and umpire for us, Dr Brown, pleeease! I just wish you would and you must know the rules as you must've played before – I mean, everyone knows the rules.'

'It grieves me to disappoint you, Miss Van der Mann, but a closed book, no less. Alas for my lifelong allergy to rough games.'

George scowled into the empty glass he was about to put down. The hot little number had it coming. She couldn't know the poor chap had been Martha's best squash and tennis player, but she should have enough nous not to rub in the salt.

Belinda pouted prettily. 'Oh, well, if you won't, Dr Brown, I'll just have to rope in someone else.' Her luscious gaze rested perfunctorily upon George. 'No use asking you, Dr Ashden. Nothing'll drag you from your bridge game.'

She undulated enticingly away followed by the eyes of every man present, but only Paddy, a born actor, wore the indulgent smile the old-Africa-hands had just afforded Mrs Mellor.

Mrs Van der Mann clicked shut her lorgnette and turned confidingly, 'Such a perfect gentleman!'

Mrs Mellor looked up from studying her crochetwork. 'I'm sure you're right, dear. To whom do you refer?'

The slither of the water against the ship's sides made the sound of softly tearing silk, the slowly turning twin-screws hummed gently, the vibration of the deck was almost negligible, and from the darkness behind him came the occasional half-audible endearments, breathy fumblings and stifled giggles of the couples either – illicitly – huddled in the tarpaulin-shrouded lifeboats, or entwined in the shadows beneath. The unlit boat-deck at night was the acknowledged sanctuary of those involved in the transitory couplings that were as much a part of the passengers' lives on long sea voyages as the beef tea and dry biscuits served to them at eleven a.m. Tonight and every night, thought Paddy, calculating that certainly four and probably five couples were in his immediate vicinity, and according to Mrs Mellor, tomorrow night – back to square one. He grinned a little self-derisively at the green light on the stern of the ship ahead – and at the warning pill inside the spiced sugar.

'They always change partners after Port Said, Dr Brown. That happens every ten days at sea. The regularity is most remarkable, but understandable. The most ardent passions tend to cool after ten days close proximity with what, in reality, are total strangers. What's also remarkable,' Mrs Mellor continued, 'is the way most passengers leave their morals ashore when they come on board. I couldn't count the number of the happily married travelling alone that I've seen indulge in passionate shipboard attachments and later race joyously down the gangplank into the arms of their waiting spouses without one backward glance. Very few would have even contemplated such behaviour on land and some do get very hurt, particularly the lonely. But the combination of endless free time, being waited on hand and foot, sunshine, moonlight and duty-free liquor can prove irresistible to all but the strong-minded, or just old. I've seen much less of this on the Atlantic run, but it is so short and so often demands a strong stomach. The sudden need to throw up over the side is scarcely conducive to pleasurable dalliance, wouldn't you say?'

He laughed. 'I would, indeed.'

Mrs Mellor smiled. 'Fortunately, on this run at this time of the year now we're out of the Bay (of Biscay) we're unlikely to meet rough weather until well down the east African coast, if then. The monsoon season will be on, but we may miss them. I hope so. They spoil people's fun.'

'Mrs Mellor, you're a lady of tolerance and charity.'

'My dear young man, I am neither! I've seen far too much of the damage both can cause. If I had to approve all that amuses me, I'd be a sour old dragon. I've no objection to being a dragon and am deeply grateful to have lived long enough to be old, but I would object strongly to being soured. Embittered. Bitterness—' she paused looking at him searchingly 'is a boomerang. Keeps coming back, so one's friends start dropping away and though one's relatives may have to suffer it, they will do so as little as possible. What's far worse, is that one has to suffer oneself. Can you imagine a more unpleasant companion for life? Of course you can! This is one of the battles you've had to fight, isn't it?'

That unexpected insight jerked out the truth. 'Aside from your use of the wrong tense – *mea culpa*.'

'Most understandably.'

'No,' he said, 'no. Not as I'm qualified to know my own luck in re-achieving mobility. Gratitude should have written it off.'

'Yes, if you were a saint,' she retorted. 'I'm told they exist but never having met one keep an open mind on that. But I have observed that for the majority of the human race – including myself – gratitude can be both a burden and a bore. Frankly, Dr Brown, though happy to be grateful to the Almighty, I'd run a mile to avoid those to whom I owe most. Since I can no longer run – she smiled wickedly, 'I take long sea voyages.'

His face lit with laughter, and relief. 'Your honesty is as refreshing as your common sense.'

'I'm gratified you should think so. Most people do not.'

Not so mobile right now, he thought, easing back the chair to outstretch his stiffening, aching, legs. The couple of hours spent walking around before taking the gharri were sending the bill. A long soak in a hot salt water bath would fix them later. Plenty of time for baths; only now for this glory. He lit another cigarette but before he finished it heard quick steps coming up the nearest companionway and towards him over the deck. He glanced round and cursed mentally. He was in no mood for Nanny. 'Up for a spot of air, Doc? Good party ashore?'

'Er – yes, sir, and great, thanks.' Morgan came closer to add in a murmur inaudible from a yard away, 'Old Bert on the lift told me I might find you here after I tried your cabin. Could – er – could I have a word, please, sir?'

Paddy looked at him more closely. He was back in

uniform and had on his cap at the correct angle that he only assumed when escorting the Captain on his daily inspection of the ship. Paddy nodded before saying audibly, 'Thanks, Doc. Getting down in the dark is hellish trickier than getting up.'

'Any time, sir.' The automatic response hid Morgan's surprised relief that the poor crock had caught on so fast. He was very worried and the interview he had just requested and had with the Captain had been no anodyne.

They did not speak again until on the illuminated upper promenade deck and several yards from the nearest passengers leaning on the rail.

'Just come from the bridge, Doc?'

'Aye, aye, sir.' Morgan hesitated, then had to ask, 'How did you guess?'

'Spot diagnosis,' drawled Paddy to contain his impatience. Mother of God, boy, he thought, if I'd a quid for every time I heard – or made – that scream for help during my twelve years' hard as a Martha's resident I'd not be freeloading round Africa – I'd have bought the bloody ship. 'My cabin first, as it's only one deck down, your surgery's two and presumably—' he tilted his head at the shining desert, 'a few more minutes won't signify. Damn all you can do about putting a patient ashore until out of the canal.'

'Damn all,' echoed Morgan absently. He was struggling to adjust to this reversal of their previous relationship. Though an intelligent, conscientious young doctor, he was still too inexperienced to be aware that he shared with most doctors the patronising element within their paternal – or maternal – attitudes to their patients and from Tilbury he had bracketed Paddy in this category. He knew the latter's prestigious higher qualifications and former appointments, but as he had been on the scrapheap for over two years, was so easy going and – through no fault of his own – lethargic, he had seemed to Morgan one of those lightweights that were somehow good at exams and had the knack of hitting it off with those in high places, that in Benedict's, as most British teaching hospitals, often resulted in their getting the high-powered jobs over more deserving heads. And, of course, being Irish and not subject to being called-up for the war or National Service had given him a head-start in Martha's since he qualified. But as he was the only consultant physician on board – and even he, Morgan, had better qualifications than Ashden – sheer desperation had made him ask the Captain's permission to consult him.

They went on in silence and during the short descent in the lift Bert, the liftman, who like the Captain, First Officer, purser and majority of the older crew, had served in the Royal Navy during the war, pretended to be an automaton and pleasurably tossed up between cholera and black water fever. Plain to him as the nose on his face that the young shaver had not got his nibs in tow for a bit of fluff from tourist with Gyppy Tummy.

They left the lift at the Reception Hall on the lower promenade deck where Paddy's cabin was the first on the right down the port-side inner corridor. A minute private vestibule, off which lay the small bathroom, opened into the fairly spacious cabin furnished with solid mahogany, brass-knobbed, fitted wardrobe-cum-dressing closet and dressing-table, well-sized single beds, not bunks, and two large chintz-covered arm-chairs. Morgan closed the vestibule and cabin doors and checked that the smallish window in the bulkhead that overlooked the deck was closed before opening his mouth.

'Before the request I wish to make, sir, I've got to give you a message from the Captain. The Captain presents his compliments and particular assurances that you are under no obligation to—'

'Thanks. Taken as read.' Paddy switched on two air-blowers, sat on the bed against the deck-side bulkhead and waved Morgan to the spare against the inner. This was no moment for demonstrating the difficulty he had getting out of armchairs. 'What ails whom and is bugging you as you don't think it's what it looks like?'

Stone the bloody crows, next he'll call me 'laddie', thought Morgan, with such an unexpected upsurge of relief that his anxious face looked younger. He perched on the edge and dropped his cap on the bed.

'She's a young woman from tourist that I've just admitted to the ship's hospital.' (Two four-berthed sick-bays that adjoined the surgery.) 'She looks like an acute peritonitis probably caused by an appendix abscess. Appendix *in situ*, no question of pregnancy and I'll swear she's not a food-poisoning.' Paddy nodded and pulled off the sweater he had put on to go up on the boat-deck. 'Specifically, sir – she is a Mrs Irene Valerie Venner, age twenty-one, British, C. of E., travelling alone to Mombassa to join her husband. No kids yet. Venner works in a bank in Nairobi and is coming down to meet her.' He paused and pushed a hand through his short dark hair. 'As I've said, she looks a typical surgical emergency but I'm not convinced that she is and would very much like a physician to look at her, so—'

'Of course.' Paddy lit a cigarette and threw over the case and lighter. 'Go on.'

'Thanks, sir.' Morgan lit up, got up to return the articles and glanced at the neatly stacked books that converted to a bookshelf the top of the low dressing-table bolted to the bulkhead between the two bedheads. He had seen the books daily on the Captain's inspections but never before bothered to notice the titles. Some were classic and modern novels, others recent editions of medical textbooks. Being a fair-minded young man – and a fast learner – he sat down again wanting to kick himself. He gave in lucid detail his very thorough examination of Mrs Venner.

Paddy's quick, dark eyes narrowed. 'Give me the pulse and respirations again.'

Morgan's eyes quickened. 'Yes. Bugging me too, sir. But the poor kid is dead scared – she seems a very young twenty-one – never been out of England before, only married five months, never been in hospital and is scared of doctors and nurses and terrified of being left behind in a hospital in Egypt. Also—' he shrugged helplessly, 'she is thick as three planks.'

'Blind terror can have that effect, Morgan.'

'Actually, I haven't overlooked that, but – hell, sir! Beat this. She now admits to feeling lousy all yesterday and having a "nasty little tummy pain on and off, Doctor".' Did she come to the surgery or send for me or Sister? One of us is always on call and on board in port. Not she. All yesterday she lived it up with her gang and last night went midnight bathing "to cool off a bit, Doctor".' Paddy momentarily closed his eyes. 'She shares a cabin with three Rhodesian girls going home from holidays in the UK. All travelling alone – quite a bunch in tourist – and solid wood between the ears. This morning Mrs Venner horsed ashore with them soon as we berthed and didn't get back until an hour before sailing when she was in such a bad way they almost had to carry her to their cabin. Still didn't strike 'em to shout for medical aid. They'd convinced themselves all that ailed her was too much sun and gin and that she'd be fine after sleeping it off.' He paused to collect his thoughts and watch Paddy put on a tie and dark jacket. 'Luckily they've got chummy with a sensible type sharing the next cabin with three English girls going out to new jobs in Nairobi. Typists, I think. Anyway, Mrs Mackenzie heard the row next door, looked in, and promptly sent two for me or Sister, got rid of the other and Mrs Venner into her bunk. I'd just come back on board so Sister West and I went along together.' He smiled wanly. 'Probably still be there if Mrs Mackenzie hadn't managed to persuade Mrs Venner that as soon as I had her in a hospital bed I wouldn't pick up a knife with one hand and slap on an anaesthetic mask with the other.' He was too absorbed to notice that again Paddy's eyes had narrowed. 'I whistled up a stretcher and got her into hospital. At least no problem there. Pro tem she's our only bed-patient.'

Paddy nodded non-committally. 'How does she know there might be a possibility of her being taken off to a hospital ashore?'

Morgan gave another helpless shrug. 'Her idiot oppos (friends) were hanging about outside when we wheeled her out and one began blurting it out until silenced by a look from Mrs Mackenzie that would've shattered a pyramid at fifty paces.'

'Useful old body.'

'Damn useful to us tonight, sir, though not exactly old. Actually,' a momentary smile touched Morgan's anxious eyes 'rather decorative. War-widow, I think.

But to get back to Mrs Venner – the Captain says that if in my professional opinion she requires major surgical treatment he'll arrange to stop the ship at Suez and have her taken to a shore hospital. I had to tell him I wasn't yet ready to give my opinion as I'm not sure of her diagnosis. Whilst he digested this in silence, I asked his permission to consult you.' He tugged unhappily at his hair. 'I'm afraid the Captain's not best pleased with me. I can see his angle. The Owners aren't too keen on those that ring up unnecessary harbour dues – but I'm even less keen to hand over a patient in this set-up until I'm convinced it's necessary, and I'm not.'

'Nor would I be from what you've given me.' Paddy paused for thought and Morgan had the impression of seeing the brain ticking over in the dark eyes. 'It could be any of several different diagnoses. Query acute abdos can be so hellish tricky to diagnose correctly that it was a Martha's rule that all had to be seen on admission by a physician and surgeon. And from what you've given me, she could as easily be medical as surgical. Well, now—' He reached for his stick, stood up, combed his hair and took a worn briefcase from the bottom drawer of the dressing table. He pulled out his old stethoscope, pushed it into one jacket pocket, and the familiar gesture gave him the sensation of a small, not unpleasant, electric shock. 'Let's take a look at her,' he said, and as they left together for the second time in the last several minutes, for a split-second his mind returned to the British War Cemetery in Genoa.

About an hour later Paddy left the surgery on his own and looked up and down the long, narrow, empty inner starboard corridor of B-deck that at the far end led to the lift and stairs and at the shorter, to heavy, metal deck doors opening on to the tourists' deck. It

was just after two a.m. and from the quiet, the occupants of the first-class cabins lining that corridor had
retired for the night. He looked up and down again,
then limped to the metal doors and out on to the deck
and into moonlight so bright that it dimmed the gentle
deck lighting.

The middle of the stern half of that deck was blocked
by the tourists' reception room and the swimming pool
beyond, and the lights streaming from the former
further illuminated the strips of open deck that on both
sides ran round to the stern. There was no sound of
voices nor sign of anyone else around and he backed
to sit on a high-backed, wooden-slatted settle bolted
against the bulkhead a few feet to the left of the doors
he had used. Directly in line with the settle was the
nearest starboard companionway running up from the
tourists' cabins on A-deck; another was parallel on the
port side and the heads of both were lighted. He looked
from one to the other, and again all round, and then
his gaze was diverted to the exquisite panorama of the
desert now in such brightness that the barely percep-
tible movement of the dunes was visible.

Shifting sands, he thought, but not just shifting times
in medicine, a couple of avalanches. Penicillin in '44;
the antibiotics in '48.

'It's the acute pneumonia in her lower left lobe and
the localised diaphragmatic pleurisy that's responsible
for the similarity to the clinical picture of an acute per-
itoneal inflammation. Your medical instincts were on
the ball. She isn't surgical.'

'Thanks, sir, thanks very much. Thank God it's only
pneumonia and a touch of pleurisy.'

'And for the antibiotics.'

'Oh – er – yes, sir. I suppose things must've been a bit dodgy before you had 'em or penicillin.'

Just a bit, he thought. Just enough to freeze the blood at that diagnosis when pneumonia was one of the greatest killers in and out of hospitals and so frequently fatal in the elderly that it was called 'the old man's friend'. But he had said nothing of this to Morgan having long learnt how incomprehensible it was to anyone qualified since 1948 just how much those two towering allies had revolutionised modern medicine. Had I attempted to explain, he thought, and thrown in, 'this is why I'm on this ship tonight,' he'd have trundled me back to my cabin in a wheelchair.

His mind returned to the relief in Mrs Venner's very pretty, greyish, tear-stained, childish face, and he felt again the inexpressible pleasure of being able to make the kind of firm diagnosis that removed a patient's worst fears. That pleasure and the brief recall to his profession had left him much less tired than earlier. And he dwelt intentionally on the past hour to avoid thinking of his present in a part of the ship he had not visited before.

It was a strict shipboard rule backed by the conventions of the old British Empire that still obtained on board, that passengers should not trespass out from their respective classes. This rule was scrupulously obeyed by all the first-class passengers and the majority in tourist. The minority was solely composed of the young women travelling on their own or with girl-friends, who joyously discovered that, if only after dark, and with the assistance of one of the junior officers off-watch and co-operation of his peers, the rule could be safely circumnavigated to ensure their attendance at the parties one or other of the juniors held almost nightly in his cabin. The cloak-and-dagger element enhanced everyone's pleasure and, though well-known to their seniors, was largely overlooked as, owing to the proximity to their own cabins, these parties were innocuous as church-hall bun-fights.

Paddy had obeyed all the shipboard rules with a stringency those who had known him in youth would have found incredible, and that owed far more to his continuous consciousness of being a guest on the *Rose* than to his physical condition or any change in his character. He knew very well that no one on board would now object to his trespassing. It was over twenty minutes since Morgan, looking downright schoolboyish in triumphant relief, had left to report to the Captain and he had finished the cup of tea pressed upon him by the beaming young nursing sister. It was a safe assumption all the ship's company not asleep now knew how he had spent the last hour and Mrs Venner's diagnosis, and that it had already reached all still up in both classes. His using the nearest open deck for a short rest before returning to his cabin wouldn't raise one eyebrow.

He held up his watch to the moonlight. Two-fifteen.

'. . . and she insists on coming back to ask after Mrs Venner tonight, though I tactfully suggested the morning would do just as well, Dr Brown, but we all know what patients' relatives and friends are like . . .'

Had Sister put her off? Not if she was Ellie. No nice kid half a dozen years her junior would deflect Ellie in this context. And it could have been her back in Genoa. That had been her walk – figure – legs – black hair, he recognised in hindsight, and whether or not she then knew he was on the *Rose*, for both their sakes she would have walked on by. That was neither the time nor place for the big reunion scene, he thought guardedly, but the guard was not strong enough to prevent his face from turning rigid and in the moonlight presenting a black and white caricature of a man in great pain.

In Genoa it had not occurred to him to associate the young woman walking towards the steps with Elinor Mackenzie, as a self-defensive amnesial block had, from the last Monday in October, 1952, removed her and the preceding weekend from his thoughts. Suddenly, the block had evaporated but, as ever, memory was selective. He recalled that weekend to the last minute he had spent with Elinor, but not that the Saturday afternoon on which he had been admitted to Luke's only single-bedded small-ward as a query acute influenza under observation, had come exactly five weeks before his intended wedding day. But if he had remembered this it would have been only with the sardonic amusement afforded by the Christmas cards he had received for the last two years from his ex-fiancée and her husband.

In the early afternoon of that last Monday in October, 1952, pathological confirmation of the revised diagnosis of poliomyelitis had reached Luke and in the early evening he had been transferred to a London fevers' hospital, as Martha's, being a general hospital, was not allowed to treat diagnosed notifiable disease. Elinor had gone with him in the ambulance and worn a white linen face mask and long-sleeved white surgical gown over her new sister's uniform. Throughout the journey she had sat by him, holding his hand, imperceptibly taking his pulse and watching the rise and fall of the little green rubber bag attached to the base of his green rubber oxygen mask, and from time to time gently stroking the damp forelock from his hot forehead and burning, aching, fever-glazed eyes. When the ambulance finally slowed to its final stop, her hand-clasp had tightened and she leant over him and looked into his eyes as she whispered, 'I have to leave you now, Paddy. I'll be seeing you. You'll do. You will! I know you!'

A few hours after being lifted out of the ambulance he had felt himself being lifted into an iron-lung. He had never before let himself recall the throttling panic and terror that had then gripped his informed mind despite a crashing headache, soaring temperature and drugs. His eyes squeezed shut, his forehead and upper lip glistened in the moonlight and his whole body tensed, as that of a patient in too terrible pain to risk breathing, and he needed a conscious effort of will to reach for a handkerchief and open his eyes. It was then that he saw Elinor slowly emerging from the nearest companionway.

FOUR
Red Sea
June 1955

'Elinor Mackenzie,' reiterated George, as if thinking in another language. He mopped his heavy, red, dripping face. 'When did you say her husband bought it?'

'Sometime in '44.' Paddy flat on his back on his bed under the window blew a smoke-ring. 'She only heard after the war.'

'Bloody hell.'

'Yep.'

George got off the side of the spare bed to pour himself another glass of water from the vacuum mug that an hour ago had been refilled with iced water. It was now tepid and the clean bath towel George had been sitting on for the past few minutes to protect the white cotton quilt was soaked with sweat. Paddy's cabin was presently one of the coolest places in the ship. The window was wide open, all the air-blowers were full on at COLD, and the cabin's temperature was 99°F. Outside it was 125°F in the shade.

They had just come from lunch and Paddy had used this first opportunity to tell George in private of this meeting with Elinor three nights ago. George's addiction to bridge and dislike of mixed company and Paddy's preference for the latter and passion for reading his illness had finally allowed him to indulge, were resulting in their meeting mainly at meals and for pre-dinner drinks. This suited both since, as so often when friends in youth meet again in maturity, the more they saw of each other the more they recognised that the mined gap between them could only be traversed with a care that was hard to maintain in the inescapable proximities of shipboard life and particularly in the blistering, draining heat of the hot season in the Red Sea on an un-air-conditioned south-bound vessel whose maximum speed of fifteen knots equalled that of the prevailing north-south wind.

Paddy had just sounded as if the meeting lasted a couple of minutes. In reality it was over thirty before Elinor's, 'Paddy, I should push off to the surgery and then get below decks with the good news. The poor kids are in a terrible tiz.' She rose quickly from the settle and stood smiling at him and looking to him as young, but much prettier than in her girlhood. The new chrysanthemum hair-cut, the light woollen-lace scarlet stole over her pale bare arms and tight-waisted full-skirted black seersucker dress enhanced her femininity and gave her an elegance that he had never seen in her before. 'It's lovely to see you again and sweet of you to hang around with the good news.'

'I had to, Ellie.' He stood up. 'I had to find out if you

were you. I'm so glad I did.' He waved at the moonlit desert. 'Not precisely where we came in.'

'No bread-bin,' she said and in the moonlight they exchanged a smile that, momentarily for both, demolished twelve years.

'Before you vanish, am I right in thinking you haven't told Morgan or Sister you're trained?'

She nodded. 'Kiss of death if I had. Where's the young medic or nurse that wants to know an ex-ward sister's watching from the sidelines?' She looked around. 'No one seems to have come by, but as someone's bound to have seen us nattering, I'll tell Sister that we met in Martha's in the war. Thanks again and sleep well.'

'And you, Ellie. See you around.'

She had turned to go, but turned back smiling. 'Across the barricades. I'll bring my knitting and you bring the food-parcels.'

He laughed and she disappeared through the heavy metal doors, without, he noted, having made one reference to his present health, past illness, or the ship's call at Genoa.

George sat back on the side of the bed. 'Was she one of your old flames?'

Paddy stubbed out. 'No.'

'Then how in hell did you remember my running into her in '45?'

'I didn't. She reminded me about it after I'd told her you were on board.'

George scowled. 'Why in hell should she remember me?'

Paddy looked at him for a few seconds and thought of Elinor's, '. . . reminded me of Alistair.' He said, 'You had just got out of the bag and she didn't then know that her husband was six feet deep.'

George's scowl deepened. 'Should've worked that out. Too bloody hot.' He hesitated. 'Why hasn't she married again?'

Paddy shrugged. 'I never saw much of her after the war. She vanished first to do midder for a couple of years and then to staff in Hope down at the Hut. I started running into her again when she shifted back to take over as Sister Luke in the summer of '52, but then I was no longer in residence.' He grinned reminiscently. 'She was one hell of a break for the medical side after old Sister Luke and a bloody good medical nurse.'

'Then why pack in Martha's?'

'No alternative to resigning after her mother-in-law's first massive cerebral last year. Ellie and her old man were onlies, her own parents died either just before or early in the war, her mother-in-law was a widow, they were each others only close relatives and I always gathered, pretty fond of each other. The old lady eventually died this March. Ellie was still dealing with the aftermath, and I'd say whacked on all counts after home-nursing a paraplegic for fourteen months, when one of her old set cabled an invitation to come out to the Cape for her tenth wedding anniversary and stay on for a couple of months. Ellie was her matron-of-honour and is the godmother of her eldest kid. She told me that she hadn't had a holiday in ages and always wanted to see Africa, she thought – why not? – cabled back by return and got cracking.' He fell silent, then thought aloud, 'Another on the run.'

'Run?'

Paddy felt the outline of the mine under his foot.

'The Africa Run on the good ship *Rose* plying her trade ferrying exiles to and from the Empire.'

'Huh! Bugger-all left. South Africa's out this year. Kenya's on the skids. This Mau-Mau business is just the tip of the iceberg. Once Kenya goes, Uganda and Tanganyika'll follow suit.'

'You'll still have Rhodesia and Aden.'

'Christ, who wants Aden?' George mopped his neck, 'If she's sharing with three others two decks down their cabin must be the Black Hole of Calcutta.'

'Dante's inferno, no less,' Paddy drawled. His mind returned to the problem he had been working on since handed an item of shipboard news with his morning tea.

George shot him an irritated glance. 'I suppose she had to go tourist.'

'Literally, she said. This was the last ship from London that could get her there on time and she booked too late to get a first.'

'Tell that one to the Marines!'

Paddy looked at him quickly and recalled the odd note in Elinor's voice when explaining this point. 'Think so?'

'God, yes! Women'll tell any lie to save face. Can't bear to admit being skint. Unless the old girl left her a packet – and doesn't sound likely as she obviously couldn't afford a nursing home – she's bound to be on her uppers. She can't have saved anything out of the pittance nurses earn and won't have much of a pension. What was her husband?'

'Captain. Gunners or Sappers. Forget which.'

'Huh! Without kids she'll be lucky if she gets two quid a week. Probably less. If you ask me,' added George dogmatically, 'she's off to the Cape to hook another husband. Bound to be getting desperate now she's getting long in the tooth.'

'Younger than us. Thirty-three.'

'Different for chaps. All women are over the hill at thirty,' insisted George. He needed the reassurance of that long-held conviction. He was sweating as if after a hard game of squash, his chest burnt with prickly heat, the bath towel was chaffing the backs of his bare legs and he was perplexed and infuriated by his inability to stop talking about the wretched woman. Bloody tough luck – bloody bad show – but these things happened and anyway water long under the bridge. And aside from this Godawful heat, life on the old *Rose* was bloody good value – first-rate grub, decent chaps, wizard bridge, no post-mortems from his partner nor catty remarks and sulks about his playing late into the night, skipping breakfast and having a good lie-in – if not pro tem as the heat in his B-deck starboard cabin was having him under a shower at sunrise. He was sorry for any wretched popsie having to sweat it out on A-deck, but no concern of his.

He glared at Paddy's prone figure. They had both changed for lunch, but where his shirt and shorts were already hugely sweat-stained and crumpled, Paddy's short-sleeved, open-necked white cotton shirt and white cotton trousers only looked limp. And though his grey hair, deeply-tanned face and arms could have been oiled, he was so relaxed that his face looked younger. George reminded himself of the heat's ability to relax muscular tension, and that he needed the reminder heightened his irritation with the temperature in general and Paddy in particular for running into the wretched popsie.

'I need a wash.' He stood up holding the shirt from his chest. 'Use your bathroom?'

'Help yourself.'

'Thanks. Next time out I'm booking a billet with one. Only another twenty-five pounds on the ticket, isn't it?'

'Thereabouts.'

'Worth it.'

'Why not fly to Johannesburg and on by short hops?'

'Hell of a long haul by air. Prefer the sea when not frying to a crisp.' George glared around the cabin. On the first morning out from Genoa he had heard the first-class' explanation of Paddy's round-Africa trip without comment having had Paddy's version the night before. It had not occured to him to wonder how Paddy, in his present circumstances, could afford the £500 ticket, as even though in youth they had been equally impover-ished, owing to the inate lack of self-confidence conse-quent upon being the averagely intelligent son of an academically brilliant and adored father, he always assumed his contemporaries were earning far more than he and probably subsidised by private incomes. He had long-forgotten – if he had ever taken it in – that Paddy had been the fourth son and child of his late parents' eight children and self-supporting since the day he qualified.

He said abruptly, 'Trust you to get old John Whatsit to pull a string. You always were crafty as a cart-load of monkeys.'

Paddy ignored the charge and waved languidly at the spare bed. 'If you want to kip down on it, go ahead.'

'Not in this heat. Kip down and I wake with a mouth like an old sock and a cracking head. Best on the move.' George backed out to the bathroom.

Paddy glanced after him, turned the hot wet pillow under his head and lay back listening to the salt water rushing from the bath's cold tap which from the accompanying stream of blasphemies, was running hot. And for the next few moments he thought upon mad dogs and Englishmen and what the English would do when they had no colonies left to retreat to and the chips were down at home, and Elinor's face in the moonlight. 'I need this break, Paddy. I need time to think out what I want to do with my life. I thought I'd have plenty of time for that on the voyage, but—' and she laughed 'not for the first time – I was wrong . . .'

The ship had entered the Red Sea on the night before last and from early yesterday morning the boat-deck had been awned, but only before breakfast or after sunset could Paddy tolerate the heat up there. All day yesterday, as today, the power of the sun had cleared sunbathers from the open decks around the swimming pools that few used before nightfall. Only up to mid-morning and exclusively on the port side were deck-chairs in daylight use and the limply slumped occu-pants, if first-timers-out, belatedly recognised that com-monsense and not snobbery, underlay the old maxim of Empire exiles sailing to and from India and the Antipodes; Portside Out, Starboard Home.

Now before every meal in both dining saloons clean towels were spread on the chairs of the ship's officers to save the seats of their 'whites' being stained by the red leather and face-mopping had become an accepted social convention. And even at dinner in the first-class, sartorial elegance was as rare as a male passenger's tie. The majority of the men wore short-sleeved, open-necked cotton shirts loose over knee-length shorts; all the women and teenage girls had abandoned shorts and slacks for their loosest cotton dresses over a minimum of underwear and only used face powder. Foundation cream, rouge, mascara and lipstick smeared within minutes of application.

'We are now seen without artifice, Dr Brown, and only in the Red Sea,' confided Mrs Mellor on this second morning in the Red Sea, 'am I seen without my corsets. Oh, the relief of getting them off!' She waved to and fro the large, painted paper fan in one hand and mopped her face with the handkerchief in the other and wore a navy, cotton, sleeveless tent floating from her shoulders and just a wedding ring. 'How fortunate you are to tan like a Latin.'

'The less kind would say to be thick-skinned.'

'Very probably. The world is full of fools.' She smiled benignly at the young nursing sister coming in through the hooked-open door. 'Don't let me keep you, Doctor! Here's Sister.'

Mrs Mellor always breakfasted in her cabin and on the morning the ship left the canal and anchored briefly in the Bitter Lakes, Mrs Van der Mann, fresh from the hands of Mavis in the ship's hairdressers, came in with the news of what had transpired in the night.

'. . . and Mavis says he's one of the best chest men in London . . . yes, Harley Street . . . no, he wouldn't have told you – great men are so modest! . . . Yes, just pneumonia that Mavis says these anti-whatever they are will clear up in a few days – wonderful what doctors can do these days – and it seems this little Mrs Venner is really very attractive and has been turning all the men's heads in tourist! I'm afraid she sounds a little fast – but isn't it intriguing!'

'In what way, dear?'

'Well – of course we all know how careful doctors have to be about these things, but as he hasn't taken up with one girl since we sailed and my Belinda says that though he couldn't be more gentlemanly she's sure he is a wolf in sheep's clothing . . . you know how girls talk! And he is so attractive . . . well . . . men are men.'

'So I have observed. And that Mavis has given you a very nice firm set. Will you forgive me if I now go along to see if she can fit me in today?'

About an hour later Mrs Mellor was amused and the lounge disappointed by the sight of Dr Brown and Sister West sharing a sofa and iced lime-and-sodas.

Mrs Van der Mann lowered her lorgnette in dismay. 'So that's the way the wind's blowing!' Then she brightened. 'The Third Officer won't like it.'

Mrs Venner was making the expected rapid recovery and Dr Morgan kept Paddy informed of her progress, but as he had not requested it, Paddy had not again visited the women's sick-bay that now had a second patient, a Mrs Agnew from 'first'. And by this morning his new friendship with Sister West had ceased to interest the lounge unless the Third Officer happened to look in when he was discreetly watched in the hope of seeing him grinding his teeth.

'I've no sympathy with the Third,' said Mrs Van der Mann. 'He has no business to be chasing an engaged girl and I'm sure she's given him no encouragement. Far too nice and sensible and really quite attractive in a way,' she allowed in a tone that implied that way lacked sex-appeal, since as many women, but no men, she equated feminine sex-appeal with beauty.

Mrs Stevens, a youngish, widowed grandmother who shared a cabin with Mrs Agnew, said archly, 'Dr

Brown seems to think so. And how nice to see him feeling strong enough to enjoy himself a little.'

Mrs Mellor nodded benignly and thought of her second husband.

Across the lounge, Paddy laughed. 'The whole pack, Sister?'

'In full cry, Dr Brown,' replied Sister West in her quiet, brisk voice. She was twenty-seven and had the healthy, open, tanned face and lithe sturdiness of a young games mistress and exuded efficiency and an aura of impeccable rectitude that particularly endeared her to the female passengers. This was her third voyage on the *Rose of Africa* and in September she was resigning to marry a young farmer and friend from childhood. She sat straight-backed, her knees and feet together, capable hands in the lap of her white American-style uniform, and the flowing white muslin Army cap framing her neat fairish head and shiny tanned face. 'Now our glamour girl's temp. is normal and she's allowed visitors I've every wolf in tourist and the ship's company yowling at the surgery door. Mrs Agnew's sprained ankle is my salvation. Means I only have to pop in and out to chaperon. Even so, I only let 'em in in pairs.'

'Very prudent, Sister. Another?'

'Thanks awfully, my kidneys would adore it!' And when their drinks were replenished, 'Honestly, Doctor, though, as I've told you, she's a good patient, she's so dumb it's not true! She thinks the chaps are all being ever so kind!' He grinned. 'She honestly doesn't know she's the hottest little trick on the *Rose*. When she hits Kenya she'll leave the Mau-Mau standing – my heart bleeds for hubby. You know what they say on the east-African coast. "Are you married or do you live in

Kenya?" ' She sipped more lime then looked professionally down her nose to add, 'I even had Mrs Mackenzie's missionaries in the queue last evening.'

She had never before mentioned Elinor to him, but being metaphorically on home territory, Paddy demanded eagerly, 'Missionaries? New one on me. Tell me all, Sister! How many has she got?'

Sister West smiled professionally and mentally nodded. She and Bill Morgan had agreed that those two could never have been more than ships that pass in the night, or Mrs Mackenzie wouldn't have let out about knowing him. Who anywhere wanted to dig up their murky past? And as he not only was the Owners' oppo but had the Old Man' ear, no careless talk on this one.

She said, faintly apologetically, 'Only two, Dr Brown. Nice old chaps. They're going back from home leave to their mission stations in up-country Uganda. They've been in Africa years and are yellow as Japs, poor dears – recurrent malaria and probably black water fever. Our glamour girl,' she went on chattily, encouraged by his amused interest, 'says those three ganged up at Gib and always go around together and that Mrs Mackenzie must be a missionary-type as she doesn't drink or go to parties. Was she a religious type in Martha's?'

He shrugged. 'I honestly don't know. Martha's used to be a rather religious hospital – every time Big Ben struck eight all the ward nurses fell on their knees for morning or evening prayers – but I never saw all that much of her. We'd been knocked about and the nurses kept coming and going between London and our evacuated branches. But now I think back, no, I don't remember her as a party girl.' He offered cigarettes and when, as always in uniform, she shook her head, lit his own.

70

'From what you've told me, tourists go in for parties in a big way.'

'Non-stop, even in this heat. My heart bleeds for Mrs Mackenzie sharing with three of the wildest in a wild bunch. But harmless wild. On the whole.' She flicked from her bib pocket the watch that with her engagement ring was pinned to the inside. 'Oh, woe! Do forgive me, but must cast off. Passengers' noon surgery in ten minutes and we'll be innundated again with prickly heats, burnt soles of feet, incipient heat-exhaustions – they won't remember not to play in bare feet on hot decks and to take their salt tablets – stiff necks – seven at this morning's surgery! Never remember not to sit or sleep directly in the path of their blowers – peeling faces, shoulders, backs – you name it, Dr Brown – it's peeling. Thanks awfully for the limes! My kidneys adored them! Please don't budge – cheery-bye!'

After George left, Paddy spent some time cursing the ship for having no inter-passenger telephone system. But the *Rose of Africa* had been built in an era when passengers no more expected private telephones and air-conditioning in their cabins than in the bedrooms of their homes. The recognised methods of inter-passenger communication were either to go along in person to the other's cabin, send a verbal message or note with a cabin steward, or hand in the last at the assistant purser's office, and since all had roughly the effect of putting it out over the Tannoy, to use any to contact Elinor would make her the automatic target of gossip in both classes. But, somehow, he must talk to her privately and today – Mother of God! The heat was softening his brain! That announcement during lunch meant a general post tonight!

'. . . will be held as usual after dinner on the upper promenade deck for the benefit of all first-class and tourist-class passengers. We hope you will all come and enjoy *Rose Marie* in glorious technicolour starring Howard Keel and Anne Blythe and as it may have slipped your minds, ladies and gentlemen, the chilly white stuff you'll see lying about in the film is called snow.' The assistant purser's voice paused for the expected laughter. 'The film will be shown in the customary two parts with a fifteen-minute interval. Thank you, ladies and gentlemen.'

And this, thought Paddy, after sinking enough straight limes to rejoice my kidneys and refloat the *Titanic*. He fell asleep smiling and was still smiling when woken at five by Dixon, his cabin steward, coming in to refill the vacuum jug.

'You've had a good kip, sir.' Dixon's lined, leathery face was greyish and glistening above the hooked collar of his spruce white jacket. 'Always best to kip off the heat same as the Arabs. Know what's what, they do, and should seeing as it's their sun.'

Dixon dealt with the jug then unnecessarily straightened the books on the dressing-table that were his particular pride. During the war when the *Rose* had been a troopship, Dixon had served in the Royal Navy, but in all, pre- and post-war he had had fifteen years on the *Rose*. But not once afore, he told his oppo, Dusty, on the starboard cabins, had he had a single 'first' with the more than the one or two books from the ship's library. But this run never the once fetched in the early tea without catching his bloke with his nose in one from his own bleeding library. No surprise to him what the lads was now saying of his being one of the Harley Street nobs. He could've told 'em and that for all he was the Owners' oppo, being a proper gentleman, no side to him, nor leaving off his tie for dinner nor his underpants now it was on the warm side – which was more than he could say for most this bumped-up lot in 'first' that by rights should be down 'tourist' seeing the old *Rose* didn't carry passengers steerage.

'Good picture tonight, sir. I see it last time round. Going to take the look or give it the miss same as the last two?'

'I'd seen both of them but not this new version of *Rose Marie*. Maybe I'll watch from the pool.'

'Not see much from there, sir, seeing the operator's platform that's going up now backs on it. But a nice bit of music for a hot night.'

'Scorcher like last?'

'Got to expect that till we're round the Horn of Africa, sir. Cool down a mite then. Not that that'll worry the sharks.'

'Many in the Indian Ocean?'

'And the Red Sea, sir. Shadowing us like U-boats they are. Nasty things, sharks. Nasty minds.'

Paddy's lips twitched. 'And teeth, I'm told?'

'You never said a truer word, sir. What them teeth can do—' Dixon shook his balding head and launched into a detailed anatomical description of the limbs and lives former shipmates had lost to sharks. 'Not as there's need to worry, sir. Never lost the one passenger to a shark, has the old *Rose*. Run the cold bath for you now, sir? If you leave it the mite it'll cool to tepid.'

'Thanks, Dixon. That'll be fine.'

Dixon vanished to the bathroom leaving Paddy wondering whether Dixon's attempt to lower the temperature by chilling the blood and the purser's choice of tonight's film were fortuitous, or calculated psychiatric therapy. And then, as sleep had cleared his mind, he wondered if what he hoped to arrange for Elinor would eventually prove the right or wrong therapy, and not only for her. And the flash of personal insight provided by that ambiguous conclusion so absorbed him that unthinkingly he swung his legs to the floor and stood up on bare feet and went into the bathroom.

Dixon watched woodenly until alone in the cabin when he winked at the stick jammed between the used bedhead and dressing-table before stripping off the damp bottom sheet and pillowcase and replacing them with clean.

The huge screen was hoisted above the open entrance to the veranda café that was in darkness for the performance to avoid the lights distracting the audience in the deckchairs ranged on the open deck. The geometrically straight rows were divided by a middle aisle and flanked by strips of deck running round to the swimming pool at the aft end. Once the film started the deck lights in that portion would be turned off. These were already lowered when the audience began arriving to enhance the impression of an auditorium before the curtain rises. And overhead the navy-blue, star-massed sky was alive with distant sheet-lightning and the golden streaks of falling meteors. The ship was at full speed and the hot night air motionless; the sea was smooth, black satin and in the ship's wake the white foam split the blackness like a Roman road in the making.

Mesdames Mellor, Van der Mann and Stevens were early arrivals and being experienced shipboard filmgoers chose seats near the aisle in the third row from the back as these provided excellent views of the screen and the audience coming round the deck from the first-class and up the nearest companionways from the decks below. Mrs Mellor, the oldest, took the aisle seat, and settled back to watch the incomers whilst her companions continued discussing the problems of the white settlers in Kenya. Mrs Stevens and Mrs Agnew were amongst the little group of widowed grandmothers in 'first' going out to open-ended visits in Kenya at the request of their married children with young families.

'It was only when my son wrote asking me to come out,' said Mrs Stevens, 'that I realised what a difficult time they are having. My son says these dreadful Mau-Mau attacks on isolated farms are increasing and he and Isobel are constantly on edge and his heart is in his mouth when he has to leave her with the baby. But he has to get on with his work on the farm and he says what is so sad is that they had always thought they got on well with their house-boys and farm-workers. But now he daren't trust any, as if they've taken this secret oath and they can't help themselves. I don't know what he means by that but—'

'Good gracious!' Mrs Mellor interrupted. 'Our clerical movie fans have acquired a girlfriend. Why haven't we seen her before?'

Mrs Stevens was uninterested in the tourist-class though she made a point of exchanging the time of day with any she met in the ship's shop, hairdresser's, surgery or when visiting Mrs Agnew in the sick-bay. But she was momentarily interested to see the nursing sister and Third Officer sitting down in the still empty, as most unpopular, front row.

Mrs Van der Mann glanced severely at the three tourists taking the last empty seats at the far right end of the row ahead. She disapproved of missionaries of all denominations; she considered they did a great deal of harm in their foolish attempts to put ideas into the Kaffirs' heads. 'Kaffirs' being her term for all black Africans. 'Probably the wife of one and been poorly. Missionaries' wives are usually sickly creatures,' she added not unkindly, as, though of limited understanding, she was in many ways a kind woman. She turned back to Mrs Stevens, who continued as if uninterrupted.

'What else could I do but shut up my house and come out? I told my married daughter – had your dear father been spared he would say, as so often in the war, "You must do your bit, Dorothy!" But he would have been shocked at the thought of Tom's promise to teach me how to shoot. I've never held a gun in my life. But Tom says he never leaves Isobel without his revolver, and when she's feeding and changing little Melanie, she needs someone to hold it that she can trust . . .'

No, thought Mrs Mellor, pursuing her observations, the wife of neither from the attention both were paying her. Stylish hair – pretty profile – quite young – nice little figure – and so wise to have kept out of the sun. Nothing aged a woman like sunbathing – ah! Her sharp eyes softened and followed Paddy's slow progress up the starboard side. After dinner he had changed back into a cotton shirt and trousers and had swimming-trunks underneath and a towel over one shoulder. He exchanged waves with Sister West and two or three others, then paused at the far right end of the row ahead. Good gracious! The girl was introducing him to the two Anglicans!

Mrs Van der Mann tapped her arm. 'That young woman talking to Dr Brown is a friend of that little flibbertigibbet in the hospital. Mrs Stevens has met her there and says she's a lady,' she whispered, disapprovingly, being a firm believer that all should adhere to the station in life to which God had called them. She made no allowances here on financial grounds since she regarded money as a sordid subject of interest only to men. She returned to Mrs Stevens. 'What you should have in Kenya, my dear, is the new law we are now bringing in in South Africa. We call it "apartheid". That means "separateness" ' – and there she had to stop. The deck lights had gone off and over the Tannoy one of the two assistant pursers was welcoming the audience to the film that was about to begin.

It was so dark in the pool that Paddy had slid into the invisible water before he discovered the several swimmers floating on their backs and watching what they could see of the screen above the operator's platform. He swam silently around them rejoicing in being cool and at the lightness of his legs in water and listening to the soundtrack that, owing to some quirk of the acoustics caused by the pool's sides, undulated like an ill-tuned wireless. He judged the interval would be made when Rose Marie was packed off to be turned into a young lady, and climbed out at the first Mounties' chorus to have more time for thought. He sat on the high, still-hottish rail around the pool with his back to the screen. He watched the sky and the sea mentally turning over how best to persuade Elinor to let him help her change her ticket and refusing to dwell on the contrast between the pleasure seeing her had just given him and his reaction to this three nights ago.

The hot air dried him in minutes. He re-dressed in the flickering shadows of the deck around the pool then strolled to the aft rail and sat on one of the chests that contained deck games equipment. That rail overlooked the aft portion of the lower promenade deck, the stern of the tourists' deck below, and the broad, straight swathe of foam in the ship's wake. The soundtrack was clearer and softer than in the pool, the opening bars of the 'Indian Love Call' floated over his head and a star fell so close it seemed he could have reached out and caught it.

It was a long time since he had sat waiting for a particular woman, but never before, he thought, in this ideal Hollywood setting for the big seduction scene. It was then he heard steps behind him and glancing round, rose without his stick. 'Thanks for coming out, Ellie, but I didn't mean to drag you away before the interval.'

'You didn't, Paddy. Curiosity did and I'm enormously grateful as this sky's even more glorious with the lights off.' She smiled up at him in the flickering darkness that hid the joy in her eyes after seeing him stand un-aided. 'For God's sake, man, sit down and ask me tenderly "Happy, my darling?" so I can simper, "So happy, my darling," and the cameras can home in on the close-up.'

He laughed and sat by her. 'Mother of God, Ellie, with your talent for mind-reading in another age you'd have been burnt at the stake.'

'If I had, you'd have been at the next. You catch on quicker than radar.' She inhaled gratefully. 'One can breathe up here! Bliss!'

'That's why I want to talk to you.' But he hesitated. 'Won't those chaps object to your walking out prematurely?'

She looked at him quickly but their backs were to the

screen and it was too dark for her to see more than the angular outline of his long, narrow, face. 'Not they. Far too sensible and too hooked on movies as they can so seldom afford, or get the chance, to see any.'

'They struck me as decent old chaps.'

'They are, though not that old. Mid-forties, but both have had twenty-odd years in Africa.' She did not add, where their wives are buried, but she went on talking of the missionaries to give him more time for what he really wanted to say. He never stopped talking, she thought, but always in the past when unsure how something would be taken, he'd prevaricate for ages. And when straight bad news had to be given, whenever possible, he left that to others, and when not, after giving it, often there were tears in his eyes. She had remembered this so clearly three nights ago, that immediately she saw him sitting on the settle she had known that whatever his motive for being there, it had not been to break bad news about Irene Venner. And as she talked on she thought, it then took him a few minutes to put on a superb act of being pleased to see me, but now, thank God, he's climbed back out of the pit – and so have I, she belatedly recognised – so this really is where we came in.

'I like and am grateful for them,' she continued, 'since by association I'm labelled as God-squadder and able to opt out of all the fun and games without giving offence. Thanks.' She accepted a cigarette and in the lighter flame her eyes laughed. 'I'm far too old for jolly shipboard jinks.'

'Not visibly, and that's no line. One of these fine days you must tell me your secret of eternal youth.'

'Thanks, but you haven't seen me in daylight.'

He did not answer for a few seconds. Then, 'Not face

on. But that was your back in the war cemetery in Genoa, wasn't it?' He heard her quick intake of breath. 'Proxy for Alistair?' he prompted gently.

She breathed out. 'Yes, that's why I was there. I can't take flowers to his grave. I know vaguely where it is, but one of his friends in the camp told me – years later – that the jungle had taken it over long before the Nips surrendered. So I put my flowers on one of the UNKNOWN dead. I thought that almost certainly somewhere, some woman, still desperately wanted to do that.'

'Yes. Oh, yes,' he breathed and they fell silent and shared the same sense of despair that had consumed him when standing by the white graves in the Italian sunshine.

'This was before you saw me, Ellie?'

'Yes,' she said simply, and as their minds were in accord, no more was needed. Then she asked 'What's bugging you, Paddy?'

'The thought of you sweltering in a starboard sardine tin two decks below my cabin. I want you to change your ticket to the Cape.'

She sat straighter and stared at him in the darkness. 'You obviously think that's possible. How? First's booked solid.'

'Not since last night according to Dixon, my cabin steward. A reliable chap. This is the way of it,' he said eagerly. 'A double starboard cabin on my deck has been empty but reserved from Tilbury for the retired couple that paid for it for the round trip. Two days before we sailed the husband had a mild coronary but they hoped later to pick us up at Port Said, or at the worst, Mombasa. But yesterday morning the poor chap had a major – all plans cancelled – and last night the purser had a cable lifting the reserve. Dixon says once the company's African agents hear this they'll snap it up from Mombasa. So I think you – we – should move fast. I say "we"—' suddenly he hesitated 'listen, Ellie. I'll not pretend it'll not be a bit pricey – no!' He snapped down her attempted interruption. 'I know it must be as it's the same as mine – private bath *et al* – and I know what mine cost. I've worked out what the extra'll be from here to the Cape – and – I would very much like it if you would let me settle that for you – no! Just listen – and stuff the umbrage and remember Victoria's dead even if none on this ship have yet heard of it! Just think how long we've known each other and that I've never even bloody thanked you for holding my hand and I'd bloody like to do so very much!'

She had kept silent as he had left her no alternative, but now had he not stopped she would have shouted him down. 'Scrub that lot, Paddy! When did you and I ever take umbrage with each other, or expect thanks for doing our jobs? As well,' she spread both hands, 'seeing how seldom any of us got thanked! But this is enormously generous and kind of you and I'm tremendously grateful, though, honestly it isn't necessary as—'

'Balls! It's bloody necessary, woman! I do not enjoy thinking of you on the wrong side of the tracks and feeling a selfish, pampered, sod freeloading round Africa in luxury handed me on a plate. That's right, you heard!' His quick-temper had flared beyond caution. 'Handed me for free, just like that.' He snapped his fingers. 'Telling you is busting a promise but the old boy'll understand when I tell him. And you're telling me we don't expect thanks! Let me tell you it was a bloody close thing the old boy didn't have to scrape me

81

off the floor of his club's dining room. "Take a trip, m'boy," he said, or words to that effect. "Do you good – leave it to me." And just because once, way back, "Chesty" Alexander shoved him into Luke's small ward with both lungs consolidating. Shoved, literally!'

Elinor had listened to his explanation of the unreserved cabin with mounting interest and only attempted to interrupt to explain that owing to her late mother-in-law's Edwardian horror of touching her capital, after her death she had been stunned by the size of her inheritance and could well afford the extra charge. But his final disclosure had entranced her for very different reasons.

'Paddy! You're talking about – what was his name – yes! Sir John Foster-Green! Don't you remember?' She urged excitedly. 'I was there!'

'Yes. I remember,' he said in another voice. And again for a few moments they looked at each other in silence and neither noticed that behind them the soundtrack had stopped and around them the deck lights had come on, as during those few moments their present was in the unknown future and they were in their shared past.

FIVE
London
December 1943

'Is Luke often this quiet, Mackenzie?'

Elinor looked up in surprise from ruling black ink columns in the exercise book that was the ward's Dangerous Drug Book. The speaker, Nurse Thane, had taken over as night senior four nights ago. The last three nights had been too busy for the two night nurses to have ten seconds' private conversation and in the previous two months not once had the former senior asked Elinor's opinion on anything. 'Not this quiet, Nurse,' she replied, in the flat murmur all the staff used at night since it carried far less than a whisper. And then as Nurse Thane, though two years older was only one year her senior in hospital time, she added, 'Nor have I known the nocturnal chorus so quiet or so many empty beds.'

Nurse Thane nodded and went on writing the inter-night report for Night Sister's collection on her two o'clock second round. On the past three nights she had not been able to start the report before ten to two, it was now only five to one but already the chorus of snores, sighs, grunts, heavy and quiet rhythmical breathing, occasional mutters, and the creaking bed-springs of patients turning in sleep, had the reassuring depths of the hour before dawn when even the illest and most restless finally slept.

The nurses sat on the left side of the mid-ward desk that was bathed in a pool of crimson light by the red shade-covered ceiling light pulled down to within a few inches of their capped heads. The darkness of the long wide ward was tinged with pink by the red night bulbs and Beds ten to twenty-seven were empty. This morning fourteen of Luke's patients had been transferred to the hospital's main evacuated base and the beds of the remaining eighteen moved into the first nine places on either side of the open entrance to the inner corridor that at night was a darkish, rose-coloured cavern.

'This morning's massive exodus to The Hut has left a strange, one might almost say unhealthy quiet over the whole medical side tonight, Nurse Thane,' said Dr Danby, the Senior Medical Officer, on his night round an hour before. 'For which we can thank the Government's latest directive insisting we transfer all medical patients fit to move out of London, and Jerry for laying off air-raids on London all this year. The Government is convinced we're about to be inundated with victims of London's current annual influenza epidemic, but as London is presently sleeping in its own bed, this is presently being kept to manageable proportions.'

'And the Tube platforms empty.'

'Precisely. No better way of spreading any virus than by packing hundreds of tired people on to cold, damp, draughty, stone platforms to a background of noise that heightens apprehension and wrecks sleep,' he said, noting her strong physical resemblance to her only and older brother who had been killed in North Africa last year. A quiet, pleasant, nippy little chap of distinct promise, David Thane . . . damned shame . . . damned waste. However . . . 'Of course this quiet won't last. And, as ever, it's contagious. Why every ward in the hospital should blow up and subside in unison – with or without Jerry's assistance – is one of the many inexplicable facts of hospital life that I first learnt to accept in peacetime. Cas is quiet as a tomb, the theatres in darkness, the surgeons have already retired to their beds in the Doctors' House and I hope to be in mine, shortly.'

'I hope you can, Dr Danby. And stay there till morning.'

'I share your hopes devoutly, Nurse. Goodnight.'

Nurse Thane belonged to a junior third-year set that had been moved to London from The Hut earlier this week and sent on duty as night seniors for their first time. This premature promotion would never have occurred in peacetime, but the insatiable demands of the Forces and evacuated branches of the hospital for newly State Registered fourth years, had left the Matron of Martha's no alternative to using as best, the best at her disposal. But as Nurse Thane was a very perceptive, intelligent and efficient student nurse – which was why she was in charge of Luke at night – she was acutely aware that from nine p.m. to eight a.m. her patients' lives were literally in her hands. The Night Sister had the final responsibility for the whole hospital, and one Night Assistant Sister (a fourth year), but they were the only two SRNs on duty and had to cover eight above-ground and six basement wards, and Casualty, that was open all night, in a hospital that, owing to the vast amount of bomb-damage it had already suffered and its geographical position in the heart of London, now only admitted acute cases, the majority as emergencies.

Nurse Thane's glance rested on Elinor. It was part of the junior's nightly 'routine' to keep the D.D. Book ruled up at least five clear pages ahead and usually she had no time to do this until taking over the ward for the senior's thirty-minute 'midnight meal' after Night Sister's second round. Poor kid looks dog-tired, thought Nurse Thane. Long time on nights – and longer still since Singapore fell.

Elinor sensed the glance, looked up, and had the impression Nurse Thane's small ears were twisting like an Alsatian's scenting danger. 'Think we're too quiet, Nurse? They all sound flat out.'

'They do. And were when I last went round ten minutes ago. And bound to be quieter now all our chests are coughing their guts out down in William at The Hut.' She hesitated, looking up and down. 'Snag is, I haven't been in Luke long enough to get the smell. How does it strike you?'

Elinor had to inhale consciously. She had long stopped noticing the atmosphere of the bricked-in ward at night. This was the first week of her third of the three-months night duty worked – in peacetime annually and wartime bi-annually – by all the second, third, and, when available, fourth-year student nurses, and it was nine nights since she had last had three off given after every twenty-one on duty. She was so chronically tired that always at the onset of the small hours her mind felt stuffed with cotton wool, eyes sand-papered and head too heavy for her neck. She had to force her concentration on the mixed reek of carbolic, methylated spirits, talcum powder, stale tobacco smoke, hot red rubber undersheets, human sweat and exhalations, wax polish and anthracite in the stuffy air.

'Just smells like Luke to me, Nurse – no.' She sniffed. 'Linctus missing.'

Nurse Thane smiled slightly and thought of the rider in the customary confidential report on the ward at night left for her by her predecessor. 'NB Re: Mackenzie. Bit green, wizard memory, doesn't flap. Good luck . . .'

She capped her fountain-pen. 'I'll go round again, then you eat. What've we got tonight?'

'Quite decent. Shepherd's pie that actually smells of mince, jam tart and an apple.' Elinor reached for the red ink pen to deal with the column headings. To collect from the main kitchen before coming on duty the mess tins containing the meals the night nurses ate in turn in their ward kitchen or dutyroom, and prepare the food for serving, were other items on her junior's 'routine'. 'Hot or cold, Nurse?'

'Got yours in the slow oven? Right. Shove mine in when Night Sister shows up – dammit! I'll cope,' she muttered and fled soundlessly to silence the ringing of the ward's only telephone that was on a wall-shelf in the inner corridor on the nearside of the duty room, the first door on the left from the ward.

Elinor had automatically risen and moved to stand in the ward between the twin rows of sleeping patients. Though not yet as quick a mover as Nurse Thane or her predecessor, she was quiet, having had this dinned into her from her first night on-duty.

'Get this and get this stat., Mackenzie – oh – know what "stat." means?'

'Medical abbreviation of the Latin, "statim", English, "at once".'

'Right. So get this, the first duty of any night nurse is to ensure her patients' sleep. God help you if you wake up any of our men. I won't, nor will Sister Luke or Night Sister . . .'

Thank heavens the phone doesn't seem to have woken them, thought Elinor, looking from side to side and out of the corner of her eye watching Nurse Thane's small, trim back. Elinor couldn't hear the one-sided conversation, but she knew instantly why her senior was scribbling in ink on the up-turned hem of her apron skirt. Admission, she thought desperately, and at this hour bound to be a coronary and setting either ten or twenty-seven for a D.I.L. will wake some before the rumbling trolley wakes them all.

Nurse Thane hung up and gestured to Elinor to rejoin her at the desk.

'Admission, Nurse?'

'Yes. Acute double lobar pneumonia, fifth night from onset and not responding to sulphonamides, but as the ambulance is coming from the far side of Esher and unlikely to be here for another half hour, I'll take two ticks to brief you. Bit complicated.' She flicked up her apron hem and read, 'Sir John Michael Foster-Green, age fifty-nine, C. of E., stockbroker, one of our gover-nors, next-of-kin, wife – not bringing him in as very arthritic.' She smoothed down her apron and looked at Elinor. 'Dr Alexander's with him in the ambulance.'

Elinor's mental cotton wool evaporated. Dr Alexan-der was Martha's senior thoracic honorary consultant and Elinor had only seen him in Luke at night when one of his patients was on the Dangerously Ill List. 'Is this because the patient's coming in on the D.I.L., Nurse? Or because he's a governor?'

'The first – and they're old friends. Night Sister's just told me that's why Sir John has refused to allow his GP to contact Dr Alexander until an hour or so back. Apparently he objects strongly to using old friends and his position, but tonight his wife overruled him. He's been nursed at home. Private day and night nurses. The night nurse is bringing him in to hand over as Martha's doesn't use outside trained staff, or, since the war, take private patients. He's coming in as a G.W.E. (General Ward Emergency) and going into our small-ward. Far less disturbing for our other patients on all counts as Dr Alexander says he's going through to crisis.' She saw the alarm in Elinor's eyes. 'Seen that yet?' Elinor shook her head. 'All the pneumonias in here since you came on nights responded to sulphas.?'

'All the "acutes". But we had five that developed hypostatic pneumonia as secondary complications and—' Elinor looked at the open D.D. Book 'and they went in sleep. It was very quick.'

'What were they?'

'Three had head tumours, two carcinomatosis.'

'Quick and kind.' Nurse Thane was brisk. 'Would you want to linger with either?' Elinor had to look up and shake her head. 'Now listen. I know your set haven't yet had medical lectures but I'll have to make this snappy and you must read it up for yourself. When an acute pneumonia doesn't respond to medication and takes its own course, this generally reaches a crisis on the ninth day or night from onset. The exact time depends upon the time of the onset. Got that? Right. Now – from onset the patient is obviously ill, distressed, has a high temp. and needs good nursing, then, usually on the fifth day

89

or night, the temp. starts soaring and goes on rising until it reaches the crisis peak on the ninth. Then, one of three things happens. One,' she raised her left hand above her head, 'the temp. starts falling rapidly and in a few hours is down to normal.' She dropped her left hand silently on to the desk. 'That's called a fall by *crisis*. Two,' again her hand shot up, 'the temp. starts dropping jerkily, over a day or two, but each new peak is lower than the one before, until down to normal.' Her left hand traced a descending peaked graph to the desk-top. 'That's a fall by *lysis*. Got that?' Elinor nodded intently. 'Right. Now, three,' she raised and held her left hand poised, 'the temp. doesn't drop,' her hand rose higher 'it shoots higher and beyond the heart's toleration,' She sliced down her hand and flattened it on the desk. 'That's why it's called "crisis". If the patient can't come through it, that's the end. Clear?'

Elinor's mouth was dry. 'Yes. Thanks.'

'That's OK. Now, one break. As Cas is quiet and the only department with two night seniors, Night Sister is shifting Nurse Hardy in my set to be Sir John's night "special".' She glanced into the corridor. 'One of my ideas of nursing hell is to have a D.I.L. out of sight and sound of the ward and particularly an acute pneumonia needing constant watching and real nursing.' She half-smiled. 'We're going to have every medical pundit in Martha's in and out of Luke in these next four days and nights, but they – and we – know that all that can really help him now is good nursing. Nurse Hardy's done a lot of "specialing", but she'll need a lot of help from us both. Shove a muffler round the kitchen door handles to keep it ajar, as you'll have to keep one ear on the small-ward and the other on the ward.' She flicked out her watch. 'I've used up five minutes. Get

cracking setting the small-ward for a D.I.L. "chest",
Mackenzie.' They had both risen. 'I'll do a quick round
then get the cylinders and flow-meter into the corridor
for you. OK?'

'Yes, Nurse.'

The small-ward lay off the far left of the corridor from
the ward and pre–1922, when Martha's sisters ceased
to live in their wards, had been Sister Luke's bedroom.
It was now the only extant single-bedded small-ward
in the semi-ruined hospital, normally reserved for sick
members of the all-male qualified staff or senior male
members of the lay; junior lay staff and medical
students went into the general wards. It was always
left ready for an immediate admission but not for one
on the D.I.L., since the additional equipment this
required was far more frequently needed in the main
ward. It took Elinor a little over a minute to switch on
the overhead and bedhead lights, remove and fold the
white cotton quilt embossed with the arms of Martha's,
neatly roll back the top bedclothes for the admission of
a stretcher-patient, and check all the basic equipment
was in place. When she shot out to go into the stockroom that was next door, already lined up just outside
the ward entrance were a tall, heavy, black iron oxygen
cylinder in a taller, black iron, low-wheeled stand, with,
hanging from the cylinder's neck, the green linen bag
containing the rubber face mask and tubing; a smaller
black iron cylinder of carbon dioxide in a similar stand;
and a large, rounded, flat-bottomed glass flow-meter
half filled with sterile distilled water through which the
oxygen passed before reaching the mask, standing on
a lowish wooden stool. All these had been moved by
Nurse Thane from the spares against the wall on the
inner left of the entrance. She could not take them into

the small-ward, as a strict hospital rule ordained that not even for seconds at night, must the ward be left without one nurse in the patients' sight and hearing.

Quickly, quietly, Elinor trundled the apparatus to the right bedhead, connected it up, checked the gauges, and tested the mask on her face. Then she raced to the stockroom for three pairs of wooden bedblocks in rising sizes to be used to raise the foot of the bed; a tall thin, white metal, portable transfusion-cum-drip infusion stand; a large iron bedcradle to take the weight of the top bedclothes; and two Edwardian stone hot water bottles that she filled from the simmering urn in the kitchen – Martha's having run out of the now irreplaceable, rubber bottles.

In the linen room, two doors up, were the extra pillows essential for chest conditions and the extra blankets that might be needed hastily. The metal, lidded, sputum mug and enamel urinal she got from the sluice off the far left of the main ward. The sterilised drums of swabs, and small white enamel bowls and kidney dishes, and the spare long-handled bowl for forceps in a large jam jar filled with carbolic solution, were stored in the duty room. The last was essential for removing articles from sterilised drums, as sepsis was still one of the great enemies in all hospital wards and the 'no-touch technique' that forbade touching anything sterile with bare hands, was rigorously taught and enforced.

She checked the setting breathlessly. What else? Yes. Drinks tray from the kitchen – red shade covers for the lights – a scarlet D.I.L. label drawing-pinned to the outside of the door and a muffler over the handles. She dealt with these swiftly, re-checked, then hurried quietly back into the ward.

'Set, Mackenzie? OK. Take over here whilst I check.' Nurse Thane vanished and returned shortly, smiling quietly. 'Nice work. All there in ten minutes flat. Go and eat and I hope you can get most of your break. Leave mine cold. I'll eat later when I can.'

Before starting the meal that she ate sitting on the kitchen table, Elinor hooked open the tall, wide, mahogany doors that opened into the main ground-floor corridor and were only closed at night or during air raids. She had just taken her first bite out of the apple when she heard the rumble of a high metal stretcher-trolley turning out of the inner entrance to Casualty that was roughly forty yards down the corridor. She tore back into the ward shoving the apple into one of her dress skirt pockets under her apron. The night senior had to admit in person every patient coming into her ward at night, and a few seconds later, Elinor, standing at the desk, watched wide-eyed the stretcher-trolley being whisked into the small-ward by Angus, the junior night porter and the grey-haired, black-jacketed and pinstriped Dr Alexander, with the escorting Night Assistant Sister carrying the honorary's medical bag, and Nurse Hardy, the patient's small suitcase. Elinor had no chance of more than a glimpse of the heavy figure under the grey Casualty blankets and only after the small-ward door closed identified Nurse Hardy as the chubby, baby-faced, redhead she had seen sitting on Nurse Thane's left at the senior table in the dining room. And then Dr Danby, and Dr Roberts, the medical registrar and Mr Brown, the SHP, and Mr Evans, the SMO's houseman, swept in from the corridor, jumped aside to let Angus swish out the empty trolley, then vanished in the small-ward.

It was another ten minutes before Nurse Thane ushered out the Night Assistant Sister and came quickly back into the ward.

'Anything to report, Mackenzie?'

'No, Nurse. None woken. How is he?'

'Not too well.' Which meant, 'very ill'. 'Make tea for five and shove the tray on to the duty room table – and keep your ears flapping for Nurse Hardy.'

It seemed to Elinor that she had spent the second half of that night and all the next four, dodging between the kitchen and small-ward; kitchen and main ward; and fighting the clock instead of the longing for sleep. She lost count of the times she carried tea trays into the duty room and later discovered these being washed up by the SHP. 'Thanks awfully, Mr Brown.'

'All part of the service, Nurse. Mother of God – ' he tilted his black head to listen – 'that "Chesty" back again?'

'Wrong steps. Prof. Medicine.'

'No peace for the wicked.' He hastily dried his hands. 'Not that there's one damn thing he can do either,' he muttered under his breath, streaking away.

At other times: 'Mr Brown, thanks a lot! You've cut my breakfast bread!'

He shrugged mournfully. 'Better than hanging about doing SFA. (Sweet Fanny Adams.)'

She looked curiously up at his pale, tired, blue-chinned face. 'Then why hang about?'

He glared at her. 'Doing penance, no less.'

'What do you – sorry – that's Nurse Hardy—' and she catapulted from the kitchen.

Throughout those four and a half nights the small-ward door kept opening from the inside; 'Sorry, Mackenzie, need help lifting him higher . . . need help shoving in higher bed blocks . . . Sorry, Mackenzie, oxygen's down to its last quarter – another cylinder . . . more glucose lemonade, please . . . more drinking straws . . . another sputum mug . . . another bottle (urinal) . . . cope with the BP (bedpan) please, . . . refill this hottie (hot water bottle), please—' and, which sent cold chills down her spine, 'Get Thane, stat!'

Being the junior, she was allowed to help her seniors with the D.I.L.s, but the heavy skilled nursing was their responsibility. And, as all his nurses, she grew very fond of the large, elderly, bushy-browed and unfailingly courteous man fighting for breath and his life.

From his second night, when she took the first night drinks round the main ward that now had twenty-four patients, in bed after bed, the occupant shook his head. 'Seems the poor old bloke out the small-ward's proper poorly, but got to keep hoping, Nurse Mackenzie. And how you keeping, Nurse? Had a good kip today? That's nice and reckoned you would seeing you weren't off your feet the once last night – and here's the SMO and that Mr Brown, back. If you ask me, Nurse, in and out like Yo-Yos all day and all night, they are.'

In the small hours of that night, she asked Nurse Thane, 'They do nothing but stand looking at Sir John, Nurse, so why do they keep haunting us?'

'The SMO because he's a good SMO and responsible for every medical bed in the joint and Mr Brown because he's browned off at having to leave it all to us and wants to watch how we do it. Actually, though he'd kill me for saying this, he's a pretty good nurse. Some physicians are. Not surgeons. How's your routine?'

'Bit behind.'

'Then get cracking and catch up or Sister Luke'll give us both hell again in the morning.'

At the junior table at breakfast on those four mornings, 'What's his temp. this morning, Ellie?'

Every morning the figure was higher.

'Crisis Monday night, Ellie?'

'Small hours, Tuesday.'

On Monday she slumped into her seat and her set exchanged glances.

Then, 'What, Ellie?'

'105.8 this morning. His cough's agony to hear, even from the kitchen. Every expiratory grunt has me wincing for him – and his delirium's been coming and going all night. Thank goodness they can't hear him in the ward, but they know everything that's happening. Thane says the patients always do and no one knows how, no one tells them, but they just do. They're being wonderful – they always are when we've D.I.L.s in the ward. Even our gastrics have stopped binding about their mushy diets and lashings of milk and are swearing blind nothing they'd fancy more than a nice drop of cold milk.' She yawned exhaustedly. 'Thank goodness no lecture this morning.' (For the benefit of the night nurses all the second and third-year student nurses' lectures were held from nine to ten a.m.).

Although exhausted she slept badly that day and in the early afternoon lay awake whilst the short, damp December day faded into the soaking darkness of blacked-out London by four-thirty. She dreaded the coming night, as always, when she feared a patient would die. Normally, despite the long hours and constant tiredness, she infinitely preferred night-nursing, as this allowed juniors far closer contact with the patients than on days, when there were many more seniors on duty and the juniors spent hours on the non-stop cleaning that was essential to keep the ward and outhouses in the spotless condition insisted upon by the ward sisters, and a necessity to combat sepsis. She had come to know all Luke's patients as friends and to cherish the smiles that accompanied their nightly greeting, 'Here come OUR night nurses!' and the little smiles that so often appeared in the sunken eyes above green rubber oxygen masks when she arrived at the D.I.L.s' bedsides to assist a senior. Last night Sir John had been too delirious to recognise her, or any of them. And in her handing-over report Sister Luke said that again Lady Foster-Green had spent all day in her wheel-chair by his bed, holding his hand, and had only been persuaded to go home by the explanation that to see her there all night would distress her husband. 'Lady Foster-Green will be back in the morning though far from well herself,' said Sister Luke. 'I fear the loss of their only son at El Alamein last year has caused a marked deterioration of her condition and is not presently assisting her husband's.'

Elinor, as all the night staff, had heard of David Thane's death, and she and Nurse Hardy had stared fixedly at their folded hands in their laps.

But lying there watching the afternoon die she forgot David Thane, and even Alistair, and that she had ever had any other life than this unnatural upside-down existence in perpetual darkness that would have been unbearable were it not so continuously brightened by the discovery that her patients returned the great affection she had for them. If it weren't for the patients I couldn't take nursing, she thought, just before dropping into an uneasy sleep.

During the first half of that night once more she

repeatedly took over the main ward that now had thirty patients but was as quiet as the first half of the night of Sir John's admission.

'Ever so comfortable, ta, Nurse. Don't want nothing. Be off, pronto,' said the patients and those in the left beds furthest from the entrance covertly watched the small-ward door and with nods and humourless winks passed on their observations to their fellows. At a little after eleven, when Nurse Thane was helping Nurse Hardy and Elinor at the desk, she saw the patient in Bed Fifteen suddenly raise his head and, glancing into the corridor, saw Matron and the Night Sister going into the small-ward.

'I'm sorry you've been woken, Mr Cook.' She turned his pillows, straightened his drawsheet. 'How about a hot drink?'

'Not for me, ta, Nurse. Be off again sharpish, you'll see.' He was a foreman fitter in his early fifties with an extensive gastric ulcer and a hard, shrewd face. He looked up at her kindly. 'I'm sorry as the poor old gent down the way's not too good, Nurse Mackenzie, but don't you fret. Like my old nan used to say, got to be worse before you're better. Proper fighter that old gent, seemly. And in the best place. He'll be up before the count's out. You'll see, Nurse.'

Often before the patients' kindness had had her close to tears that she had always managed to control. Not now. She kept her eyes downcast and pretended to ignore her wet cheeks as she thanked him. Matron's come to say goodbye, she thought, and that's why all those pundits came in earlier – and have now gone.

'Thanks, Mackenzie. Anything to report?'

'Mr Cook woke. Off again. He – he saw Matron.'

Nurse Thane nodded, her eyes blank and too big for

her small face. She raised a hand to acknowledge Mr Brown's return to the small-ward. 'Get cracking Mackenzie,' she said mechanically.

About an hour later whilst Elinor was cutting the breakfast bread, Mr Brown raced silently into the kitchen. 'Ice, stat!'

Elinor flung open the refrigerator door, grabbed a large china bowl and, as together they emptied the ice trays, breathed, 'Higher?'

'106.8. If it can't be got down he's had it,' he muttered grimly and vanished with the bowl.

She opened wide the kitchen door and returned to cutting bread and listening painfully to the soft incoherent mumbles of delirium and the terrifying rapidity and shallowness of the expiratory grunts.

Nurse Thane stopped on one foot in the doorway. 'Take over. I've to help Hardy tepid sponge.'

The four or five patients awake and feigning sleep closed their eyes and breathed deeply as Elinor went slowly from bed to bed and, when she sat down at the desk, exchanged thumbs-down. She was still too inexperienced to recognise their deception, or to be allowed to tepid-sponge a dangerously ill patient. She began ruling up the D.D. Book, and her mind kept switching from what was now going on in the small-ward, to the numerous occasions that she had practised this technique on lifesize waxen dummies, first in the Preliminary Training School and later in the Senior Tutor's classroom. 'Watch me closely, Nurses, and always remember that this procedure demands skill and care. When a tepid-sponge is required to lower a patient's high temperature, sponging down that patient's body must be performed very gently as a too precipitate chill can cause the shock that can result in

heart failure. Watch me closely, Nurses. Gentle sponging movements, like this . . .'

'Anything to report, Mackenzie?'

'No, Nurse.'

'Good.' Nurse Thane uncapped her fountain-pen and
wrote on the blotter, '105.4.'

Hope flared in Elinor's eyes. 'What now?' she
mouthed.

'Just nursing. Most of the pundits have left the hospital. The SMO's still up. He'll be back and Mr Brown,'
she nodded at the corridor, 'still *in situ*.' She paused,
frowning. 'I'll say this for him, he's a quiet fly on the
wall and obviously, as he's keen on medicine, this is
very useful experience even if one, he, and all of us,
dread seeing. My third and I hope my lot. His second,
he says, but the first was in the '41 blitz and he had to
keep rushing back to Cas. He'll help Hardy with lifting
and changing sheets, so with luck, you can get on with
your routine. But, first, you must have your meal break
– and make a small pot of tea. Mr Brown'll collect
Hardy's and his cuppas, and have one yourself.'

'Bring you a cup in here, Nurse?'

'Please. I've nothing like finished my inter-night
report and Night Sister'll show up for her second round
in two ticks.'

A few minutes later, in the kitchen, 'Mother of God,
but you're an angel no less! No need for saucers!'

After another hour, 'Take over, Mackenzie. I've to
relieve Nurse Hardy for her meal break.'

Thirty minutes later, 'Thanks. Anything?'

'No, Nurse. Temp. still dropping?'

Nurse Thane's deeply shadowed eyes smiled for the
first time tonight. '103.2.' She flicked out her watch.
'We'll start work at five.' ('Start work' – the early morn-

ing washings, bedmaking, temperature-taking and treatments rounds.) 'Get their early tea in at five to.'

At ten minutes to five Elinor had set the large twin-shelved wooden food trolley for the patients' early morning tea. She was just making this in the largest brown metal pot when Mr Brown came silently and very slowly into the kitchen. He lounged against the dresser and, pushing back the black forelock off his greyish, unshaven, face, grinned euphorically.

'Normal.'

She nearly dropped the filled pot. 'Normal!'

'98.4 and sleeping like a babe in arms!' He lunged for and held wide the kitchen door. 'Will you just listen to those splendidly peaceful, normal respirations you can't even hear?' He closed the door on the muffler and swung round to her. 'I suppose I couldn't scrounge —' but she was holding out a steaming saucerless cup of tea. 'Mother of God, but you're a lovely girl, Mrs Mackenzie! You're all lovely girls and the old boy's a lovely old man and he's come through crisis and I love him for it for all he's just aged me fifty years! Who needs youth? Can I scrounge another for Nurse Hardy – ' he accepted the second and put the first cup on the kitchen table to blow her a kiss. 'May the holy angels and saints bless you, Mrs Mackenzie – and is it any wonder I love you though I've no conception why I should seeing you're not my type at all!' He retrieved the first cup, and she held open the door and he backed out both cups aloft and still grinning euphorically. And a few minutes later she pushed the laden trolley with one hand as the other was flattened over her mouth to stifle her euphoric laughter.

SIX
Off Mombasa
June 1955

The party's over, thought Elinor, hovering in surprise in the entrance to the first-class lounge. The party's over and reality hasn't waited for the gangplank to go down. It's come aboard before the pilot.

She had just been driven from the deck by a sudden equatorial downpour that was hammering the ship and blocking out the dark green Kenya coastline. The ship was due to arrive in Mombasa in under two hours and disembark two-thirds of all the passengers. She had gone straight out on deck from breakfast; the dining saloon had been near-empty and she had expected to find the lounge even emptier. But it was so crowded with men that she did not at first notice Mrs Mellor, the only other woman present, sitting crocheting on a sofa against the far bulkhead. The men were sitting round coffee tables cleaning and checking the hunting rifles, shotguns, and old British and German Army revolvers that, with their ammunition, had been locked in one of the purser's safes since they boarded and just returned. They were unusually silent and the tension in the atmosphere contrasted sharply with yesterday's euphoria and last night's singing of Auld Lang Syne'.

The day before the ship had awakened in party mood and the morning's traditional Crossing The Line ceremony in the swimming pool – 'Stand by for the bump as we go over the equator!' – was the curtain-raiser for the official and unofficial end-of-voyage festivities that went on into the small hours. The Children's Hostess stopped Elinor as she came away from breakfast and Paddy stepped out of the lift. 'Mrs Mackenzie I need you for the Children's Entertainments Committee. Please, rally!'

Paddy looked amused and stopped to listen as Elinor protested, 'But Miss Dawes, I'm not a member.'

'Father Gerachty, our Chairman'll fix that,' insisted Miss Dawes, a tall, tanned, engagingly plain young woman with the authoritative voice of a first-class nanny. 'I must have you as I've got to have at least one lady judge for this afternoon's Children's Fancy Dress Parade and being mums all my Committee ladies have chickened-out. They know every mum whose little angel isn't in the first three is going to hate the judges' guts, but as all are leaving us tomorrow, couldn't you bear it?'

Elinor tried again, 'But having no children—'

'Makes you ideal! No axe to grind, young and married. I must have someone young or all the mums'll protest that she's too old-fashioned to know what children like dressing-up as now, and they'll be even more snooty if she's a spinster. And as Father Gerachty's just told me you did a little nursing in the war you shouldn't be too shattered by thirty-odd children in full cry. Do, please, rally . . . you will? Thanks a million! Our other judges are Father Gerachty and Mr Yates (the senior assistant purser), and the Committee is meeting in the veranda café in fifteen minutes. I can't be there as I'm due in my nursery, but will you show up? Great! I'll just nip aloft and give Father Gerachty the good news!' She raced off up the ornate mahogany main staircase.

Elinor looked at Paddy and he came closer. '*Mea culpa*. But when he asked what you were doing in the war—' he shrugged and left his sentence unfinished.

She smiled. 'I'm glad it was only a little. Was I a VAD?'

'I didn't specify as you said you wanted to avoid this particular kiss-of-death,' he drawled, thinking how enchantingly desirable she looked in a blue and white candy-striped sundress with a matching bolero, and how far removed from the crisply-professional young ward sister he still couldn't bear to remember. 'Before you vanish to do as England expects, seen George this morning?' She shook her head. 'He's keen to rope you in to the farewell do he's throwing his bridge chums in the smoking room after dinner tonight.' He read and partially answered the expression that flickered through her eyes. 'No. No way out as this apparently equates with VE night. You'll just have to—'

'Think of England and smile prettily?'

His smile was guarded. Their knack of picking up each other's thoughts was beginning to disturb him rather badly. 'What else, on this floating last out-post of Empire?' He limped on into the saloon, cursing George for a tactless myopic.

Elinor looked briefly after him. The tremendous heat

in the Red Sea had suited him clinically and his face now looked his real age and so remarkably attractive that the teenage girls haunted Paddy as they formerly had Dr Morgan. In this last week she had more than once seen him stand unaided for a minute or so, but from behind he still had the walk of a frail, lame, old man. Suddenly his left foot slipped on the polished parquet; he righted it immediately, but not before she had grabbed the carved bannister to stop herself rushing to help him. She went on up the stairs thinking that the day he no longer passionately resented being helped would be the day he was mentally over his illness and how bitter for him had been this long time at the receiving end, even though there was no trace of that bitterness in his face. That thought reduced to a triviality George's insensitivity in obviously seeking Paddy's permission to invite her to his party tonight.

She took the stairs as quickly as Miss Dawes and having a few minutes in hand, she went on deck thinking how much Paddy, and how little George, had matured, and that beneath the latter's seedy, middle-aged exterior still lingered the naive, vulnerable boy in an outsize battledress. She walked slowly up the port side, keeping in the little shade provided by the bulkheads of the reception rooms, as she had no hat. She wondered uneasily if Alistair would have remained so immature. She had repeatedly heard from her mother-in-law's friends how alike had been mother and son, and to the end of her life Helen Mackenzie had seen only in black and white and never even suspected that shades of grey existed.

The ship was at full speed and there was some movement in the hot, bright, morning air. The equatorial sun, though a little less remorseless than in the Red

Sea, still cleared the deck of sunbathers and converted the pool at the aft end to a hot-water bath. The water in the pool mirrored the blue of the cloudless sky and the smooth, clear green Indian Ocean met the empty skyline all round the horizon. There were no other ships in sight and the smooth green was broken only by the white foam in the ship's wake and the black fins of the little posses of sharks keeping pace with her twin-screws.

The sharks diverted her from the thoughts she was trying to avoid. She walked to the rail to watch the black fins breaking the surface and grey shadows beneath swimming straight as torpedos. A scrawny, teak-tanned, middle-aged man striding up the deck, eyed her hesitantly, then stopped. 'If you'll forgive my saying so, Mrs Mackenzie, you are ill-advised to linger hatless in the sun.'

She turned smiling and was touched that the speaker should have broken his rule of never speaking to anyone when taking his daily five-mile walk round the deck. 'Thank you, Mr Carter, and you're quite right. Not that I should be lingering,' she explained quickly.

Mr Carter's dour, lined, face relaxed into his rare one-sided smile. 'You're a brave lady, Mrs Mackenzie. Morning.' He raised his greenish jungle hat and strode on.

She smiled after his khaki shirted, shorted back. He was a colonial civil servant returning from leave to his final tour of duty in Bechuanaland, and previously had only spoken to her when they met daily in the ship's library. She had heard from Paddy that he had been widowered years, had married children in England, and kept himself to himself since Tilbury. She had been a little surprised when he first addressed her in the library and then discovered they had similar tastes in books. She liked him for that and for the way that he seemed to take her changing cabins as based fundamentally on her desire for privacy and not for some ulterior motive. Which puts him and Paddy in a minority of two in 'first', she thought, as she turned into the awned, open entrance of the veranda café.

Father Gerachty, the only cleric in 'first' was on some mission from the Vatican to South Africa – shipboard gossip insisted he would be the next Pope – and looked a cheerful, youngish, middle-weight boxer in T-shirt and jeans. He welcomed Elinor as the Prodigal Son, the other passengers with the glad cries the British reserve for friends and foes on the last day of the holidays and Mr Yates with practised gallantry. Mr Yates was twenty-four, darkish, thickset, quite attractive, and in his own opinion, irresistible to women. He covertly eyed Elinor as the sharks the ship and before the meeting ended replaced her on his mental list of future conquests. He had previously removed her name from Gibraltar on the grounds that two Holy Joes and a shared cabin were too dodgy to be navigated even by a bloke with his technique. And during this past week he had agreed with his junior colleague that a bloke had to tread softly when poaching on an oppo of the Owners. But since – in his opinion – none trod more softly than he, it was another four weeks to the Cape and she was still sleeping alone – he made it his business to know such things – he replaced her name at the top of his list. Elinor gave no sign of noticing his new attentiveness, and whilst smiling with the composure she had found invaluable since changing her ticket, resisted the urge to pat him on the head and say, 'Sorry, kid, no dice. Even though you've finally caught on that I'm not your VIP's mistress.'

Elinor changed cabins late afternoon on the day following the showing of *Rose Marie* and that evening Paddy re-introduced her to George. After a pre-dinner drink, both men escorted her down to the vast dining saloon that had a domed glass roof two decks high, a musicians' gallery, and was as lavishly appointed as any pre-war first-class London restaurant. Pre-war, as still in London as elsewhere in the UK, the cold hand of austerity had not wholly released its grip. There had been no new faces since Port Said, and the news that some woman from tourist '. . . they say a childless war-widow and one knows what that usually means . . .' had moved into one of the most expensive cabins, had flashed round before the first sundowners. When the three walked in, only the Captain, Dr Morgan, and a handful of passengers had still to arrive; the heads swung in their direction and buzz of conversation so subsided that for a good two minutes the four musicians sweating through the 'Thunder and Lightning Polka', had the rare illusion of an attentive audience.

Paddy, on Elinor's left, murmured, 'Our Captain is the stuff that builds empires. He likes a lively opening number, a good waltz with his soup and fish, a gavotte with his cut off the roast, Noel Coward or Cole Porter for afters, and no nonsensical pandering to the heat.'

George mumbled, mopping his red face, 'At least these fans cool it a bit.' He avoided looking at Elinor. He didn't believe in bloody mirages or like the smell of this turn-up, but knew when a chap had to close ranks.

Elinor looked around with the composure she had

last needed when attending her first Sisters' Meeting. 'Personally,' she said 'this Christian likes music with her lions.'

Paddy's mouth twitched and George's tightened. The purser came forward to usher Elinor to her pre-arranged seat at his table and introduce her new companions. One was Mrs Stevens.

'Mrs Mackenzie and I have already met, Mr Weaver.' She smiled thinly across the table when Elinor was seated between the portly brick-red Major Shaw and leathery, greying Mr Frobisher. 'Such a surprise, Mrs Mackenzie! You said nothing of this when we met in the hospital last evening.'

'As I was then still unaware there was any possibility of my changing cabins, Mrs Stevens.' Elinor smiled at the purser. 'Thanks to Mr Weaver and the Wireless officers, it was all arranged today.'

'Goodness! You are a fast worker – oh dear – that sounds so – but you know what I mean.'

Elinor smiled composedly. 'Of course. And how nice to find I'm at your table.'

Mrs Snow, on her husband's left, put in tartly, 'And how nice that you've already made other new friends in first-class, Mrs Mackenzie.'

'Very nice, indeed, Mrs Snow.' Elinor recognised more than the yellowish tinge of Indian suns in the baked, lined, petulant, fifty-ish face that had once belonged to a chubbily pretty blonde. 'But not new friends. I first met both doctors in the war.'

'Oh. Really? Your husband a medical man?'

Elinor shook her head. 'British Army, Regular. Gunners. Weren't you in the Indian Army, Major?'

Major Snow purpled with pleasure. 'By gad, Mrs Mackenzie, spot on! Twenty-five years' service before the memsahib and I moved on to Kenya in '48. Gunners, eh? Great chaps! Gentlemen of the Artillery . . .'

The purser smiled urbanely and relaxed imperceptibly. He was good at his job that in addition to other abilities demanded business acumen, diplomacy, a fathomless fund of cleanish jokes, a keen understanding of human nature and cynical tolerance for those human failings that infringed neither company rules nor maritime law. He could spot a potential troublemaker from his or her first meal and disliked seeing blood spilled at his table as it upset his appetite. He turned jovially to Mrs Stevens, 'How gratifying for us all that Mrs Agnew will be well enough to return to her cabin tomorrow.'

The Captain had arrived and musicians begun 'The Blue Danube'. And at all but the purser's, the doctor's, and the Captain's tables – where protocol forbade gossip to Mrs Mellor's private chagrin – the assembled company settled down to the happy prospect of a five-course meal spiced with slanderous speculations. Before dinner ended the generally agreed odds were 5–1, Brown; 125–1, Ashden.

It was a couple of minutes before Elinor noticed Mrs Mellor was beckoning and she joined her solely because common courtesy left no alternative. She had been avoiding Mrs Mellor, as George had confided that 'Paddy and the old dragon are thick as thieves' and she had been determined to show both he and Paddy that she had no intention of intruding upon their shipboard friendships, or of being regarded as the social responsibility of either. Nor, in that disturbingly altered atmosphere of the lounge, was she in any humour for the kind of searching personal questions and barbed references to Paddy that she had been receiving from her own sex since changing cabins.

Mrs Mellor lowered her crochet and said without preamble and very quietly, 'Yes. An uncomfortable spectacle.'

Elinor looked at her quickly and sat down. 'Does this always happen before Mombasa?'

'Not in my experience. But my two previous post-war voyages down this coast were—' she faced Elinor to mouth 'pre-Mau-Mau.'

Elinor's nod concealed her surprise that Mrs Mellor should recognise that although the Mau-Mau attacks on white settlers and their own people had been continuously discussed in both classes since the ship sailed, to voice the subject audibly now seemed as crass as talking of death in the hearing of soldiers about to go into action. 'Shook me.'

'So I observed.'

They looked at each other and then back at the men in tropical shirts, knee-length shorts and socks, or safari suits, or carefully preserved British blazers over cravated shirts and drills. Major Snow puffed importantly over an old Luger and wore his 'Left to me, dear lady, and I'd settle the Mau-Mau's hash in five minutes . . .' expression. Mr Frobisher wearily oiled a hunting rifle and his leathery face looked years older than yesterday. He had told Elinor he had been born in Kenya one year after his parents emigrated from Devon in the final decade of the last century. 'I cannot tell you how much my wife and I are looking forward to retiring to dear old Devon, Mrs Mackenzie . . .' Only from Paddy and others had she heard that neither of the Frobishers had family or friends left in England. 'Sad,' she murmured.

'Lost causes always are, my dear.' Mrs Mellor glanced

at Mr Frobisher. 'Especially for the very few with the foresight to recognise their cause is lost.'

Elinor looked more closely at her companion's sharp-eyed, intelligent, old face. 'And no ties in the country they call Home with a capital H.'

'Quite.' Mrs Mellor sighed. 'I feel so sorry for the older white settlers. The young have the energy and time to start new lives in Rhodesia, South Africa, Australia, New Zealand, or back in the UK. A very different prospect for those that have lived all their lives on land they have loved and regarded as their own – though, of course, it never was.' She paused to exchange farewell bows with several men leaving. 'The Empire only took a lease on the land and the Empire ended on the day the British left India in '47.' She smiled drily. 'Not that that news has yet reached many on this ship or in British Africa. Be prepared to step back in time when you go ashore in Mombasa. And the further south you go, the further back.' Elinor's eyes widened. 'I do not exaggerate, my dear. Kenya is roughly twenty years behind the UK and down in the Union – more like forty. The South Africans still have no television and call the cinema the bioscope.'

'No!'

'Yes, indeed. And white South African women discuss the servant-problem as much as my mother when I was a girl. Possibly,' she added briskly, 'they discuss other subjects, but not in my hearing. Nevertheless I'm sorry the Union is leaving the Commonwealth, though I approve of republics. That's why I love the States with all its faults. Dr Brown says despite my English birth and upbringing, I'm a republican under the skin – and that reminds me! Now I've got you alone there's something about him I've been longing to ask you. May I?'

Damn, thought Elinor, I was beginning to understand why Paddy likes you. She smiled politely and made the expected response.

'How did that passionately republican Irishman survive the war in London without breaking a blood vessel?'

Surprise shed Elinor's composure like an old coat and her face lit with laughter. 'Probably as he hadn't time for it. He never stopped binding that our something war was none of his something business, and when asked why he didn't just beat it back to Ireland, said how could he wangle time to cross the Irish Sea when he'd none to get a hair-cut? And when not blowing all fuses, he made us all laugh a lot.' She paused and her eyes looked backward and the laughter went out. 'By all, I mean patients and staff and I think the patients loved him even more for that than for being a good doctor, which he was – is.' Again she paused and thought of Irene Venner's returned health and ecstatic welcome when she ignored shipboard rules and joined the party in the tourist lounge last night. She thought aloud. 'Laughter has tremendous healing properties.' She heard herself, and added, 'I'd say his sense of humour saved his own and quite a few others' blood-pressure.'

'I'm sure you're right.' Mrs Mellor nodded to herself and recalled the brief account she had been given of Alistair Mackenzie's captivity and death. 'A long time that cast a long shadow,' Dr Brown had said, and in his dark eyes had been the expression she had just seen in Elinor Mackenzie's. That shared experience has forged an unbreakable bond, she reflected, though I doubt either yet recognises its strength. What is beyond

113

doubt is that they are not, and have never been, lovers. His eyes wouldn't give that away, but hers would.

The ship had stopped to pick up the pilot and the lounge was suddenly emptying.

'Time to put away my tatting and make my final round of farewells.' Mrs Mellor tucked the crochet into her handbag. 'I do dislike farewells, but mercifully on a ship the sting is removed by the certainty that the departing will have forgotten one's existence before halfway down the gangplank. Before I go – good time last night? . . . Splendid. Please, don't move—' but Elinor had risen with her. 'Thank you for joining me, Mrs Mackenzie. Cheered me up. I shall look forward to continuing our conversation when we sail. I'm moving to an hotel ashore for the next six days. A ship dies in dock and I'm too old to enjoy the reminder of mortality and fortunately able to indulge myself.' She looked very kindly into Elinor's face. 'And I disapprove most strongly of the unnecessary wearing of hairshirts. Enjoy Mombasa. *Au'voir*.' She sailed off through the empty lounge and towards the lift.

Elinor sat down again and belatedly noticing the rain had stopped took her library book from her straw handbag to give Mrs Mellor time to get clear before going back on deck. The book was an omnibus edition of Edgar Wallace's African novels that Mr Carter considered gave the best description of pre-Great War colonial Africa written by a white man. She opened but didn't read the book. She stared down at the printed page wondering why she had allowed unreasoned prejudice to dismiss Mrs Mellor as an autocratic, garrulous, pampered old woman whose ideas had remained unchanged since instilled by her Victorian parents. She knew she should have remembered Paddy's low boredom tolerance, how always in the past he and she had liked the same people, and how much she had liked the several Mrs Mellors she had nursed for their courage, fortitude, and often, irrespective of social background, bawdy humour. She was troubled and confused by her misjudgement. Myopic as George, she thought, with far less excuse as he's still in his hell.

Her mind returned to the few minutes private conversation she had with Paddy in the smoking room last night.

'I'm glad you showed up, Ellie,' he said. 'Upset George like hell if you hadn't. He's always needed to show the chaps that he's a popular chap and been a damned nice chap. But as Shaw said of – can't remember whom – if he wasn't so damned nice he wouldn't now be so damned.'

'New one on me, but fits him.' She hesitated. 'Why did his marriage go wrong?'

'He's told you it did?' he demanded, oddly. She shook her head. 'Nor me. Never mentioned his marriage or wife's name. I've forgotten it, but I saw the announcement of her death in *The Times* or somewhere. Car smash. Driving alone . . . what's that, George? Will I have another whilst Ellie's dallying over hers? You have to ask when I've an empty glass?'

At lunch-time the previous day she found in her cabin a note signed by all her former cabin-mates and Irene Venner, inviting her to their farewell party. Before leaving George's, she drew him aside to explain this. He was shocked.

'I say – should you? Rather bad form. I mean – not done.'

She smiled soothingly. 'Relax, George. I won't be

drummed out of the regiment. I haven't taken the Queen's shilling. Thanks for a lovely party and—'

'You will come back?'

'If it's not too late and thank you again.'

After the tourist party she spent a long time in the comparative quiet of the stern of the tourists' deck talking with two missionaries. When she parted from them with her first genuine regret of the night she felt incapable of facing another glass, drunken embrace, promise of eternal friendship and to 'meet up on our next leave in dear old England'. She went on quickly, almost furtively, back to her cabin, undressed in her bathroom and went to bed in the dark to avoid showing a light behind her bulkhead window curtains. She fell asleep listening to distant laughter, slurred voices, the soft hum of the engines and slither of the sea against the ship. All night her dreams were haunted by George with Alistair's young face; George with the fair, aesthetic, mature face of the only other man she had loved, who was George's present age, and despite three years as a prisoner of the Japanese, still looked the younger man – unless he talked of his wife.

Two of the three had had unhappy marriages, she thought, staring down at the open book. Coincidence? Or one not uncommon consequence when a girl married her first boyfriend and was too young and ignorant to see beyond the white lace, church bells, walking down the aisle and riding off into the sunset. And – as me – too green to know what she was supposed to do in bed and her embarrassed, fumbling young husband had to show her? Alistair was so sweet – but the poor darling had been dead over two years before I discovered how little he had known about sex – or me. We never had time to be more than loving strangers, but had he lived, would things have soured for us, and at their age, would his face have aged when he mentioned me? Or would he have just silently hugged his desolation, like George?

'Morning, Elinor. May I join you?'

She looked up quickly, forcing a smile. 'Morning, George. Sure. How's your hangover?'

'Top of my head's just about back on.' He sat by her and smoothed his fading fair hair. His eyes were badly bloodshot and pouched and jowls sagged but he was well-shaven and wearing a clean, long-sleeved white shirt Martha's tie, and khaki drills. 'I'm afraid I got a bit lit-up last night.'

'With half the ship. Why not? Party night.'

'Some – er – some women get hellish shirty when a chap gets smashed.'

'Some do, some don't, but not many trained on hospital parties. Any man off call and sober when one ended was regarded as a blot on Martha's. Remember?'

'Actually – er – never went to 'em. Never been a party man like Paddy. This is why I wanted to catch you alone this morning. Thing is – ' he flushed slightly 'I'm hoping you'll rally.'

'My God, not another Fancy Dress Parade!'

He frowned. 'Sorry. Don't get you.'

Her involuntary smile was unconsciously maternal. 'Just waffling. What's on your mind?'

That smile comforted and perplexed him. He had never seen her smile like this at old Paddy – didn't add up – nothing about her did – and nor could he stop thinking about her. He had spent the whole week telling himself that whatever smut was flung around the smoking room was none of his bloody concern and that old Paddy had a perfect right to lash out for his own purposes and been bloody generous even when skint. Hell of a facer that she should be willing – hadn't looked the type – didn't look it now – but women were all the same – trust Kipling to get it right. And she was still such a hellish snappy piece. Knocked him for six on her first evening – daren't believe his eyes – been sure she'd look her age, harder, in daylight. She just looked better – dammit!

'Thing is,' he repeated, and then went on to explain he had just had a cable from an ex-POW friend now living in Nairobi, due in Mombasa this morning, offering to show him the local night spots that night. 'Hellish good chap, Toby Thomas. Sapper. We're always kept in touch. His cable says bring others and make up a party. How about you and Paddy coming along? There's no other woman on board I want to ask anyway, she'd make it dodgy if there's dancing. Tough on Paddy having to sit it out but different with you as you know the score. What do you say?'

She didn't answer directly. 'How long was your chum in the bag?'

'Three years. We first met up in Italy and then again in my last camp in Germany. We – er – walked home together.'

She had heard too much about that forced march and other POW forced marches to follow her instincts and turn this down bluntly. 'What does Paddy say?'

'Haven't asked him yet. First I wanted to know if you think he's up to it. I do. I think it's time he had a night on the town. Do him good.' He watched her fixedly and very hopefully. 'Don't you?'

She was honest. 'I'm not sure he's up to crowds of strangers yet – though for God's sake don't tell him this.' She looked around the empty lounge. 'After twenty-two days at sea the ship's become his home territory. But he's never yet gone on one sight-seeing tour ashore with anyone but you.' She turned back to him. 'He'll know if he is or not. And this is a very kind thought of yours, George. Why not ask him then get back to me?'

'I suppose that means his thumbs-down goes for you, too,' he said, looking sulky as a schoolboy forced to stay in during play period. To cover his disappointment he picked up and scowled at the title of her book. Then suddenly his face altered to that of a younger, happier man, and he grinned. 'Good old Edgardo Vallarchy!'

She did a double-take at his transformed face. 'Say again.'

'Edgardo Vallarchy.' He gripped the book as if it were the hand of an old friend. 'Saved my sanity when I was warded in that Jerry hospital in Rome.'

Her expression quickened. He had never talked of his war to her or Paddy. 'When were you there?'

'Forget exactly.' He frowned unseeingly at a point in mid-air. 'August – no September, '43.'

'Why were you warded?'

He did not answer at once and she waited in silence and without moving, just as she had so often waited when sitting on bedside lockers for the kind of revelations wounded soldiers gave their nurses, especially at night, and often, no one else. He said at last, 'A few months earlier the Italians had shifted me from an officers to an O.R. (Other Ranks) camp near Genoa. This wasn't too long before Italy packed it in and they needed a British MO as their only had croaked of dip. (diphtheria), poor sod. It wasn't a bad camp as camps go, and our chaps were good types. I liked them a lot.'

He faced her but didn't see her. 'No one ever told us what was happening to the war. One day all the Italians got shifted out and the Jerries took over.' He slapped himself for cigarettes. She took a packet from her hand-bag, put one between his lips and help up a lighted match. 'Thanks,' he muttered, still staring into her face and seeing only the past. 'None of us much liked the change. First thing the Jerries did was bring in more rolls of barbed-wire and set up a machine-gun post on the perimeter. They were hot on test-firing from that post – sometimes into the camp. Accidentally, they said, when I complained to the Commandant.' He smiled faintly. 'A few days later another bit of acciden-tal test-firing got me a bellyload in the right buttock.'

'Bone or flesh wounds?' She asked professionally and as she anticipated he responded with the medical details.

'Not that I then knew much about it,' he went on. 'Next thing I really knew was that I was in a German military hospital in Rome. Still no recollection of getting there. But there I was in a bloody great ward filled with Jerry O.R. wounded. Decent chaps on the whole and the Jerry surgeons knew their stuff and weren't short of drugs or anaesthetics. That was a break as the Italians had run out of both long before they packed it in. Another break was that all the medical orderlies that dealt with me were Italians. Nice little chaps – not too heavy-handed. I could have struck it much worse, but what had me browned off as hell was the boredom. I didn't then speak or read German. None of the chaps in beds near mine spoke English – or if they did didn't let on – and every book in the ward – weren't many – was in German. And then – ' he broke off and his face was illuminated by a boyish smile that she had last seen on him ten years ago, and one she had last seen in Alistair's face after he kissed her goodbye and leant, waving, out of the window of a train pulling out of Waterloo Station. She looked down into her lap and did not see Paddy watching them from the lounge entrance then turning and going back out on deck.

'And then,' repeated George dreamily, 'the old boot came round.'

Elinor blinked. 'Matron?'

He shook his head. 'Some Jerry brass hat's wife. Flat as a board fore and aft, flat feet in shoes that could have doubled as Army issue and a face like an old boot. She stopped to chat with most of her chaps but marched by my bed eyes front. I wasn't surprised she ignored me. The Gestapo was always breathing heavily down the *Wehrmacht's* neck'; fraternising with the enemy was not just *verboten* but bloody dangerous. But the next day – next morning – one of the Italian orderlies – kindly chap needing a shave – charged up to my bed waving a brace of aged books over his head and shouting joyfully, "Edgardo Vallarchy! Edgardo Vallarchy!" '

'George! She sent them to you?'

'God save the kind old boot, she did! Two of Wallace's in English. *The Ringer* and *The Four Just Men*. I never knew how she swung it, but she took one hell of a risk. I've never forgotten her or those books. Knew them by heart when they shifted me off to Germany. I tried to take them along but the Jerry guards took them off me before loading us on to the train.'

'Ambulance train?'

'Huh! Cattle trucks, stretcher-cases and walking wounded for the use of. Straw on the floor wasn't too filthy for the first couple of days.'

Elinor's throat was tight. She had heard other first-

121

hand accounts of such trains and of rotting jungle huts converted into prison-camp 'hospitals' with no beds, bedding, medical equipment, drugs, anaesthetics, nurses and only rarely, one British MO. 'How long were you on that train?'

He had to think and before he could answer 'Hands to stations fore and aft!' sounded over the Tannoy. He blinked as if waking and the youth faded and the lines deepened in his face.

He said abruptly, 'God knows why I've bored you with all this. Never told anyone before.'

Not even though you were married nine years and must have loved her more than you knew to be still so hurt, she thought sadly. 'You haven't bored me.'

He was unconvinced. 'Women like to forget the war.'

'Yes. We do. Even when we can't.' She looked down at her wedding ring. 'But I don't think people should be forgotten, or can be, by those that loved them.' She looked up wet-eyed. 'I'll never forget Alistair.'

He was appalled. 'Christ, I've upset you.'

She said gently, 'Upset is too trivial a word in this context. Of course this hurt to hear, but not for me, for you, Alistair and all the others that were shut up for what should have been some of the best years of your lives. Shut up in the nagging uncertainty of ever getting out, on low or no rations, with no privacy and no women. Tough on all men; toughest on young men.'

He muttered incredulously, 'You – understand.'

'George, I've been around.' She took the book from his hands. 'Go and sound Paddy about tonight. I'll be somewhere on deck.'

He rose obediently, 'Can I tell him you're for it if he is?' She had to nod. 'Good show! Thanks Elinor.' He shot from the lounge as if it were on fire.

The ship had just emerged from the Channel into a wide, natural, recently enlarged harbour when she lent on a rail a few yards from her cabin window. The hilly dark green land was dotted with large, white houses and backed by distant mountains that were black etchings on the sky. The crumbling grey ruins of a fort tipped the headland that guarded the northern entrance and ranged along its inner side were cars parked as if for an English point-to-point. The white houses had red, sloping roofs and private gardens and there were clumps of what looked like English oaks. And standing by, or sitting on the roofs of the parked cars, were groups of people waving, smiling and calling greetings to the incoming liner in British voices.

Mr Carter joined her at the rail. 'Reminding you of home, Mrs Mackenzie?'

'Very Surrey-ish.'

'A misconception no doubt aided by the well-tended gardens.'

'And the oaks.' He shook his head. 'Not oaks?'

'Marshmallow trees.' He gestured with the stem of his empty pipe. 'The trunks look solid, but are soft and spongy. Use an axe on one and it just sinks in. Can't be cut down. Only way to get rid of them is burn them down and burn out the roots, but even so, sooner rather than later new seeds will take root.'

She rested her hands lightly on the hot brass and mahogany rail. 'I could've sworn they were oaks.'

He peered at her over the top of his dark glasses. 'If I may offer a little more gratuitous advice—' she gestured assent, 'never in Africa allow yourself to be deluded by any transient impression of a resemblance to the UK. Nor, at any port on this coast, go ashore on your own after dark.'

She looked in surprise from the white crowds on the headland and the white crews of the little fleet of sailing and rowing boats coming to escort in the ship. 'But all right in daylight?'

'Possibly, though I wouldn't advise it. Should you go shopping or sightseeing with two or three other ladies and stay together, you should suffer no disadvantage. But after dark, for a white woman, a masculine escort is essential.'

She thought of the girls in tourist going out to first jobs as typists and nannies and eagerly anticipating exciting social lives, and of the darkness that fell like a curtain at six p.m. 'Quite a restriction.'

'No doubt. Particularly for women previously only accustomed to the freedom of movement they had in the UK. However—' his half-smile appeared 'since presently in Kenya the ratio of British men to British women is roughly five-to-one and rises to ten-to-one where young women are concerned, possibly for the latter, their greater problem is which of the queue to pick for escort.'

She smiled, glad for those girls. 'I see what you mean. May I ask, how long have you worked in Africa?'

'Since '24. I was born in Nyasaland. My late father was a District Officer. My brothers and I were sent home to school shortly before the Great War and that kept us from returning to our parents. Being sixteen when that war ended, I missed it. My two elder brothers were less fortunate. Killed on the same day in '17. A not uncommon occurrence at that time. It was an unpleasant time,' he said mildly, 'as, no doubt, was your war.'

'It was,' she said, as mildly, and for about a minute they stayed silent and watched the British and American sailors waving to the *Rose of Africa* from the decks of their respective destroyers that were anchored parallel with each other on different sides of the harbour.

'Courtesy calls or showing the flag, Mr Carter?'

'I would surmise a little of both.' He used his pipe stem to gesture from the sleek grey lethal warships to the anchored armada of brown-sailed Arab dhows and the ruined fort. 'Mombasa was a cluster of mud huts when that fort was built, but already the dhows had traded here for centuries. And they will continue doing so for centuries after the last western navy has upped anchor for good, and the remaining dust of that fort been blown away by the wind. Man and man-made buildings are finite. Africa is infinite.'

She heard the rare warmth in his voice. 'And you love Africa.'

He hesitated. 'I'm not sure that I am capable of loving the unknown, but mysteries have their own attractions. I am always glad to return to Africa and when I finally have to leave I've no doubt it will be with regret – and the mystery of Africa still beyond my understanding. Morning.' He raised his jungle hat and drifted away.

Elinor stayed to watch the figures waving from the headland, and as they lined the docks ahead. The smiling crews of the little boats shouted joyfully, as if the *Rose* was bringing their hearts' desire. She had never known the ship receive such a warm welcome. She sensed the element of homesickness this contained and suddenly understood why Mrs Mellor, George and Mr Carter had confided to her in the last hour. She had that starboard side of the lower promenade deck to herself; the disembarkers were queuing one deck down; and the other 'goings-on' were on the two above. She glanced at the empty deckchairs behind her as her sub-

125

conscious thrust up the long-forgotten memory of her boarding-school on the last day of term after all the girls going home had left. The handful staying on for the holidays had drifted aimlessly around the empty classrooms swapping confidences, sharing the sweets the headmistress handed round from the tuck-cupboard immediately the last station bus left, forming temporary bosom friendships, and maintaining the absolute taboo on any mention of 'mummy and daddy' in Africa, India, Ceylon, Burma, Shanghai, Hong Kong and the Antipodes. She had not often had to stay at school in the holidays; just often enough now to recall vividly the children in the empty classrooms mutely recognising that homes were places that belonged to other girls and not them.

One of the prices generations of British children had to pay for the Empire, she thought, when there was no widespread immunisation therapy, penicillin or antibiotics, and too often the alternative resulted in another child's grave in the British cemeteries in the pink splashes that ringed the map of the world. She thought of her parents who had died in India within eighteen months of each other during her last two years at school, and of the infant brother who had died there three years before her parents returned to England for her birth. Her father, a Martha's man in the Indian Medical Services, had then gone back to India when his leave ended, and her mother had eventually rejoined him when Elinor was five and considered old enough for boarding-school. From then on she had only seen her parents for a few months every three years, and spent most of her school holidays with the married childless cousins of her father who had become her joint legal guardians in England. They had shown her great kindness and meticulously observed their responsibilities as proxy-parents, and when they were killed together by the high-explosive bomb that destroyed their Chelsea house in May, 1941 during the second London blitz, she had grieved for them as she had for her parents. By then, at Helen Mackenzie's insistence she had been living with her in Northumberland. 'This is Alistair's home and your rightful place until he returns and can give you your own home, Elinor . . .'

She had never forgotten the comfort Helen's insistence had then afforded her and it was only now, fourteen years later on a ship entering Mombasa, that a flash of self-insight illuminated the vital part played in her life by the childish longing for a home born in those empty classrooms during the school holidays.

She needed the certainty of privacy to think this over and went quickly back to her cabin. It was hot and airless. She opened the window, half-closed the curtains, turned on all the blowers and lay on the bed under the window whilst her mind juxtaposed past and present like a jerky 'stills' camera. She saw Helen's tear-swollen face in late September, 1945. 'I know you've got your work – but you won't forget this is your home and that you are all I've got left and leave me to get old and die alone amongst strangers. Promise, Elinor – promise . . .'

Then her lover's set, angry face in early 1953. 'You can't do this, my darling! I won't let you give up your career – your ward. You love it! She has no right to expect this of you and can well afford a nursing home!'

She heard her retort, 'You have no right to forbid me anything, Richard. You'll just have to accept that Helen matters to me, as I've had to accept your religion does to you. Matron has accepted my resignation and been very sweet. And perhaps' she added gently, 'this is right for Helen, and us.'

'I can't bear – I won't lose you!'

'My dearest man, you're a lawyer. You tell me how you can lose something you have never owned?'

She closed her eyes to black out memory and in a few minutes fell deeply asleep. When she woke in mid-afternoon the engines were silent. The near-empty ship echoed with the vibrations of the ventilating plant: hammering; the squeaking of derricks; the shouted orders of the bridge officers supervising the unloading; the soft patter of the bare feet of the African dock labourers and their deep voices calling and singing from the black depths of the open holds over which the bedraggled kites hovered and wheeled like airborne beggars.

Her cabin steward had been in and closed and locked her window and left on her dressing-table a sealed envelope that contained a note from George written at noon:

> Your steward says you are sleeping. Writing
> not to disturb you. Toby T. just come aboard
> and we're off ashore. Paddy lunching ashore
> with Mrs M. – expects back around tea-time
> and all for tonight. Hope it will suit if we call
> for you at eight. Dinner booked for nine.
> Great to have you along. Regards. G.
>   P.S. T.T. says black ties in order.

She smiled slightly and thought aloud. 'To rephrase Paddy – what else, when dining with the ghost of the Empire?'

SEVEN
Mombasa
June 1955

The African waiters wore long white robes and green sashes; the Egyptian wine-waiter, a red fez; the Belgian head waiter, a black imperial; the Scottish solo pianist, a white tuxedo; and thousands of insects hurled themselves to death against the great plate glass window behind Paddy's back.

'More room for your long legs that end, old boy,' said Toby Thomas, seating Elinor on his right and George on his left at the oval table he had particularly reserved for its panoramic view of the coast and the hotel's dance floor on the beach below.

The brilliantly lit and appointed dining room was larger than the first-class dining saloon, all the other diners were in dinner-jackets or floor-length dresses and on their slow progress to their table, the new just-above-ankle-length A-line style of Elinor's black silk taffeta briefly diverted all the other women's eyes from

Paddy's long, elegant, limping figure. Only Elinor was close enough to see the slight beading on his upper lip.

Toby Thomas was forty, but looked younger. His pleasantly pugnacious face was deeply tanned and he had a neat military haircut and moustache. He enjoyed hosting a well-turned-out, top-drawer party from Home and showing them that out here they knew how to live. He pressed upon them his choices from the extensive menu and South African wine-list and expounded on the good life in Kenya without mentioning the gathering shadows. George listened with growing optimism for his future in Rhodesia and the other two with a smiling interest that cloaked their individual awareness of the rumblings of the distant volcano and that the only black faces around belonged to the waiters. On the dance floor below the floating skirts and trousered legs of the dancing couples merged upwards into swirling, headless, shadows. The floor was only lit underfoot; on the invisible dais, the lights on the stands of the five-man band, were small as throat-torches; the lighted ends of the cigarettes of the sitters-out at the tables circling the floor were clouds of fireflies in the darkness. The surrounding white sand had a ghostly glimmer and the calm, navy blue Indian Ocean shimmered in starlight so bright that it dimmed the waning sickle moon. And in the soundproofed dining room the Scottish pianist played selections from '20s and '30s musicals as if in the Palm Court of an expensive English seaside hotel in those decades.

They were finishing their Gateau Mombasa, when the ex-POWs briefly relapsed into a private, 'What happened to old . . .'

Paddy leaned towards Elinor to murmur gravely, 'Do you think the King will marry Mrs Simpson?'

She was equally grave. 'Only if he abdicates. Once the story breaks the country won't stand for a divorcee on the Throne.'

His eyebrows rose, 'But do you think the English will ever get their heads out of the sand?'

'What's that about sand, old boy?' Toby demanded. 'Do forgive me. Missed the rest. Inexcusable! But if you like good white sand you'll see plenty down this coast. Just don't walk on it in bare feet. Jiggers aren't all you'll pick up in a few paces. And stick to the pools for a swim. Sharks'll take a man waist-deep – but this is not the subject for a dinner table with a charming lady present. Something I've been meaning to ask you, old boy. George mentioned you were at Stoneyhurst. One of my best mates and nearest neighbours – Penny and the kids are shacking-up with them tonight – Dan Desmond, must have been around in your time . . . By God! Good mate of yours, eh? Old Dan's going to be sorry to miss running into you again. And Penny—' he bowed to Elinor 'distraught at missing you, dear charming lady. Penny loves meeting girlfriends from Home and having long girlie talks about fashions and hair-dos. She always used to come down to Mombasa with me, but – right now – we don't leave the children without one of us. Joan, our English nanny, is first-rate and our house-boys splendid chaps – but Joan hasn't been out here long . . . How about dessert? Cheese? May I suggest . . .'

Again the conversation became general. Toby and Paddy did most of the talking, George listened contentedly, drinking quantities of wine, and Elinor obeyed the conventions of her girlhood by putting in an occasional deferential remark and otherwise providing an admiring audience to the men. Toby exuded approval of her attitude, George glowed with a near-proprietary satisfaction, and Paddy's eyes glittered with sardonic amusement. Their coffee and liqueurs had arrived when the subject moved to Rhodesia.

Toby said, 'You'll enjoy it, old boy. We were down there for our last leave. Beautiful country, the Rhodesians are rattling good types and the place is just like pre-war England. But as for England—' he smiled deprecatingly '–mine own country and all that so I trust I'll be forgiven for saying that in my humble opinion it's changed beyond belief and not for the better. On our last home-leave in '51, we couldn't wait to get back. The whole place was in a shocking mess – nothing but bomb-damage still lying about – shortages – rationing – talk of welfare state and Jack being as good as his master. All those Labour so-and-sos' fault, of course – nuff said! Mustn't bore our charming lady with politics! No, no!' He dismissed Elinor's disclaimer. 'You don't have to pretend so fetchingly to me, Mrs Mackenzie. Old married man. I know you ladies prefer to leave such tedious matters to us mere males. More coffee? . . . Another liqueur? . . . No takers? Then shall we move on and take in another aspect of Mombasa by night?'

Toby was dealing with the bill and George draining his glass when Paddy murmured to Elinor, 'But such a pretty little head.'

She fluttered her eyelashes, 'Fiddle-de-dee, Rhett. How you do run on.'

George hurried to draw back her chair and lay her black lace shawl over her shoulders as if she were made of glass. He couldn't remember when he had last so enjoyed a good night out. Old Toby hadn't changed – always been the life of the party when all they'd had

132

to drink was much-stewed esartz coffee dregs. Paddy was in great form and not a woman around to hold a candle to Elinor. She'd clean bowled old Toby. When they stopped first for drinks at the old British Club and she and Paddy were waylaid by the Frobishers spending the night there before returning up-country in the morning, Toby said she was the most fetchingly elegant little filly to set foot in Kenya since he and Penny emigrated from Kent in '47, and that he didn't buy what he, George, had said about those two this afternoon.

'I'm not saying the chap hasn't an eye on her – more than a spot of the old Adam in that chap notwithstanding the dodgy pins – bloody tough luck that – but if she's his property I don't know my own name. He – or any chap – could do a lot worse than hitch up with a pretty little widow straight out of the top drawer, who, from that little black number alone, can't be short of the odd bob. Hallmarked Bond Street, old boy. And she knows how to wear it and what a chap needs . . . nuff said! Time to join the ladies . . .'

And old Toby, reflected George, following the others into the waiting hired car, had always had the knack of getting dead on target from his first spot recce.

Toby sat in front with the African driver and George between the others on the back seat. He leant forward to peer through the closed windows at the long, neon-lit, main street.

'Reminds me of the Great West Road,' he said approvingly.

Paddy said, 'If that had this superfluity of cinemas.'

Elinor looked at the huge posters of Humphrey Bogart and Ingrid Bergman, Katharine Hepburn and Spencer Tracy, Clark Gable, Judy Garland and others, advertising films she had first seen in the war. She thought of Mr Carter and Mrs Mellor and stayed silent.

The main road and neon lights ended abruptly. The narrowed grey road ran on into the darkness of the open bush and the driver switched on the wipers to clear the windscreen of bombarding insects as automatically as a London taximan in a sudden squall. They met no other traffic and their headlights transformed to headless, limbless, white torsoes the African men in singlets and shorts backing off the road to let the car pass.

Toby lit a cigarette, 'Just in case the odd mosquito gets in.' He turned back. 'This spot's not far out of town and worth the look-see for a glimpse of the seamy side of Mombasa and – according to Penny – for the music. Penny's a bit of a jazz fan. She's always got the gramophone going and no prizes for the name of the muggins that has to keep winding it up. Place fascinated Penny and, if a spot seamy, I'll make sure we've a table with our backs to a wall. With three chaps as escort party, no cause for alarm, I hope, Elinor – if I may?'

'Please, Toby. And, none.'

'Bless you! Just one word of warning. Dancing *verboten*. You'll see why.' He turned back and in Swahili told the driver when to return for them.

George thought aloud in a mutter, 'Wouldn't have suited Brenda. Couldn't ever bear talk of the seamy side.' He didn't notice his companions' quick sideways glances at this first mention of his dead wife's name.

Paddy said, 'Don't come seamier than in Martha's backyard. Ellie's been around.'

'So she's told me,' George retorted quietly but the challenge was as unmistakable as the suddenly electric atmosphere in the back of the darkened car. None of them spoke again until after it stopped and when it slowed Elinor adjusted her shawl to shroud her bare arms and cowl her neck.

The size of Toby's tip procured them a table against an outer wall by removing it from four amiably co-operative, slightly drunk, American sailors. The three sitting on the long bench that lined the wall, squeezed out grinning, the fourth, a gangling, fresh-faced boy, offered his cane chair to Paddy. 'I guess it'll be easier on the butt, sir – pardon me, ma'am—' he blushed and swayed off to join his buddies and the group of US sailors at one end of the long bar that was eyeing and being eyed by a similar group of British sailors at the opposite end. The bare wooden table was badly scratched and charred by cigarettes, but reasonably clean and, as the bench, was nailed to the floor. There were other tables against that wall and many more around the smallish dance floor that was backed by the bar that ran the length of the opposite wall. All the tables were taken and all the walls covered by life-size paintings of girls in leis and grass skirts, or sarongs, with skins that varied from *café-au-lait* to black. The eyes were enticing, the figures seductively posed, but far more decorously covered than the average chorus line in London or New York, and the skins mirrored those of the girls sitting together at two tables jammed against the musicians' platform that looked too rickety for the upright piano and shirt-sleeved African quartet taking a break and downing beers.

The wall-paintings relieved George. 'Scarcely porno-graphic.'

'Of course not, old boy. The Africans know more about sex than any nation on earth and that nothing's more exciting than the veil.' Toby glanced at Elinor's shrouded shoulders and George's mouth tightened. She sat between them and was looking around composedly and Paddy was ostensibly watching the sailors at both ends of the bar.

'Odds on shore patrols'll be busy tonight,' he said.

'Standard form when either Navy's in port, old boy. Can't blame the chaps. As Kipling didn't quite put it – single chaps on lower decks don't grow into plaster saints. Big problem out here is the shortage of girls. Never enough to go round. The Africans marry their women young and once married, no messing about. Man's country, Africa.'

Paddy's gaze was on the girls at the two tables. 'Those kids are very young.'

'Always the few that slip through the net, old boy. As well for the chaps, one might say.'

Paddy nodded impassively and looked away. George smiled uncomfortably, Elinor glanced at the back of Paddy's head, and suddenly recalled one nightmarish evening in Casualty in the last winter of the war when one of the innumerable girls and young women wheeled in half-dead after back street abortions, had died on a stretcher trolley before she could be wheeled to a ward. Paddy, the only available registrar, had held one end of the trolley, one of the medical students working as Casualty dressers the other, and after they had whisked it into one of the empty clinical rooms and he helped her cover the pretty, childish face with a grey blanket, his face had been white as his then less controllable temper.

'Mother of God,' he snarled. 'If I could right now castrate every man in London including myself I'd bloody do it!'

136

George discovered their table and bench were nailed down. 'Standard form in this joint, Toby?'

Toby nodded. 'Only the chairs stand free. Cane can't do much damage to a man's head.'

Paddy looked round. 'Providing the legs don't gouge out his eyes.'

'I say, steady on, old boy. Alarm the lady. Not alarmed I hope, Elinor?'

'Merely wondering who'll make the first entrance. Glenn Ford or Rita Hayworth.'

'By God, you're right! Knew you were a good sport soon as I clapped eyes on you. Must pass this on to Penny. Right up her street! Great film fan!'

A waiter arrived with four bottles of beer and four cleanish glasses. Elinor used the diversion for a more comprehensive look around. There were several others in evening dress at tables nearer the floor and all had the tan of white settlers. The women looked tired and bored, the men's hard faces were flushed and their voices a little too loud. The only other women were the girls at the two tables. They wore western evening dresses in cheap bright materials and their uniformly beautiful and unsmiling eyes were too old for their young faces. All were smoking but none drinking. They sat either in silence or chatting to each other and ignoring the men watching them from the bar, the tables, or from against the walls. Most of those men were in their early twenties or younger and their hot eyes were hungry and wary. One old seaman sat alone at a table on their far left; his lined bitter face was mahogany-tanned, his eyes slid from side to side like a cat's, his hands clutched a half-empty beer bottle and he sat so still that he could have been nailed down.

The double bass player picked up his instrument and

began plucking the strings, the drummer took up the beat and the girls at the two tables lifted their heads like flowers after rain. The pianist tapped out the beat with his feet and sat stiff-backed for about half a minute before his hands exploded on to the keys and the trumpeter raised a shower of notes. The floor was packed in seconds and the sailors' white uniforms, clutching holds, and mainly awkward feet, enhanced the brightness of the girls' dresses and the innate grace of their movements. The numbers followed without break and with continuous improvisations from the trumpeter and pianist. The steady, sensuous beat had even the bad dancers swaying in rhythm; the wooden floor vibrated; glasses and bottles jangled; and the watching men's faces grew more flushed and slurred.

'Christ.' George mopped his face. 'Hard to keep one's feet still.'

'No harm there, old boy, so long as you keep them under this table. Stand up with Elinor and you throw her to the wolves. Law of the jungle once she's seen dancing and the refusal to a cut-in can be answered by anything from a fist to a jab from a broken bottle.' He gestured imperceptibly. 'Watch the luscious filly in yellow with the little civvy.'

The tall, very lovely girl in clinging yellow satin danced like a ballerina and as if dancing alone and oblivious to the young white man in a limp duck suit, collar and tie, grabbing her more tightly and glaring at the large American sailor tapping his shoulder. Then the latter dropped his hand and closed it into a fist. The little man dropped his arms, the American clutched the girl and was a good dancer, but again she danced on as if alone for the few seconds before an equally large British sailor tapped her partner's shoulder.

Momentarily the two men's eyes measured each other, then the American shrugged and released her.

George was jubilant. 'Trust the Navy to take the Yanks down a peg. The way they still brag about having won the war for us makes me want to puke.'

Paddy raised an eyebrow. 'But, didn't they?'

Elinor said conversationally, 'Of course they did and God bless 'em for it or none of us could have had tonight's superlative dinner or the chance to hear this shatteringly good jazz. You wife's right, Toby. This quartet is superb.'

George's colour had risen. 'Damned amazing. Good as Yank jazz.'

Paddy said drily, 'Hardly amazing. Where did New Orleans get it from in the first place?'

'Christ, you don't change!' George snapped. 'Always had to know all the answers.'

'And where's the Irishman that doesn't? Or—' Paddy nodded slightly towards the bar, 'can't smell an incipient punch-up at fifty paces?'

Toby looked at the bar. 'Dead right, old boy. Time we moved on – if that's all right with you, Elinor?'

She smiled. 'Whenever you say, Toby,' and mentally breathed out. She was conscious of being an object of discussion amongst the American group and guessed what could be coming. She knew that Paddy, and she was sure Toby, would deal with this tactfully, but doubted that George or the British sailors would do the same. She had nursed scores of Royal and Merchant Navy seamen in the war and liked them enormously, but learned that whilst, in general, the most peaceful of men, when confronted by any real or imaginary affront to their uniform, ships, Navy or nationality, they took action first and dealt with the consequences later. And since they sat down to dinner she had sensed the change in George's attitude towards her which now that his blood-alcohol was lowering his defences, was as obvious as his resentment of Paddy.

Toby checked his watch. 'Our boy should be back with the car. Just take a quick recce. Don't want to keep you hanging about outside. Back on the double.' He squeezed out and Paddy slid into his seat.

George said. 'Bit cramping for you, I'd have thought, Paddy.'

'Not really and the view's better.' He flicked open his cigarette case, glanced up and added under his breath, 'Or was,' and exchanged a fleeting and deeply communicative glance with Elinor.

George had turned puce. 'If those bloody Yanks dare—' He was silenced by Elinor's sharp kick at his right shin as their table was surrounded by six Americans pushing forward the one who had given Paddy his chair and was grinning with the bravado of a boy determined to prove his manhood to his peers and himself.

'Umm – pardon me, sir – ma'am – umm – would you care to dance, ma'am?'

Elinor smiled up at him and then at Paddy whilst her left hand held George's stiffened right wrist under the table-top.

Paddy said pleasantly, 'Perhaps I can persuade my wife to dance with you, son.' He turned to Elinor. 'My darling, you love dancing and now I can no longer dance with you, you mustn't let my feeling a bit off colour spoil your own or this young man's pleasure—'

'Dearest, this is sweet of you, but no.' Her voice was warm with concern and she laid her free hand on

Paddy's on the table-top. She gazed up in appeal. 'Sailor, thank you very much for asking me, but I know you will understand I must stay with my husband. He's not at all well and needs to get out in the air. Our friend has just gone to see if our car's there.' She turned anxiously to George. 'We shouldn't wait?'

George nodded dumbly. He had caught on but was too incensed for speech.

Paddy smiled bravely into Elinor's anxious face. 'My darling, I hate to spoil your evening, but I'm afraid you are right. I could use some air.' He attempted to stand, slumped back and looked up at the now confused, embarrassed Americans. 'My legs have a nasty habit of going AWOL every now and then. If one of you chaps wouldn't mind giving me an arm up—' Six pairs of arms lunged for him and from somewhere behind an Englishman's voice demanded, 'Yanks giving trouble, sir? Need any help?' The speaker was the RN Leading Seaman who had cut in on the girl in yellow and in the next couple of seconds he had thrust through to Paddy's free side and his oppos had surrounded the Americans.

'Far from it, thanks, old chap,' Paddy replied amiably, but the order was clear. 'These good chaps are just helping hoist me off this bench. It could be said—' his voice weakened, 'not a moment too soon, as—' and his voice stopped as he sagged forward and closed his eyes.

George had risen but was too hemmed in to do more than watch impotently whilst Paddy was lifted into a chair-lift formed by grasped British and American hands, and Elinor fluttered helplessly, as if she had never seen a man faint. The combined Navies cleared a path and escorted them through the tobacco and beer-fumed hall vibrating to the uninterrupted, steady, sensuous music. Elinor held Paddy's stick and clung to George's supporting arm, and the returning Toby stopped aghast.

She said quickly, 'I'm afraid Paddy's had one of his turns, Toby. These gentlemen are kindly taking him to the car. It's there?'

'Present and correct.' He shot a glance at George who nodded imperceptibly. 'Thanks, chaps. This way. Follow me.'

Elinor tightened her grip on George's arm, paused to let the procession get ahead, and murmured. 'Quid to each Navy. You'll cope?'

He grunted in assent. He didn't need her to tell him the form, nor like her knowing how close he had come to making a fool of himself, and discovering that she was as good a bare-faced liar as Paddy. He was relieved when directly they were outside she let go of him and rushed to join Paddy in the car. Toby had closed the door after her then turned back to thank the sailors; and their driver, on Toby's instructions in his seat, switched back on the inside lights. Paddy lay back, closed-eyed, in the far window seat and George watched her lay a hand on Paddy's forehead and take his pulse before she jumped out.

'Gentlemen, you've been wonderful. Thank you all very, very, much.'

'Anytime, ma'am!'

'Glad to be of service, madam,' they chorused and in turn shook her offered hand and nearly wrecked her knuckles. Then one re-opened the car door for her, the driver switched off and on the lights, and turned to watch what was happening in the back as avidly as the combined escort party.

Paddy did not stir when again she reached for his wrist and with her other hand stroked the grey forelock from his damp, high, brow. She forgot the watchers and studied his closed, strained face in genuine concern. She had guessed, and his pulse-rate confirmed, what this act was costing his pride. Then he sighed deeply and blinked open his eyes exactly as someone coming out of a faint. Their faces were very close and for a few seconds each saw the unguarded truth in the other's eyes. And then his eyes lit with reminiscent laughter and he slowly shook his head and protested plaintively, 'Eleven years no less, Ellie and you've still not told me if we'd a boy or girl.'

EIGHT
London
November 1944

There were no patients waiting on the benches when Nurse Eyre, the senior Casualty staff nurse, crossed quickly from Room One to the porter's lodge that overlooked the whole department and the entrance from Casualty Yard. A double row of heavy blackout curtains closed off the always open entrance and for the past four years all the windows had been bricked up, but wisps of fog cobwebbed the overhead lights and the dust cloud hovered like ectoplasm just under the high ceiling of the great hall that could – and often did – accommodate one thousand patients. The dust was a mixture of the grime, soot, and plaster that coated all air-raid victims. During the last five months the smell of that dust had become as constant in the Casualty air as the fumes of ether, carbolic, iodoform, chloroform, and surgical spirit coming from the nineteen assorted, medical, clinical and surgical dressing rooms that lined and opened into the hall. Now, for the first time since early morning, all but three of the rooms were in darkness and the air had lost the additional sickly-sour scent of fresh-spilled blood and ugly reek of human fear.

Nurse Eyre stopped at the glassless window, buttoning her long sleeves and putting on her starched cuffs. 'I'm off to supper, too, Jackson.'

'Righty-oh, Nurse.' Jackson added her name to those of a student nurse and the two medical students working as Casualty dressers, whom she had just sent to supper. Jackson was a slight, pale, greying man temporarily deputising for the senior Casualty porter on his half-day that should have begun at one p.m. It had been six p.m. before Jackson had taken over the lodge to his infinite relief, as the necessity to keep within reach of the battery of telephones that was literally the heart of the hospital's lifelines, allowed him to sit down for the first time that day. He said feelingly, 'You'll be glad of the breather, Nurse Eyre.'

Nurse Eyre nodded wearily. She was in charge over the weekend, had been Sister Casualty's deputy for two years and had long grown accustomed to the kind of day they had just had, but her normally pink cheeks had the pallor of a night nurse. She had been on duty since seven thirty a.m., and when she came on, the long, pew-like mahogany benches ranged down the hall on either side of a wide aisle, were thick with air-raid dust and filling with slumped, seated, figures, huddled under grey Casualty blankets.

At five forty-five a.m. another V2 rocket had landed in Martha's zone and by noon thirty-four severely injured victims had been carried in and sixty-eight minor-injured had brought themselves in for treatment. All the 'minors' had now been discharged home; the severely injured were either in the wards or basement theatre, where four tables were in simultaneous action. There were still eleven waiting in the theatre queue; in all the above-ground and basement wards the surgical sides had overflowed into the medical; and in the last hour the theatre had borrowed two of Casualty's six dressers to act as theatre porters. Martha's, as every hospital in the country, was so desperately short of porters that the few they managed to employ – who were all either over the age or physically unfit for military service – were too valuable to be spared from their respective departments. Jackson was presently the only one in Casualty as the colleague officially on with him had been given special leave-of-absence to search for his only sister missing since that morning's rocket landed.

'Before I go, Jackson – any word of Franklin's sister?'

He shook his head grimly. 'Bound to take time searching the other hospitals this side and the wardens' posts. The fog'll not help.'

'I'm afraid not.' Nurse Eyre hesitated, though already late for the penultimate serving of supper. Franklin's missing sister had cast a deeply personal shadow over the whole Casualty staff all day and Franklin was Jackson's great friend. But the one thing that always cheered him was Casualty-shop, as it made him feel as omniscient as Dacey, the senior porter, who knew everything without having to be told. 'Jackson, a quick run-through in case you need it.' His face quickened eagerly. 'Three of those four women on the left front bench are waiting for the three sprains-and-bruises in Room One and the fourth for the query Vincent's Angina in Three. Nurse Phillips (the junior staff nurse) and one of our two remaining dressers are in One; Mr Stewart and Nurse Mackenzie in Three. Mr Jason has seen the woman in One and the boy with the query hairline fracture in Seventeen with Nurse Dale (a student nurse) and the other dresser. The women can go home once their dressings are done and Mr Jason's just taken the boy's wet plates down to the SSO in the theatre. If you need another house-surgeon before Mr Jason gets back, get Mr Winter. I'm pretty sure the woman in Three and the boy will have to come in, though I'm not sure where they'll fit them. Basement wards, probably. I just hope the police get the boy's mother here soon. Father's in the RAF in Scotland and the poor child is only fourteen and scared stiff. Though what his mother was thinking of to let him ride his bike in this fog, beats me.'

'You can say that again, Nurse. Can't see your nose on your face outside, but should give us a bit of hush. Traffic's down to walking pace where not stopped dead and seeing Jerry dropped his calling cards on our side yesterday and early this morning, shouldn't be many around till pubs close and they'll be half-empty. Still—' he glanced at the women on the front bench, 'always be those taking the tumble in the blackout and do you wonder with all the holes and cracks lying about?'

'I certainly don't. Right. I'm off.' Nurse Eyre swept off, crackling starch and exchanging smiles with the waiting women and the last of the seven to eight p.m. Saturdays only, ward visitors making for the yard entrance that had been the hospital's main entrance for all patients and visitors since the departments on either side of the old, main entrance had been destroyed by direct hits from high-explosive bombs in October 1940.

Jackson exchanged nods and 'Nice night I don't think!' and 'Black porridge and cold as charity!' with the departing visitors, then shot out of the lodge to ensure none had displaced the blackout curtains. Not that any air-raid wardens would spot it tonight if they left them open, he reflected, returning to his high stool. When he'd nipped out not twenty minutes back to check the old hurricane lamp was functioning proper, he'd been in touching distance before he'd seen the red glow. That particular lamp hung under a makeshift tin-and-sandbag ledge at the far end of the twelve-foot long, ten-foot high, sandbag wall that guarded the right side of the entrance. There was a duplicate wall on the left and the lamp was there to guide ambulance drivers backing up to the doorway. The lamp had long been officially passed as invisible from the sky, but from this last mid-June, in the general opinion of the ambulance crews and Casualty staff, it should have been replaced by a searchlight, since neither the V1s, that had then started coming, nor the V2s, that had joined in since September, had human eyes and old Jerry, sitting snug over France or Holland pressing their buttons, couldn't see London, could he?

The waiting women watched Jackson's movements without interrupting their conversation. Their bench directly faced Rooms One to Five; Seventeen lay opposite One across the hall; and by unspoken arrangement they were seated to keep the open doors of One and Seventeen, closed door of Three, the lodge, Yard entrance and exit to the ground corridor, under communal observation. One was elderly, the others youngish, and they all looked tired and wore shabby headscarves and worn winter coats and carried bulging string-bags, but no longer the long-forgotten cardboard civilian gas-mask cases. Though strangers to each other, they chatted like old friends. They had been born and lived within walking distance of Martha's, ·and as their parents, grandparents and more distant ancestors, regarded Casualty Hall as their personal property and a cross between a family doctor's waiting room and social club.

A stocky, red-haired, freckled young man in a short white coat came out of Room Three, closed the door and walked slowly to the lodge.

The older woman eyed his back knowingly. 'That new doctor's fetching down a proper doctor to our Nellie.'

Her companions nodded. They knew all inter-hospital messages to and from Casualty had to go through the lodge, that proper doctors (the SMO, SSO, registrars and pathologists) wore long white coats; new doctors (housemen, all of whom doubled as junior casualty officers) short; and the young doctors (medical students) leather-patched tweed jackets or rolled-up shirt-sleeves with tie-ends buttoned inside their shirtfronts. One asked, 'Your daughter, missus?'

'Nah. Me sister's eldest. Bombed out Clapham this last January blitz, she was, and seeing her two kiddies gone for evacuees down Taunton way, moved in with her mum and me. Well, got a good job cleaning up Whitehall, so it's handier, you might say. Widow, she is, same as her mum and me. Lost ours last do, but Nellie, she lost hers Anzio and seeing me sister's legs is poorly I says I'll step over the road with our Nellie. Nasty throat she's got and the fever with it.'

'Lots of nasty throats about, missus. Now, you take my neighbour . . .'

They spent the next few minutes swopping medical horror stories as avidly as they had bomb stories in the earlier years of the war. But in this sixth wartime winter in London, too many emotions had been hammered numb for those still at the receiving end of air-attacks to want to discuss what had happened last week, yesterday, or early this morning, when it could happen again in the next hour, or five minutes. Familiarity had bred not contempt but a stoic acceptance of situations that in peacetime would have been regarded as beyond human endurance.

Mr Stewart leant on the lodge window, stifling yawns. He had been called up twice last night, and, as the whole resident staff, on duty since five fifty a.m. 'Has the SMO left for his free weekend yet, Jackson?'

The porter shook his head. 'Anaesthetising for Prof. Surgery down the basement theatre, but he's handed over the medical side to Dr Brown. Fetch him down for you, Mr Stewart?'

'Please. I think the woman in Three should come in.' It was a hospital rule that only the SMO, SSO or, when off, their deputies, could admit. He rubbed his eyes and read from the notes in his hand. 'Mrs Helen May Benton, age thirty-six, acute streptococcal throat, query Vincent's Angina – oh, yes – she's had dip. (Diphtheria).'

'Righty-oh.' Jackson picked up the internal receiver. 'Casualty wanting the acting-SMO, Dora, luv.'

'In Alex, Jacko. Putting you through.'

About a minute later, he put it down. 'Dr Brown's setting up a blood transfusion and'll be along soon as he's done – hullo, hullo!' He stuck his head out of the window like a tortoise from its shell. 'Here comes another,' he muttered, between his teeth.

'Yes,' sighed Mr Stewart. His head had jerked up and his freckles were suddenly more marked. He was twenty-three, a house-physician in his sixth week since qualification, and it seemed to him five years and not five months since the day in June when he had been a final-year medical student and, with three others, had gone up on the roof of Block Three for a better view of the strange little aircraft streaking jerkily across the sky, spitting fire from their tails and emitting odd chug-chug-chugging roars. They had thought the machines piloted by the Luftwaffe, and when the engines suddenly died, assumed they had somehow been soundlessly shot down and cheered as each dived and exploded on the ground. Then an irate message from Casualty that had the hospital's only direct line to the police, had catapulted them down the five flights of stone stairs to the ground floor. Mr Stewart had never forgotten that June day, but he no longer remembered when he had learnt that the flying-bombs that London immediately nicknamed 'doodle-bugs', and other parts of the country 'buzz bombs', were officially called V1s, the abbreviation of *Vergeltungswaffen Eins* – Revenge Weapon Number One.

The women on the front bench stopped talking and sat motionless, listening intently to the still distant, brick-and-fog muffled, chug-chug-chugging. In Room One, Nurse Phillips said firmly, 'Too fast for our side, ladies,' and her eyes smiled over the mask that hid her tightened face as she went on dressing her patient's sprained ankle. The dresser had paled under his mask, but he picked up the cue and said it was obviously the other side's turn today as they had had the only two doodles that had got through. The three patients forced smiles and said the RAF and the ack-ack had got real nippy shooting the nasty little things down hadn't they? In Seventeen Nurse Dale and the dresser exchanged brief glances over the frightened boy lying under grey blankets on a stretcher-trolley, and went on talking football with him. And in Room Three Elinor moved closer to the head of the free side of the examination couch that was backed and lined against the inner walls and reached under the grey blankets for Mrs Benton's right hand. The bomb was louder and coming fast and she wished passionately her mask was round her face and not her neck.

'How old are Norman and Doreen now, Mrs Benton?'

'Oh – er – Norman, he'll be eleven come January and Doreen's just turned eight.' Mrs Benton's hoarse voice quavered and her careworn, feverish face was whitening patchily. 'Miss 'em cruel, I do, Nurse, but glad as they're out safe.' She swallowed painfully. 'My Gawd, he don't leave off do he, Nurse?'

'I'm afraid not, but from the speed, this one's going over the river.' Elinor swallowed imperceptibly. 'And such lovely country around Taunton.'

'Yea – pretty – ever so green—' Mrs Benton's voice stopped and her face flushed with fury. The bomb was almost overhead and she glared upwards and yelled above the roar, 'Shift ye bleeding arse, ye bugger! Shift ye bleeding arse!' She heard herself and was horrified. 'Oh my Gawd, Nurse, I'm ever so sorry – I didn't ought to have said that with you there.'

'Not to worry, Mrs Benton, please. I couldn't hear what you said,' she lied, 'but whatever it was, it heard you. It's gone over.' She took the conversation back to Norman and Doreen and surreptitiously dried the palm of her free hand on the back of her apron skirt. She refused to let herself think what was about to happen on the opposite bank, and succeeded in that mental discipline from a combination of long practice, and the hammering numb of so many of her emotions.

The departing visitors groping and stumbling over the wet flags of Casualty Yard to the nearest gateless entrance to the main road, heard the oncoming bomb before it was audible in Casualty. They paused momentarily then groped and stumbled on through the impenetrable, icy, soaking blackness. The thickness of the fog made it hard to gauge the bomb's height and precise course, but from its speed, the engine was not yet about to switch off. Experience had taught them that until that moment, which heralded the dive and, roughly nine seconds later, the explosion on the ground, they were in no danger. Only around three or four were now getting through to London daily owing to the RAF and anti-aircraft guns' efficiency in shooting them down in flight over the sea or open country, but in the first several weeks from mid-June, roughly one hundred had hit London daily.

The visitors were Londoners and, as all London, they hated and feared the V1s but had learnt to take them as they had formerly taken the old high-explosive bombs, incendiaries and land-mines dropped by manned enemy bombers. When a V1's engine switched off either directly or nearly overhead, London fell flat on its face on whatever was underfoot and remained prone until the roar of the explosion and hurricane of the above-ground blast had faded. Out of the immediate danger area, London went on with the job, the shopping, the queuing, the cooking, the washing, or downing a pint. 'Life's got to go on,' said London.

Paradoxically, though in reality and politically the V2s were far more deadly, they aroused far less hatred and fear amongst the civilian population than the V1s. The rockets came too high and too fast to be heard; neither the RAF nor anti-aircraft guns had any means

153

of shooting them down; nor was there any warning of their approach. The first sign that one had landed was a blinding flash that a few seconds later was followed first by the rocket's thunderous explosion and then the roar of great buildings crumbling as dust into a great new crater. There were no survivors from a direct hit; all rocket victims came from the periphery of the pre-set target areas. That morning's was the fifth rocket to have hit London in the past twenty-four hours; they were arriving in steadily increasing numbers and caus-ing increasing concern in high places. But owing to the strict wartime censorship, the concomitantly rising figure of rockets' victims was officially known only in high places, even though it was common knowledge amongst London's ARP and civil defence workers, police, firemen, ambulance crews and general hospi-tals. But London, at ground level, shrugged stoically, and agreed there wasn't no sense fretting over what you couldn't do nothing about, and if one got your number on it you'd had it afore you heard it, so why worry?

The visitors had reached the nearside pavement of the wide main road running parallel with the hospital when the bomb roared by overhead. They breathed out and groped and stumbled on and in about a minute heard the engine stop and perhaps ten seconds later, the fog-muffled roar of the explosion echoing over the Thames. And on the opposite side of the road eight members of the crew of a USAAF B17 (Flying Fortress) who had just heard their first flying bomb, began pick-ing themselves off the cold, hard, wet pavement. Their aircraft had been badly damaged during yesterday's daylight mission over Germany but their captain had managed to fly it back to their Lincolnshire base and this morning they had all been given forty-eight hours leave whilst their aircraft was being repaired. They had spent most of the day in cold, packed, slow trains and the past two hours trying to find their way across the river to the West End. Once on their feet they groped and stumbled on, cursing indiscriminately the Krauts, the British and their captain and his co-pilot who had stayed back at base and had sworn they knew London blindfolded and in the fog.

It was about fifteen minutes after the bomb exploded that Paddy raced into Casualty from the main corridor. Mrs Benton's aunt was alone on the front bench; Nurse Dale and the dresser had just wheeled the boy to a bed in a basement ward; Mrs Benton was asking Elinor if hubby was one of the doctors; Mr Stewart and the other dresser were in Room Five with an elderly man who had just brought himself in 'Sweating like a pig and all of a tremble so you tell me for why, Doctor . . .'; Nurse Phillips was smiling to herself and writing in the log on the standing desk on one side of the open doorway of Room One and Jackson's normally grim face had a euphoric grin.

Paddy stopped on one foot. 'Franklin's found her?'

'Guy's, sir. Just had the tinkle. Still in shock and a bit cut about, but no worse.'

Paddy's smile returned the youth to his pale, haggard, face. 'Mother of God, that's the best news I've heard all day!'

Nurse Phillips had joined him, radiating efficiency and joy for Franklin. She was twenty-six, rather plain, very efficient and very tired. As all the trained nursing staff she had been on since seven thirty a.m. and her back and feet were aching badly. (Working all day during air attacks had become so customary that the Casualty student nurses had thought themselves blessed beyond belief to have been given in turn one hour off today, in place of their usual three. If possible their missing off duty would be made up at a later date, and if not possible, it would be forgotten.)

Nurse Phillips said, 'I'm sorry we had to get you back again, Dr Brown. Mrs—' she was interrupted by a raucous shout from the front bench.

'If it isn't my Dr Brown! My Gawd, and haven't you gone up in the world! Five bob to talk to you now! When they made you a proper doctor, eh?'

Paddy spun round. 'If it isn't my old friend Mrs Travis! Great to see you again!' He pushed the black forelock out of his deeply shadowed eyes. 'From the feel of my feet, one hundred years, no less. Waiting to be seen?'

'Not me, Doctor—' she explained eagerly.

Nurse Phillips waited to put in, 'Mrs Benton is in Three, Dr Brown. Notes and a nurse, *in situ*. Mr Stewart's seeing a patient in Five. Male. Sixty-four. P.U.O.' (Pyrexia of Unknown Origin.)

'Thanks, Nurse. Sorry about the hold up but I got hauled back to Luke. Tell Stewart if I want him I'll shout and if he wants me for the old boy to shout whilst I'm still here. See you shortly, Mrs Travis.'

He disappeared into Room Three, Nurse Phillips put her head round the door of Five then returned to the standing-desk in One.

Paddy had examined and signed Mrs Benton's admission form, and disappeared into Five, when Elinor helped Mrs Benton on to the newly-returned stretcher-trolley held steady by Nurse Dale and 'her' dresser. Nurse Phillips supervised from the open doorway.

'You'll like Elizabeth, Mrs Benton. A nice cosy basement ward,' she said, so cheerfully that Elinor glanced at her curiously then noticed Nurse Dale and the dresser were smiling widely. Her own eyes lit with shared relief and secret hope.

Mrs Benton reached for Elinor's hand. 'Ta, ever so, for the nice chat, Nurse. All the best. T.T.F.N.'

'And all the best to you, Norman, Doreen and your mum and aunty, Mrs Benton.'

Mrs Travis went with her niece to the basement ward and when the little procession had moved away, Nurse Phillips turned back to Elinor. 'Guy's. Shock, plus minor lacerations,' she said rapidly.

'Thank God, Nurse!'

'Yes. Now – get this room tidy then deal with Seventeen. Dale hasn't had time to get back to it and when she gets back the others should be here and you two must go to last suppers. Get a move on, Mackenzie,' she added in her normal, brisk, voice. 'If good news turns you to stone I'll keep it till you're off next time.'

'Sorry, Nurse – and thanks.'

Nurse Phillips vanished from the open doorway and Elinor swiftly stripped and sponged down the rexined examination couch with carbolic solution, re-folded the blankets, exchanged the used for a clean pillowslip, and replaced in the approved order the basic equipment for a medical examination on the glass-shelved trolley pushed against the wall flush with the hand-basin. Three was the smallest room of Casualty Hall, and only slightly wider than the large bricked-in window in the external wall, but in constant use, as both patients and staff liked the privacy it afforded. She had just rinsed the handbasin and was re-hanging the 'doctor's' hand towel when she heard a sudden inrush of heavy footsteps and Jackson's 'Now then you lads!' drowned by a chorus of American male voices.

Then Nurse Phillips' firm, 'Gentlemen I'm afraid you must have lost your way in the fog.'

Elinor, alight with curiosity shot out of the open doorway. Her appearance evoked from the eight members of the crew of a B17, a barrage of cat-calls and wolf-whistles that jolted Paddy from Room Five, which he had been about to leave. But before he was clear of the doorway the airmen rushed at and engulfed Elinor. She backed away instinctively and their momentum swept her into Room Three. They piled in after her and the last in line slammed shut and leant against the door before Paddy could get a foot in. He had been joined by Nurse Phillips, Mr Stewart and a dresser, and Jackson, puce with outrage, hissed from the lodge, 'Ring the cops, Dr Brown, sir?'

Paddy shook his head quickly, and said under his breath, 'Stay put and leave this to me. Understood.' It was an order and not a question so none answered. He knocked loudly on the closed door but the only immediate answer was the ecstatic chorus of American voices.

Elinor was backed against the bricked window from lack of space, not apprehension. She could see that none of the airmen were at all drunk, and guessed their error from their euphoric accounts of their joy in finding the 'little old red light right outside' and that from their admiration of 'the real cute little lace doo-da on those cute black curls' they had never before been in a British hospital and were still too delighted to be out of the fog to recognise her uniform. She knew that once they did, her uniform would be an inviolable armour. London had for years been filled with Allied servicemen on leave, but never in daylight or blackout, on or off hospital territory, had she known, or heard of, one

158

uniformed nurse being even verbally assaulted by any serviceman of any nationality. Nor, in the five centuries of Martha's history, had this ever happened in the hospital, or the neighbourhood, though it contained areas where the police only went in pairs.

She shouted, smiling, 'Gentlemen, please, be quiet and take a good look at me and—'

'And sure as hell you are a real cute sight, babe!'

'And sure as hell,' she retorted laughing, 'have you lot bailed out over the wrong target. This is a hospital. St Martha's Hospital, London. I am a nurse.'

The sudden silence was broken by repeated knocks on the door and Paddy's voice calling pleasantly, 'Sorry to break up the party, chaps, but this is a civvy hospital, I'm a civvy doc and need the nurse you've got in there.'

Seven of the airmen's jaws dropped and the owner of the eighth was against the door and yelled, 'She your gal, Doc?'

'Wife! Look at her left hand then open this door like a good chap.'

The impact of that reply released the pressure on the door enough for Paddy to squeeze in sideways as Elinor held up her left hand and added confidingly, 'My husband's bound to be a bit worried, gentlemen. I'm having our first baby.'

Within seconds the room had cleared of profusely apologetic airmen. Paddy waited before following the last out, he jerked up a thumb to Elinor and she did the same to him. Then he vanished and she heard his, 'Now then, chaps, what you all most need is just over the road and this chap'll guide you. The hospital pub, chaps – take them over, Pratt,' he told the dresser, 'and ask Ernie from me to look after them . . . Not at all, chaps, any time – all part of the service . . .'

159

NINE
Zanzibar
July 1955

Paddy was alone on the boat-deck when the ship anchored off Zanzibar in the early morning of the second day out from Mombasa. The hot, bright air was scented with nutmeg, cinnamon and cloves from the spice fields, and from the rail the island seemed to rise like a mirage of dark green velvet jungle, softer green velvet orange groves and banana and coconut plantations, splashed with the colours of the ripening fruit and edged with white lace.

He stood entranced for several minutes before he realised he was not leaning on the rail and his stick still hung on the back of his extended deckchair. He looked down at his legs as if he had never seen them before, then so searchingly around the empty deck that he caught the attention of the First Officer on the bridge, who saw him limp unaided, slowly, doggedly, right round the deck and mentally logged it for the Captain's benefit. Paddy went back to his chair and, as he crossed himself and lay back, he gave the long, involuntary sigh of a patient waking to find himself at last free from pain, though his legs felt weighted with lead. And the hot, scented air rushed into his lungs and removed the lingering traces of the smell of fresh paint.

Throughout the six days in Mombasa the whole ship had reeked of the paint a nine-man party had slapped on the superstructure and during daylight echoed with the noise of the new cargo of copper being loaded and lashed at the bottom of both holds. In those long, hot days and longer, hotter, lonely, airless nights when, as always in port, cabin windows and portholes were locked, he had almost welcomed reek and noise as counter-irritants to his thoughts.

His gaze returned to the view through the lower rails and his mind to the fight between his head and his heart that until the first night in Mombasa he thought had begun in the Red Sea. Had Elinor been merely a shipboard acquaintance, he would have made the first move before Aden, but their shared past, and his intuitive understanding of women in general and her in particular, had – and still – acted upon him like a straitjacket. He had sensed from their reunion in the Suez Canal that beneath her delectable exterior lay the great weariness that follows the ending of a serious love; the more he saw of her, the more he recognised this and that she was not only not ready but determined to avoid another emotional relationship. He knew her willpower – and he knew himself and how often in the past he had mistaken an overwhelming sexual attraction for love, and that in the present he was long overdue for the ten-day syndrome. Consequently, even though from that first night in Mombasa his heart insisted that what he now felt for Elinor went far deeper than sexual attraction and had been rooted in the distant past, his intelligence continued to hammer the distorting effects upon judgement and emotions of idle weeks of unbroken sunshine and starlight and calm seas and breathtaking beauty, and so often the boredom and loneliness of any passengers travelling alone down this seemingly endless, alien coast. Never since Tilbury had he felt more alien than on that first night ashore, when momentarily his guard had slipped. And then the startled recognition and touching vulnerability he had seen in Elinor's eyes, made him cover the moment with an old joke. He had spoken without thought and only when he heard himself recognised the double Freudian slip. He had sensed she had done the same and been thankful the lights had then gone out for the others to get back into the car, Toby, anxiously apologetic, George in a deafening silence. George had not spoken again until they were all back on the ship and said goodnight to Elinor. Paddy had then suggested Toby and George join him and the unopened bottle of French brandy in his cabin. They had a good party, but from that night George had stopped dropping heavy hints about this or that official tour sounding good value and not too exhausting, and last night had been openly discouraging about the one arranged for this morning.

The day before the ship had called at Tanga for a few hours and George and Elinor had gone ashore in a party that included Mr Carter. Elinor was dressing for dinner and the dance on deck that was to follow, when George came into the smoking room wearing the white tuxedo he had bought in Mombasa and an awkward smile.

'No decent bridge with this dance on tonight.' He

jerked his head at the fairy-lights that had gone up on the open deck beyond the veranda café. 'Elinor thinks she should show up for once as the Captain's pulled rank and booked her for a rumba. I – er – think I may as well look in on it.'

'Sound idea. How was Tanga?'

'Hot, but not bad value when that old bore Carter wasn't holding forth. Elinor,' George added over-casually, 'seems rather keen on one in Zanzibar tomorrow. Sounds to me a hellish hard slog. Nipping in and out of the launch, the coach, trudging round plantations and spice fields and ruins at the double, as we've to be back for late lunch as we sail at three. Still – as Zanzibar's our last call before Beira next week, I think I'll sweat it out.'

Paddy, lying in the chair, looked at the stick on the back, and smiled slightly. At breakfast he stunned George with the news that he had just bought a fifteen-shilling ticket for the tour. 'Yates says our launch'll be alongside at nine and there are no sharks here as the coral reefs keep them out. If I drop off the launch coming or going, no need to dive in . . . Morning, Doc! Enjoy the dance?'

George grunted and as usual took no part in the conversation at breakfast. He had woken with a bad headache he diagnosed as a touch of the sun and taken a couple of aspirins that were beginning to work. He was guiltily annoyed with Paddy for tagging along – step in the right direction and all that – but a chap who had danced five times with Elinor last night couldn't be blamed for wanting her to himself this morning. Still – that old bore was opting out of this one and like Paddy gave dances a wide berth. He further consoled himself by spending the rest of breakfast – as every

163

meal since Mombasa – glowering at Mr Carter now sitting on the right of Elinor's new and vacated place at the purser's right hand.

On the morning the ship sailed from Mombasa, before the last shore-based crane swung away from the newly-battened holds, the bedraggled kites dispersed, the onshore band played 'Auld Lang Syne', the coloured paper streamers from the ship to shore snapped, and the large crowd on the docks and thinner crowd on the headland waved and called their farewells, Mrs Mellor had a detailed report on the first-class in her absence from Mrs Van der Mann.

'. . . and those three only went ashore together with some English friend of Dr Ashen's on the first night. My Belinda was still up when they returned – such an exciting game of ping-pong, she said – Mrs Mackenzie retired immediately and the three men had nightcaps in Dr Brown's cabin. Belinda didn't see the Englishman leave but that nice young Fourth told her later it was about half-past three in the morning.'

'Men so enjoy swapping dirty stories together after a good night out.'

Mrs Van der Mann reminded herself she had long observed dear Mrs Mellor had the regrettable coarse streak of the English and tried not to look pained. 'After that, Mrs Mackenzie always dined on board and Dr Brown only again ashore with you last night.'

'I was his guest, dear. A charming gesture, I thought.'

Mrs Van der Mann ignored the interruption. 'Dr Ashden lunched and dined ashore every day. I can't imagine what he did. He can't have spent the whole time sightseeing and shopping. Possibly he has other friends ashore.'

Mrs Mellor concentrated on the crochet she could do blindfolded. 'Very possibly.'

Mrs Van der Mann closed her lorgnette and tapped her second left finger. 'Dr Brown lunched ashore on separate days, first with Sister, then Dr Morgan. Otherwise he went ashore on his own, but never for long or on a tour. No doubt too tiring.'

'Sightseeing exhausts the strongest and particularly in unaccustomed heat.'

'Oh, my dear, the heat – the noise – but where was I?' The lorgnette tapped her third finger. 'Mrs Mackenzie once lunched ashore with Sister West – they seem quite friendly – and this will surprise you! Mrs Mackenzie lunched twice ashore and went on tours with Mr Carter. He seems quite taken with her and has moved to the purser's table, and what's more—' she tapped her little finger, 'the Captain has taken to having little chats with her. What do you make of that?'

Mrs Mellor smiled. 'That the Captain and Mr Carter share the not uncommon masculine weakness for a pretty young woman.'

'You may be right though I wouldn't describe her as pretty – her nose is too short and mouth too wide – but she has an excellent complexion and dresses well. And there is no doubt she can afford it!' Mrs Van der Mann smiled knowingly and leant closer. 'You know my Belinda is great friends with those young fellows in the Wireless Room and the assistant pursers and how young people talk amongst themselves?' Mrs Mellor nodded eagerly. 'Well, my Belinda says that Mrs Mackenzie cabled her man-of-business in England before changing cabins and he immediately cabled back saying he had made the necessary arrangements with London. Undoubtedly her husband left her most comfortably placed and I should not be surprised if she initially booked tourist from—' she hesitated, as if about to utter a four-letter word '—socialist persuasions. Well-bred young people so often have foolish notions. I mean, I've always heard that dreadful Mr Atlee is a gentleman! But I think we should keep all this between ourselves, don't you?'

'Most certainly,' said Mrs Mellor, in the certainty that within minutes of the new passengers studying the new seating plan in the dining saloon, it would be common knowledge that the Mrs E M Mackenzie at the purser's table was a wealthy young widow and fully-paid-up member of the British Labour Party.

The ship sailed at noon. George was still smouldering over the new seating plan when he and Paddy had their usual drink before lunch in the smoking room. They had severally stopped inviting Elinor to join these sessions and come to accept, George with incomprehension, her refusal to intrude upon their friendship or allow any intrusion on her own privacy. Neither man had yet got closer to her cabin than its outer vestibule door, nor risked suggesting she visit their own. Amongst the several reasons for their individual reticence were the iron conventions indoctrinated in both in youth; the still extant convention that in this context the first move must come from the woman; and their medical knowledge that no one-hundred-percent-safe method of contraception had yet been discovered, and – as they had first learnt as medical students in antenatal clinics – how disastrous to women in particular could be just one sexual intercourse.

'Bloody nonsense her spiel about not wanting to hurt

Weaver's feelings by moving to our table,' grumbled George. 'Of course he's been so helpful to her. That's his job. What about Morgan's feelings, eh? He was all for it when I sounded him out. I should have thought far more amusing for her than to be landed with a pack of strangers and that old bore. What do you think she's up to?'

Paddy shrugged. 'Must she be up to anything?'

'Christ, yes. Women can't deal straight. Always up to something devious. And why all this hanging around with chaps old enough to be her father? Carter; those monks in tourist – damned unhealthy.' He frowned in thought. 'She show any signs of a father-fixation in Martha's?'

'I wouldn't have said so and she married a young man.' Paddy drained his glass. 'Time for another quick one?'

George brightened. 'I'll get 'em.' It did a chap good to see old Paddy back on the hard stuff and casting the old eye around the women in this new crowd, he mused, waiting for his order at the bar. Trust old Toby to have been on the ball in more ways than one. He'd seen through that bit of play-acting, played along, and later in Paddy's cabin laughed like a drain when he, George, had explained how Paddy had always been the leading light in Martha's staff shows. Rather a pity Elinor had missed it – but time and place for women and a chap only really enjoyed chewing the cud with other chaps. Still – a chap could do one hell of a lot worse – steady on! Dodgy set-up, a ship, too much time, too many women yak-yak-yakking, and anyway, though she was always damned nice she would keep a chap at arm's length. Never get herself another man if she kept this up, but obviously she wanted one.

Every woman did. And from the way these new women were eyeing Paddy and himself, they'd not be backward in coming forward – and what was far better, several chaps had the look of sound bridge players.

'Sorry to keep you waiting, Dr Ashden, sir. Same again for you and Dr Brown? Coming up.'

George's spirits rose higher as the new men crowding the bar parted for him as if he were invisible. A chap knew where he was with chaps that knew the form. This morning Morgan had told him all the newcomers in first-class were either British going back to the UK on home-leave or for good, or Rhodesians and South Africans returning home after holidaying in Kenya, Uganda and Tanganyika, and that on this second-stage of the voyage, Zanzibar metaphorically replaced Gibraltar on the first. No general fraternising until after Zanzibar, Morgan had said, though tomorrow night's dance on deck usually cracked a spot of ice. No joy there for poor old Paddy, but Toby had said there was a bloody good social life in Rhodesia so might be sound to get in some practice and this morning he had overheard the Captain telling Elinor about the dance and asking her to do him the honour of saving him a rumba . . .

'I don't like this place. It smells nasty. Can we go back to the ship, please, Mummy?'

The child's wail came from the main body of their party trailing after the guide down a long, high, narrow, dank, stone corridor in the ruins of a palace built in a clearing in the jungle in the last century. The corridor was in the women's quarters that had been least affected by the fire that had caused the building to be abandoned.

'The kid has a point.' Paddy, in a white duck suit, the panama dangling from his free hand, leant on his stick in the doorless entrance to the communal bathroom that lay off one side of that corridor. The other was lined with cell-like bedrooms, each with a longish low stone shelf built from an inner wall that had been a bed and a small, rusted-barred, single window set in the external wall too high for even Paddy to see through. Only stone had survived the fire; the guide had been hazy about its date but enthused over the once formal, beautiful gardens. The jungle had reclaimed all but the lily ponds choked with large lush lilies that looked carnivorous and engulfed the outer walls of the ruins and filled the interior with a dim greenish, under-sea light. The heat of the noon sun could not penetrate the ten-inch-thick stone walls and the air had the chilly clamminess of a tomb.

George fingered the open neck of the khaki safari suit that had been another of his purchases in Mombasa. 'Any joint left to rot in a jungle is bound to pong of rotting vegetation.'

'Stinks of far worse. Tragedy, cruelty and death.' Paddy looked up at the light-slits cut in the high, carved, curved ceiling then slowly around. The slanting greenish light gave the stone of the walls, benches and vast sunken bath, the texture of fungi that had never seen the sun. He avoided looking at Elinor. He couldn't look at any woman in this dreadful place that had imprisoned for life girls from early puberty. He looked back at the ceiling. 'The sunlight must've got in before the jungle took over.'

George's headache was returning. He was thankful to be out of the sun after the plantations and spice fields, and he enjoyed seeing round ruins. They made a chap think. 'Bloody good bath. Lose a rugger-team in it. And, anyway, nearest you and I'll ever get to the inside of a harem, old chap. Well worth a look-see.'

Paddy didn't answer. Elinor looked from one man to the other and stayed silent. She had on the white straw boater she had last worn in Genoa that now had a rose-coloured ribbon that toned with her mandarin-collared, three-quarter sleeved, tight-waisted and full-skirted cotton dress. She had changed into that dress after a Tannoy announcement at breakfast tactfully reminded all passengers that Zanzibar was a Muslim country and ladies going ashore in shorts, slacks and with bare heads, arms and legs, might give cause for offence. She stood a little apart from the men and turned away to undo the two hooks of her collar.

Paddy's temper snapped. 'In comparison those dance-hall kids in Mombasa have it cushy. At least they're free to walk where they please in the sun between lays. I'll wait for you in the coach.' He swung away quickly and the echo of his footsteps and stick down the long corridor sounded those of a three-legged man about to break into a run.

George sighed impatiently. 'Trust him to dramatise everything! Always had to! He'll never change – and if the silly sod doesn't slow down he'll bust both legs on the front steps. I suppose we'd better horse after him to pick up the pieces.'

'I expect he'll cope,' said Elinor, absently. She looked at him in a guilty wonder and almost envied the limited imagination that allowed him to dismiss as dramatis-ations any unpalatable truths that offended the code by which he lived and survived. 'Blowing all fuses when worked up is a good safety-valve.'

'Could be right,' George allowed, only as he did not

want to rush away. This was the first time he had been alone with her this morning and he was still haunted by the memory of her soft, small body in his arms when dancing last night. 'But why get worked up here? Dead history and damned interesting.'

She did not remind him that their guide had just told him there were still harems in Zanzibar and Mombasa. 'Probably his legs are playing up after all this walking and he needs to sit down but'll go to the stake before he admits it.' She didn't add – and a mental breathing space from your prep-school attitudes. She smiled. 'Him and me.' She stooped to examine the nearest portion of the broad stone rim round the bath. 'Looks free of spiders, scorpions and whatever – I'll chance it.' She sat down and rubbed her calves. 'My legs are reminding me that last night I danced for the first time in over two years – and that our Captain does a very nifty rumba.'

He looked down into her upturned smiling face and was half-deafened by his temporal pulse. He recognised – what chap wouldn't? – what it meant when a woman used delaying tactics to keep him to herself in safe cover. He hadn't expected this – hadn't even dared hope for it – and she looked so bloody sweet and enticing. He muttered, 'You're a smashing dancer. No wonder he nabbed you – three times, wasn't it?'

She laughed and spread her hands. 'Sorry. Wasn't counting.'

'I was.' He caught her hands and before he realised what he was doing he had pulled her to her feet and into his arms. 'I counted every hideous second I had to watch you in another man's arms—' His voice and face had slurred. His head knocked off her hat as he began kissing her hungrily. 'Christ – I must love you – I want

171

you so badly – I always have – never forgotten – couldn't forget you.' He went on kissing her lips, her face, her hair, until he suddenly realised that she was neither resisting nor responding. He raised his hot face to look into hers and saw the gravity in her eyes. 'Why are you looking at me like this?' he demanded urgently, breathlessly.

Her voice was breathless and gentle. 'Give me room to breathe, George, and I'll tell you.' His arms dropped stiffly to his sides and she stepped back a little. 'Thanks,' she said. She was furious with herself, not him. She reached for her handbag that was still on the rim of the bath, took out her cigarettes and a lighter, lit two together and handed him one. He accepted it with a hurt, angry nod and though she knew the truth would hurt him more, it alone could salvage some of his pride. 'You've not only always reminded me of my husband, you even kiss like him.' He winced. 'Yes. That's why. And why I've never forgotten our meeting in '45. I'll tell you now that for the first few moments then, I thought you were Alistair's ghost even though I didn't then know he had been dead nine months. You're his type – my type – so as these things generally work both ways, probably I'm yours. That's why you're now trying to persuade yourself that you love me. But, you don't. Do you?' He didn't answer. 'No,' she said, as if he had, 'you just want to go to bed with me and might enjoy it, but not the morning after. You'd be hollow with guilt at betraying Brenda's memory and, being you, at betraying me. And that—' she dropped and stood on her cigarette, 'I do understand, so please – please – don't feel guilty about this. I understand as I've been here before.' She paused, but he just went on staring at her dumbly. She glanced slowly around at the

172

stonework in the greenish under-sea light and noticed belatedly that her hat had fallen into the bath. She looked back at him. 'This place was filled with ghosts when we got here. I've just added two more. Time you and I got back into the sunlight. Would you fish up my hat, please?'

He was so confused he felt physically ill. He retrieved the hat, watched her replace it and check her reflection in her handbag mirror, then followed her through the ruins like an automaton. Suddenly his headache was much worse and when they stepped out into the brilliant sunshine he had such difficulty in focusing that he had to steady himself against a cracked stone pillar just inside the great open doorway that led on to the steep stone steps.

'Sorry. Glare.' He groped blindly for his dark glasses and the jungle hat folded under his jacket's belt.

Elinor stopped, glanced over her shoulder, and did a double-take. His heavy face was oddly mottled and the whiteness round his lips was accentuated by smears of lipstick. They were now in view of their waiting coach. She said without moving her lips, 'Lipstick on your mouth.'

George grunted with angry embarrassment. He was a bad actor but long practice had taught him how to dissemble when watched by prison guards. He took off his glasses and languidly mopped his whole, unnaturally dry face. That dryness slightly relieved him. He was not just imagining he felt lousy – his temperature was up. 'Off?'

'Yes.' She came closer. 'You've got a temp. Bad headache?'

His vision had cleared. 'Just a touch of the sun. No need to flap,' he said dismissively. He never fussed over his health and couldn't stick it from others and certainly not from her, after – what the hell! Stick to the form. He followed her back into the coach. They were the last to board and he called, 'Sorry to keep you waiting, ladies and gentlemen,' before sitting down in the triple front seat that their party, by unspoken arrangement, had left for them since they had been the last three out of the launch.

Paddy, in the aisle seat, turned from talking to the two women sitting immediately behind. 'May I introduce Mrs Mackenzie and Dr Ashden from England – Mrs Swanley and Mrs Wade from Rhodesia.'

The rest of the party had murmured the expected response to George and as the coach drove off, exchanged glances that drastically shortened the odds on George and lengthened them on Paddy. And over the tops of their glasses George and Elinor exchanged a deadpan glance that momentarily erased the last twenty minutes from their minds. Mrs Swanley was a thin, sun-dried brunette in her late thirties; Mrs Wade looked younger and the early-thirtyish prototype of all the pretty, sexy, curvaceous blonde girlfriends of Paddy's years in Martha's. They had both severally noticed her watching Paddy and heard from shipboard gossip that the two women were friends sharing a cabin on B-deck, recent divorcees, and returning from holidaying together in Kenya. That gossip had been re-born with the ship's engines at Mombasa and the enigma of the *ménage-a-trois* was again of avid interest in first, but far more discreetly discussed than formerly, since none cared to risk offending those with wealth and the Captain's friendship. And though there was some ambiguity about George's financial position, he was given the benefit of the doubt on the grounds that the rich only really chummed-up with the rich.

Later that afternoon Mrs Mellor and Mrs Van der Mann were having tea in the lounge when Elinor came in with Mrs Swanley and Mrs Wade. Mrs Mellor smiled invitingly. Elinor brought them over and after making the expected introductions and small-talk, moved with her new companions to armchairs on the opposite side.

Mrs Van der Mann clicked shut her lorgnette. 'I would not have thought they were Mrs Mackenzie's sort.'

'Possibly not. But she and that mantrap are about the same age.'

Mrs Van der Mann was too intrigued to be pained by the coarseness. 'You'd call her that? Though she's clearly past thirty and far too plump?'

'Only in the right places, my dear, and to any intelligent man, women in their thirties are far more interesting than young girls. And by that age women have learnt how to please men and that this is a man's world. Not that I would say Mrs Wade ever had to learn the former, since with her sex appeal, she has been doing that instinctively from girlhood.' Mrs Mellor thought of her second husband. 'Unquestionably, a mantrap – oh! Leaving already!' She authoritatively beckoned Elinor. 'Changed your mind about tea, my dear?'

Elinor smiled apologetically. 'Only as I've just remembered this is Monday and the library closes at five. After all these weeks out of range of a wireless and newspapers, I'm always forgetting what day it is except on Sundays because of the morning services. But I don't want to miss my place in the queue for Raymond Chandler's *The Long Goodbye* that's due back this afternoon. Do forgive me.'

Elinor hurried off towards the library until out of sight from the lounge. She went out on to the port side of the deck and down the nearest companionway to the one below. The heavy metal deck doors of the hall on the lower promenade deck were hooked open on both sides and the sound of the assistant pursers' typewriters stopped her just short of the port doors. Their shared desk faced the open-grilled window into the hall and she preferred to avoid giving them – and gossip – the interest of seeing her go along to Paddy's cabin. She looked up and down; that deck was empty; Paddy's half-curtained window was open. She strolled on, checked the deck again, then stopped, raised herself on her toes and peered through his window. Paddy was asleep on top of his bed and in sleep he looked younger, and his long thin body in cotton shirt and trousers, healthily relaxed, and his breathing was soundless. And as she looked down at him she remembered the last time she had watched him in sleep – a restless, feverish sleep, when every involuntary jerky movement of his limbs, every unconscious twitch of his pinched sunken-eyed face, had twisted deeper the knife of her professional instincts that from his admission to Luke's small-ward had suspected his true diagnosis.

She moved on and over to the rail thinking how she had wholly forgotten that dreadful weekend, and how long it was still taking her wartime mental discipline in blocking out painful thoughts to wear off. That's something else I've got to work on, she thought, but not now. Nor do I need to wake Paddy now I've seen George is so flat out that he didn't hear me knock, go into his unlocked cabin, or stand by his bunk. I'll tell Paddy when he wakes. They both need the sleep and this time, George, the most.

Earlier, when they returned to the ship, George drew her aside. 'I'm skipping lunch, taking a couple of aspirins and kipping down.'

'Good idea, but shouldn't you just see Morgan?'

'Damned if I'm telling him I was fool enough to forget a hat ashore yesterday. I'll cope. And – er – Elinor—'

'Yes?'

'I feel worse than a heel.' He had gone before she could reply. She re-joined Paddy and the two Rhodesians, and told them George was missing lunch. Paddy nodded as if no further explanation was necessary and the subject was dropped. Being a special serving they all sat together at lunch; she left first and returned to her cabin feeling as if she had just slapped a kind, thoughtless child already feeling wretched with the onset of measles. She was certain that George was cooking more than minor sunstroke, but the aspirins could help, sleep would do him more good than anything, and medical aid was literally within shouting distance of his cabin on B-deck. She decided to wait until after the official siesta time, then see George, and, if necessary, hand the problem over to Paddy. If she went over George's head to Morgan or Sister, she would infuriate him and further damage his pride, and in any illness whether major or minor, the patient's mental condition was vital. So she waited until after four and after checking the reception rooms and decks, ignored gossip and George's shocked reaction, and went down to his cabin. But neither he, nor anyone else saw her enter or leave. She was going back up the main stairs when Mrs Wade's high, sweet voice called from behind, 'Mrs Mackenzie, if you're going up to tea in the lounge, may Naomi and I join you? We've never dared have tea in there before as frankly, those two *grandes dames* terrify us! Won't you protect us?'

Elinor laughed as if at the joke of the year, mentally cursed, and remembered it was Monday.

She leant on the port rail thinking deeply, and watching the black fins piercing the bright blue sea until she noticed the shadow of the ship was growing longer. She walked round to the starboard and leant on the rail a few feet from her cabin window. She had long stopped noticing the motion of the ship, the hum of the engines, and slither of the sea against the sides, but never lost her wonder at the beauty and brevity of tropical sunsets. The great red sun was low on the western horizon and the only land in sight was the inch of palm trees and sand of a tiny, uninhabited island. The rim of the sun was just above the bright blue when she checked her watch. Two minutes to six. Then the sun dropped into the sea in a flash of scarlet, the western half of the sky turned gold, the eastern a vivid purple for two or three minutes before all colour vanished from sky and sea, the darkness closed in and deck-lights came on. She re-checked her watch. Five past. The A.P.s' office closed at six; Dixon should now have woken Paddy; and neither Mrs Mellor, Mrs Van der Mann, nor Belinda, who shared the cabin on Mrs Mellor's right, ever came down to dress for dinner before six thirty.

A shout from Paddy answered her knock. 'In the bath, George. Not locked. Come in.'

She half-opened the outer door and called quietly from its shelter. 'Sounds like your bathroom door's open. Close your eyes and I'll pull it to.'

He laughed. 'Mother of God, this teaches me the folly of leading a blameless life.' She had come in, closed the

outer and dealt with the bathroom door. 'And mean-
while back at the ranch . . . ?'

'I think George is cooking something.' She explained
why. 'You'll cope?'

'Yep. Hang on.' He still had difficulty getting out of
the bath and it was a couple of minutes before he came
out to her wearing a navy towelling bathrobe. 'You
haven't given me his pulse.'

'Didn't take it. His temp. looked high enough without my adding the coronary by waking him.'

'And when did you ever wake a patient taking a
pulse, Ellie?'

'Never. But patients in hospital beds expect to feel
fingers on their wrists, awake or asleep. Not a man
kipping in the privacy of his own cabin, and specifically
George. Shock him rigid. For God's sake don't tell him
I pussy-footed in and out. Luckily, for his sake, no one
else saw me.'

'You have a point. Right. I'll potter down soon as I'm
decent and report to you later.' He opened the outer
door, looked up and down. 'All clear, but before you
vanish, who's the third man you're about to compro-
mise?'

Her eyes laughed up at him. 'Fear not, Paddy. Your
saintly reputation is safe with me.'

He grinned. 'Get the hell out of here. My hair shirt's
beginning to itch.'

Once more no one else saw her enter or leave and
she went back to her own cabin thinking it was as easy
as Mr Yates had finally stopped hinting, to avoid gossip
at sea by keeping an eye on the clock. When she had
bathed and changed for dinner into a black lace blouse
and ankle-length black brocade skirt, on an impulse
that she refused to analyse, she put on a pair of small

diamond drop ear-rings that were amongst the few of the jewels that she had inherited from her mother-in-law that she had brought with her. Directly she entered the lounge Paddy rose from the sofa he was sharing with Mrs Wade and came up to her.

'Two things about you I don't understand, Ellie. Why aren't you in medicine? And why you've not told me you're worth a million dollars?'

She pretended to ignore the second question. 'What's he cooking?'

'Almost certainly dengue or sandfly fever. The two are so similar that at this stage it's hard to say which. Morgan's dealing. He's leaving him in his own cabin, if only pro tem, as George so objected to the alternative. Morgan'll overrule that if he thinks it necessary, with more than a little help from Sister who's already got George eating out of her maternal hand. They'll keep an eye on him and I've told him I'll look back later.'

'Poor George. Wretched for him.' She was very concerned. 'Paddy, I haven't nursed either and I've forgotten the books. How long?'

'A week or so. Maybe less. Morgan says he doesn't look in for a bad go and should be back on his feet by Beira. I go along with that.'

'Thank God for that. What's Morgan giving him?' And after he told her, 'That combination should give him a good night, but if he's awake when you look in later, tell him I'm terribly sorry and will check with Sister in the morning and if she gives the OK, look in with fruit and flowers.'

'I'll do that,' he said abruptly, as he was having difficulty fighting down more than jealousy. 'Now then – what'll you have?' He glanced around. Mr Carter had come in and was bowing to Elinor. 'Or will you take a raincheck?'

'If I may. And, Paddy, thanks very much.'

He bowed affectedly. 'And what are friends for?'

He returned to Mrs Wade, Mr Carter joined Elinor, Mrs Van der Mann lowered her lorgnette, and Mrs Mellor dwelt lovingly on the memory of her second husband, without interrupting her conversation with Father Gerachty in his customary post-sundown, elegant, clerical black.

That night's official after-dinner entertainment was tombola in the lounge. Elinor detested the game but as it was enormously popular and emptied the games room, delayed the cabin parties, and even thinned the bridge tables, she was able to retire early without attracting attention. She felt very tired and unusually depressed by her failure to foresee in the ruined bathroom that George's far from unusual mixture of masculine conceit and inferiority would make him automatically assume her reluctance to rush after Paddy meant she wanted to linger in privacy for him to make a pass. Had they been in England, he might have hesitated, but not with a rising temperature and after four weeks on this ship, where the general masculine attitude to any young woman travelling alone was that she must either be a nymphomaniac or frigid. She fell asleep fuming with irritation with herself and irritated sympathy for George who could no more help being what he was than the two men she had loved and whom he so resembled. It was only ten thirty, but when she was woken by urgent knocks on her outer vestibule door she thought she had been asleep hours and not, as in fact, minutes. She sat up, wide awake and irrationally convinced it was Paddy with bad news. She leapt out of bed hauled on her scarlet kimono, closed her window curtains, switched on the lights and rushed to open her outer door. 'Paddy is – George!'

He stood swaying unsteadily in the doorway. He was in dressing-gown and pyjamas, his puffy red face was sweating slightly and his eyes were dazed. 'Had to see you—' he muttered and stumbled forward. 'Had to talk.'

She caught his shoulders and with one bare foot kicked shut the door behind him. She said kindly, 'Duckie, you should be in bed.'

'Couldn't sleep – had to see you – apologise – oh, Christ!' He grabbed her shoulders for support. 'Sorry – bloody giddy.'

'Nothing to worry about,' she said, as if he were one of her patients and she in uniform. 'Let's get your right arm over my shoulders. That's fine.' She hung on to his right hand and got her left arm round his waist. 'Just lean on me and put one foot in front of the other – that's the form – just get you into the armchair.' They had reached her cabin. 'Now, just going to edge you round—' but he suddenly sagged. He was too heavy for her to support and the chair was too far, but she managed to heave him backwards on to her spare bed. Very quickly she lifted his trailing legs, straightened him, whisked a pillow from the other end and put it under his head, then covered him with the top sheet and single light blanket on her own bed. He was very heavy and she needed a few moments to recover her breath before she took his pulse, tested the skin of his forehead and raised his eyelids in turn. He was in deep sleep but not coma, and had begun to snore gently. She guessed he had woken, been too confused to remember he had had a sleeping tablet, got up to go along to the bathroom, and then in his anxiety to ease his guilt, stumbled on unseen up the inner stairs that ran by the aft end of her cabin's corridor; had he used the main stairs he would have been seen by some steward or the liftman and Morgan been alerted.

She went on studying him clinically whilst she stripped, swiftly replaced all but the suspender-belt and stockings she had worn earlier, re-did her hair and face and hooked in her ear-rings. She swept her kimono, nightie and slippers into a drawer, and straightened the bottom sheet and pillows on her own bed. When George eventually heard of this it would plunge him into even deeper guilt if the ship heard she had summoned aid in nightwear from a slept-in bed. She had to be quick. Any minute now Sister would discover he had been too long in a bathroom – and she must have ready a good enough story to convince George that he had not compromised her to the point of having to marry her. Oh, no! There were more, but discreet knocks on the outer door. Unless—? Play it safe. She went out closing the cabin door behind her.

That time it was Paddy, one hand on his stick, the other straightening his black bow tie. He looked very tired and politely apologetic. 'Sorry to disturb you, Ellie, but as I've just been down to see George, I rather wondered—'

'Rightly.' She jerked a thumb over her shoulder. 'Come in, please.'

'Thank you.' He came in and quietly closed the outer door. He closed it as quietly when he left to fetch Morgan a few minutes later and on both occasions she felt as if he had slammed it in her face.

TEN
The Mozambique Channel
July 1955

'Thank goodness we sail in two hours!' Sister West put her glass of lime down on the deck and hitched the damp wings of her muslin cap over the back of her chair. 'I like the Portuguese and adore Lourenco Marques, but after one day at Beira I feel a hot, soggy rice pudding.'

'Ashore this morning,' said Paddy, 'this pudding felt pressure-cooked.'

'It wasn't that bad, Paddy. Just a Turkish bath.' Elinor languidly waved the painted silk fan she had bought whilst he was buying the scarlet cotton shirt and black trousers he now wore, when they had gone ashore with Father Gerachty who spoke Portuguese well enough for them to do without a guide.

They had drawn their deckchairs to the rail of the upper promenade deck and even Sister West had her feet up on the lowest rail. The ship was anchored just outside the harbour at Beira, the sun had set ten minutes ago, and through the hot, humid darkness, the green and white lights of the port had the soft glow of jewels around the dark velvet neck of an African woman.

Sister West, sitting between them, glanced from one to the other. 'If you jump ship tonight, Dr Brown, everyone'll take you for Portuguese.'

'I've no wish to add my bones to this White Man's Grave, Sister.'

Elinor protested. 'That's on the west coast.'

'And Beira on this one, Mrs Mack,' said Sister, soothingly. She wasn't surprised they were a bit tetchy with each other this evening. They were so like brother and sister, they didn't have to pretend and everyone got tetchy at Beira. Of course they were missing Dr Ashden and though, probably, Mrs Mack was no more sorry than she that the blonde bombshell was now on the train up to Rhodesia, Dr Brown's deprivation symptoms were bound to be setting in. Not that she blamed him for what everyone knew had been going on all week. As Bill Morgan said, when a sexpot chucked herself at a chap, who in his right mind ducked and clinically, the exercise would do him nothing but good.

She went on, 'The Portuguese born out here survive – on the whole – though their infant mortality rate is ghastly. New white settlers just drop like flies. Nothing ever gets dry.' She held her bib-pinned watch up to the deck lighting. 'Good. Their train's well away from the coast now. This humidity won't have helped Dr Ashden. He's done frightfully well, but post-dengue's like post-flu – he'll be awfully tired tonight. Luckily, the others are with him and any safari with Mr Carter on board's in safe hands. And I'm sure Mrs Wade will keep a special eye on him,' she added less artlessly than she sounded. 'But am I missing my prize patient! He was a poppet – and with every respect, Dr Brown, it's not often I say that of a medical patient.'

'I believe you, Sister. The bottom, no less.'

'Nonsense!' Elinor was firm. 'Doctors can sometimes be nightmarish patients, but trained nurses always are.'

'Mrs Mack you're so right! Specially old sisters. They just lie there watching, criticising and complaining that young nurses aren't what they were when they were in training. Always scared me stiff!' She considered Elinor. 'I still can't actually believe you were a Martha's sister. You still look so young and human. How've you done it?'

Paddy's mouth twitched and Elinor laughed. 'Thanks for the kind words, Sister.'

'Not soft-soap, I mean it! That's what ghasted my flabber when Dr Ashden let it out – he did tell you?' Elinor nodded. 'Actually I'm rather glad I didn't know earlier – you'll know what I mean – though I should've guessed you'd done more than a bit of VADing in the war from the way you coped with Mrs Venner in tourist – doesn't that feel ages ago? – and poor Dr Ashden's spot of delirium.' She checked her watch again. 'Must cast off, alas! Crew surgery's early as we're sailing. Oh – you have heard dinner's an hour late?'

Paddy said, 'We have, Sister, and that there's tombola after and another boat-drill at eleven tomorrow morning. Life for a passenger on the *Rose* is a ceaseless round of pleasure.'

'That's the general idea, Dr Brown, but I wish more passengers looked on boat-drill as pleasure or even bothered to show up. You two are jolly good about that.'

'Just allergic to sharks.'

She giggled. 'I'll use that to twist arms. Please don't budge—' but he had risen easily. She beamed at him. 'Thanks frightfully for the limes. My kidneys and liver adored them.' She slapped her liver. 'Livers need watching this far south. They always keep us far busier than the sun on the next fourteen days to the Cape. See you both at dinner. Bysie-bye!' She bustled away, smiling at the several newly-embarked passengers coming out to the rail and Father Gerachty, back in T-shirt and jeans, taking his evening two-mile walk round that deck.

'A nice kid and a good nurse but only to open her mouth to make me feel old,' Paddy murmured, turning to lean on the rail. Elinor was too preoccupied to hear. He glanced back, then turned to watch the last luggage-tender pull away from the aft end of the *Rose*. This was their first occasion alone together since the night George had been admitted to the ship's hospital and he sensed, and was irritated by, the strained element in her silence.

On that night he found Morgan having tea with Sister in the otherwise empty surgery and their reaction to his news had sent higher his professional opinion of both. Morgan quietly thanked him and apologised for the inconvenience. Sister without a word, pushed forward one of the new, lightweight-metal wheelchairs.

'Sister and I'll manage him between us in the chair, thank you, sir,' said Morgan, leaving unspoken but clear, 'I'll deal with any passengers or crew we may encounter *en route*.'

Once in Elinor's cabin he politely refused their help and with Sister eased the deeply sleeping George into the chair, reiterated his thanks and apologies, and

wheeled George to the men's sick-bay. On the following morning when Paddy called socially, George had
no recollection of getting there. It was three evenings
later, on the second of his daily calls, before George
demanded an explanation. His temperature had dropped to normal, so Paddy gave the official version.

George's paler and no longer puffy face, flushed.
'Christ! Elinor hasn't said a word of this on her visits.
What are people saying?'

'Nothing that I've heard. I'd have heard. I get
around.'

Momentarily George brightened and gestured at the
three empty beds. 'Even I've heard you're shooting a
good line.'

'Is nothing sacred?'

'Not on this ship as you bloody well know. That's
why it beats me what Elinor thought she was doing
shoving me into her spare bed. Hell of a compromising
situation!'

'Haven't I just told you that either she got you lying
down or falling and possible cracking your skull? She'd
run into you blundering down her corridor looking for
me, saw you were about to keel over and as her cabin
was nearest, being a good nurse dealt with the emergency, stat., and shouted for help, second.'

George frowned. 'Suppose so. Can't remember what
the hell I was doing.'

'Who does with a high temp. and doped to the eye-
balls?'

'That's true. She still took the hell of a bloody risk.
Whole ship could've had me sleeping with her! You're
sure there's no muck being slung around?'

'Very. Nor will be.' Paddy checked both doors were

closed. 'The Boy Morgan knows his job and union rules.'

George breathed out. 'Forgotten that angle. All I've got out of him is just a spot of delirium and he thought I'd be more comfortable here. Bloody useful that – and your hot-line to the top brass won't have hurt. Bloody relief. I wouldn't like people – hell, Elinor's a damned nice little woman – bloody bad form to have people thinking that—' He broke off as the door from the surgery opened. 'Time up, Sister?'

'I'm afraid so, Dr Ashden. I know Dr Brown will understand. You still tire very easily and we want you fighting fit by Beira.' She patted his hand. 'Isn't he looking a new man, Dr Brown? We're terribly proud of him.'

'With every reason, Sister. Keep on taking the tablets, George. See you tomorrow.'

George snorted with relieved laughter and Sister West smiled maternally at him.

The stern lights of the tender had disappeared when Paddy turned and looked down at Elinor. She lay languorously, her sandalled feet on the rail, hair a black silky cap, pale, shadowed face half-hidden by the languidly waving fan, and the sleeveless blue seersucker dress she had put on clean for tea clamped to her slenderly rounded body as if wrung out. She looked, he thought, as if she had never known hard work, grief, pain, anxiety, terror, death or any but this present parasitic life. He exchanged nods with the perambulating Father Gerachty with whom he had formed the kind of unobtrusive friendship Elinor had had with Mr Carter, now on the first stage of his rail journey down to Bechuana Land. He sat down in Sister's chair. 'You'll miss old Carter and he, you.'

She lowered her fan. 'I will. Not he. Not now he's back in the Africa he loves so much he's never dared recognise it. Nothing like a great love for casting out the rest of the world.'

He had known jealousy often, but never to this extent. He offered cigarettes and when she refused, lit his own. 'That how it was with you and the chap you've left behind in body if not spirit?'

She looked for a few seconds at his face that, as always, the deck lighting transformed into a black-browed, black-eyed, angular caricature. 'In another age, you'd have been burnt at the stake.'

He shrugged. 'Many would say that's on the cards. Before the flames get me, why didn't you marry him? Obvious reason?'

She gave an odd little grimace. 'He and his wife are devout Catholics. No kids.'

'Tough. Tough all round. I'm sorry.' He had to look away. 'And for poor old George.'

She blinked. 'He doesn't need your sympathy.'

He faced her. 'Stuff that, Ellie! You know damn well he went overboard for you and now he's gone I'll tell you he did that at sight in '45.'

She said drily, 'Paddy, you've been on the lotus too long. You'd never have got this angle wrong before. Whatever happened in '45 – and the poor boy was then ripe to fall for the first girl who smiled at him – he didn't do that on this ship. He just tried to kid himself he had for a spell then realised he'd got to snap out of it, as he's the marrying and not the roving type, not yet ready to marry again, and the last person he wants to marry is one who'll remind him of Brenda and his

190

guilt for her.' She tapped her breast. 'He never said, but I'm sure I was her type.'

'Must be the lotus. I should've worked this out. I'm sure she was. He always went for your type. And you for his?' She nodded. 'Yes.' He stubbed out and lit another. 'Monotonously predictable things, hormones.'

'And misleading. Though it took George to make me realise that.'

His shadowed eyes quickened. 'In what way?'

'Being with him finally showed me that for all these years I've been looking for another Alistair and ignoring the fact that the girl he married had vanished long before he died.' She paused and he stayed silent knowing she had not finished. 'Alistair wanted a little woman for a wife. I was one when we married and without the war, might – just might – have been happy to stay one for life. But the war thrust upon me the independence I never sought or thought I wanted, then found I loved. If Alistair had come back, though he wouldn't have minded my nursing as war-work, he would have been hurt and horrified if I told him I loved having my own career. Can you imagine George's reaction? "A woman's place is in the home." Period.'

'That's for sure.' He hesitated. 'How did your ex take it?'

'With lip-service approval since it kept me near and then in London, which suited us both. But I never talked hospital-shop to him.'

He writhed inwardly. 'Mother of God – you loved him.'

'Yes. For a long time. But twice is enough.'

'Twice?'

'Trying twice to be what the man I loved wanted me to be and I'm not. Being so young with Alistair excuses

191

my not seeing it then. No excuse for what came later – and that I've only seen on this ship through George. On, and ashore. I'll always be grateful to George for this and hope to God that next time round he picks a genuine little woman – and the world's stiff with them. Nice, kind, motherly women, longing for good, solid husbands, the social and economic security they provide, who've been raised to regard any independent woman as a social disaster. George is no sexy dreamboat, but he's still got the little-boy-lost quality that brings out the maternal streak. Good, solid, family man is stamped all over him, and there are a lot worse qualities in a husband than dullness.' She thought for a few moments. 'What he really needs is someone like West. She's bright, but not too bright, kind, sensible, doesn't expect men to be saints, obviously wants to settle down and have her own home and family or she wouldn't be chucking her job – and maternal plus. It's too bad she's booked and floating out of his reach. I think she'd make him a marvellous wife. Don't you?'

'Now you've shown me the light. Yes.'

She waved her fan at the invisible coastline. 'Let's pray that somewhere in Rhodesia is another West.'

'Maybe our prayers won't be necessary.' He stubbed out but didn't light another. 'If I had a salary I'd lay a year's pay there's another in his carriage tonight.'

She stared at him. 'Angela Wade?'

'And why not? She's West's type, and if a year or two older, better to look at, very good company, loves bridge, thinks there's something wrong with a man who doesn't drink, that doctors make good husbands as they have to be solid citizens, all men are boys at heart and women wouldn't have it any other way. And one of her married sisters lives in the area of George's new principal's practice.'

She snapped shut the fan. 'My, my, you certainly covered the ground with her, Paddy.'

He looked at her in silence for a few seconds. 'Maybe you should cut down on the lotus, Ellie. That's the first cheap crack I've heard you make. We all have our off moments. Forgive me, I need a bath. See you at dinner.' He got up and walked quickly off the deck with only a slight limp leaving his stick on the back of the chair he had used earlier.

Elinor glanced from his back to the stick then lay back, absently watching the green and white lights and recalling the ironic amusement in Mrs Mellor's eyes all last week, when the latest coupling had enthralled the first-class and she had been inundated with sympathetic enquiries for George's health. Her colour and breathing had returned to normal and her thoughts to a letter from England she had had that morning, when Father Gerachty stopped by her chair.

'You appear to be having a very pensive reverie, Mrs Mackenzie. I trust I'm not intruding?'

'Not at all, Father.' She lowered her feet from the rail and sat higher. 'Done your two miles?'

'I have indeed but it seems I must try and get in one of tomorrow's later as I may not then be up to it.' He sat in the next chair and his youngish boxer's face and deceptively clever eyes glowed with the simple delight of having a red-hot tip from the bridge. 'I've just met the First round the other side. He's just had the latest weather report. The monsoon ahead of us for these past twenty-four hours has just changed course and is heading north. Unless, as I devoutly hope, it again changes course, we should meet it in the small hours. I'm a lamentable sailor. What about you?'

'The only rough weather I've ever met was in the Bay of Biscay. Lots were very sick. I felt fine. I don't know how.'

'You have been blessed with a strong stomach. Mercifully, I boarded at Genoa, as I have not.' He smiled reminiscently. 'Back in '43 on this run I was seasick roughly from Durban to halfway up the South Atlantic and then again in the Bay.'

Her mind gave an almost audible click of recall. 'On a homeward-bound hospital ship, Father?' He nodded. 'A padre?'

'No, no. A young and literally green regimental chaplain. I bought my ticket at Salerno.' He gestured to his thick, short legs. 'I sailed back to the UK in a double hip spica. (Both legs encased in plaster from waist to ankles.) I fear I gave our good, grossly over-worked sisters a dreadful time. You never nursed on one?'

'No. But during '43 I nursed lots of men from those ships when they had to sail the long way home as the Mediterranean was too dangerous. Not that the Indian Ocean and South Atlantic were then any too healthy.'

'Indeed, not. We'd to keep taking evasive action. That voyage took us nearly three months.'

'Yes. I remember others taking as long.' She paused, looking back. 'I should have remembered, but till now had wholly forgotten they came this way.'

'Memory can be mercifully selective, Mrs Mackenzie.' He noticed the stick. 'But that is a blessed sign of recovery! Is Pat coming back . . . ? I'll take it down to him. I've to fix up our chess after dinner and must get below to change for a meeting of the Adults' Entertainments Committee. You'll excuse me? See you at dinner.'

And at breakfast and lunch and tea and dinner tomorrow, she thought, with such an upsurge of irritation at the predictability of shipboard life, that she forgot all the rest he had just said. And as tonight is only a semi-first night out, at dinner I'll wear a cocktail dress, she thought peevishly, and our table will compare impressions of Beira. The British will smile indulgently and say one has always known the Portuguese have their own attitudes to the colour-bar, but are our oldest allies – such an amusing man, Charles II – and have always been great explorers and mariners. The South Africans will radiate disapproval of all Portuguese East Africa, and I'll long to say the one thing I loved ashore today was the way the Portuguese seem oblivious to the colour of anyone's skin. But I won't – as I lack the guts to take being ostracised from here to the Cape and if I came out with that truth, neither the medical profession closing ranks nor the long arm of Sir John Foster-Green, could save me from it.

She had changed for dinner when the ship sailed. She watched from the deck outside her cabin until all the shore lights had disappeared, and the ship stopped to drop the pilot. Directly the engines re-started, she felt the altered motion as the ship moved into the open sea of the great Mozambique Channel. She thought affectionately of Mr Carter, and then, guardedly, of George, and how she had glimpsed her own relief at the back of his eyes when they said goodbye that morning. A few seconds later she had glimpsed the pain he had tried to keep out when he shook hands with Paddy.

'Next one's on me, old chap. Watch your step in the Cape Rollers.'

'Safe bet, both counts. Take it easy, George. Be seeing you.'

Yes, she thought, gazing out at the smooth, shining, black sea, the black, star-filled sky and slowly rising half-moon. Yes, they'll meet again – and go on with the conversation. Not George and me. That conversation's ended. She went back to her cabin feeling as if she had come from a funeral. She re-read the letter from the Assistant Matron of Martha's that had come in the mail-bag the pilot brought aboard at breakfast-time. She was still re-reading it when the dinner chimes sounded and she went straight down to the dining saloon. All the newly-emptied places had been filled and at her table the approaching monsoon and those her companions had encountered, monopolised the conversation.

'Not many down for breakfast tomorrow, eh, Mr Weaver?'

'She may change course again, Colonel,' said the purser, with a benign smile, as the musicians began their finale, a selection from Kreisler's *The King Steps Out*.

When the screaming wind woke Elinor the ship was pitching and rolling and it was so dark she thought it the middle of the night. She switched on the bedhead light, grabbed her violently swinging watch off its special hook. It was seven forty a.m., Miller, her cabin steward had been in, shut her window, closed the curtains, switched on the blowers, cleared the top of her dressing-table and everything moveable from the floor but the armchair that was reeling between dressing-table and mahogany wall-cupboard. She crawled along her bed to open the curtains, and clung to the window to keep balanced whilst pulling down the top sash. The sky was black with huge, low, whirling clouds; the charcoal, foam-streaked sea looked on the boil; at every roll to starboard great sheets of spray soaked the roofed empty deck now cleared of deckchairs and with a rope line strung along the bulkhead beneath her window. The wind hurled spray and curtains in her face. She closed the sash, fell back on her bed, half-deafened by the roar of wind and sea and the creaking and groaning of the drunkenly pitching and rolling ship.

She thought of those wartime hospital ships that had only returned to the UK the blinded, the dying or the too severely wounded ever to fight again. All the wounded or ill British servicemen in the North African or Italian campaigns that had been expected to recover, had been taken to British service hospitals in North Africa, then given local sick-leave before returning to their units. She had to close her eyes at the belated insight into what the blistering heat of the Red Sea, and seas of this nature, must have done to men in heavy plaster splints over fractured, often splintered bones, with wounds seeping the pus that had been omnipresent pre-penicillin. Even a slight jolt would have caused them agony. And how much greater the agony of those enduring *this* in the terrible, new, perpetual darkness of blindness, and the dreadful exhaustion of dying. She thought of the always over-worked and short-staffed nursing and medical personnel that had worked on in all conditions, with always at the back of their own and their patients' minds, the lurking, hunting U-boats. And down this coast – the sharks. She had known several Martha's nurses and housemen who had later served on and gone down with their hospital ships. All, when they died, had been younger than she, now. The thought of them and those ships made her so ashamed of her last night's self-pitying irritation with the trivia of shipboard life in this luxury, in every sense, of peacetime, that it was some little time before she realised she did not feel even slightly queasy.

Miller came in with her tea, balancing like a trapeze artist on his small, neat feet. He was a small, neat man with a tanned bald head and weathered, mournful face. 'I reckoned you wasn't troubled seeing you was sleeping, madam. None alongside—' he jerked his head at the aft bulkhead, 'had the wink since afore dawn nor wanting tea. Dixon says only Dr Brown wanting his port side — a gentleman as can't be doing without his early tea, Dixon says — but his ladies is that poorly he's had to fetch up the doctor. Dixon reckons they'll keep to their bunks till she blows herself out. Not that she'll trouble the old *Rose*. Knew how to build ships, they did, when they built the old lady. But seeing she's lifting lively, if you'll pardon the liberty, madam, you want to keep close the ropes and give the deck doors and the decks a wide berth.'

'Thank you, Miller. I'll take your advice.'

'Welcome, I'm sure, madam. Just run your bath but best not more than the few inches or it'll be over the side afore you're in it.'

The high, deep bath was encased in mahogany; the few inches of hot salt water transformed into a miniature, invigorating whirlpool; but getting in and out was as difficult as standing on a swaying roller-coaster. She was so tempted to send a message to Paddy warning him either to skip a bath or get Dixon to stand by, that she decided the monsoon was affecting her brain if not her stomach. Mrs Mellor thought Dixon the best cabin steward she had ever encountered, 'Always there when one wants him and invisible when not—' and Paddy needed neither medical advice nor a mother.

She dressed in a tan cotton T-shirt, the jeans she had

only worn in the Bay of Biscay, ankle socks and plim-solls and steadied by the ropes strung along corridor walls, across halls and down the main stairs, went down to breakfast. The fiddles were up round the tables and clean white damask cloths dampened with cold water to stop crockery and cutlery sliding off and the dining saloon staff was noticeably thinner. Only fifteen passengers appeared at breakfast and the arrival of each swaying, staggering figure, was greeted with euphoric cries of congratulation and the Tannoy's announcement that boat-drill had been temporarily postponed with yells of laughter.

On her return the assistant pursers called congratulations through the grilled window and that the ship's doctor and nursing sister had been hard at it since dawn and the Fourth was a dirty shade of green.

'We've just sent him two nice bacon sandwiches.'

'Sadists!' she retorted and they shouted with smug laughter.

Dixon emerged from the starboard corridor. He stopped, feet apart, knees flexed, swaying with the roll. He had just been to her cabin and heard from Miller that she was at breakfast. 'Dr Brown's compliments, madam, and he hopes you're as well as can be expected.'

She smiled at the olive branch within the all-purpose medical euphemism. 'Thank you, Dixon. Please thank Dr Brown and say much better and – how is he?'

'Off his bacon, madam, but managed his scrambled eggs, nicely.'

'Good! But I'm sorry to hear your three ladies aren't too well.'

'Settling a mite on the doctor's tablets, madam. I'm

not saying the ladies'll be sorry when she's blown herself off.'

'I'm sure they won't. Please give them all my best
wishes and say if there is anything I can do for them
to let me know through you. I won't call. No one seasick wants to be bothered with visitors.'

'You never said a truer word, madam. Mind you,'
Dixon added woodenly, 'Dr Brown's up normal, but
berthed in his chair with his book seeing she's lifting
sharpish.' He was looking at her steadily. 'Not be the
first time he's had that anchorage, seemly, madam.'

'I'm afraid not, Dixon.' She copied his stance and
needed only one hand on the nearest rope. This was
their first conversation but she recognised the appeal
and that it would not have been made to her had there
been any foundation in last week's gossip. She had
nursed scores of Dixons and Millers; she knew the stan-
dards they expected of those they served; their loyalty
and often affection, when these were maintained; and
ruthless contempt, when not. 'But though Dr Brown
won't much like being stuck in a chair by his bedside
again, in this sea even someone with perfect muscular
co-ordination could have a bad fall. He won't want to
add to Dr Morgan's present problems or risk setting
back his own recovery by months. And whilst I'm sure
you could safely get him up to the lounge, as you'll
know, he likes to manage under his own steam.'

'As you say, madam.'

'Yes. Still – as he's up, I'll just look in for a few
minutes to thank him myself. If you'll kindly take time
announcing me, I'll slip in before he has to get out of
his chair.'

'If you wish, madam.' Dixon looked down his nose
in concealed satisfaction. He knocked on Paddy's outer

door, called, 'Dixon, sir!' and only when he opened the cabin door. 'Mrs Mackenzie to see you, sir!'

'Thank you, Dixon.' Elinor had shot by and he closed the door before Paddy lowered his book. 'For God's sake, stay put, Paddy. Hoadley East'll kill me if you bust a femur on my behalf.'

Paddy's laugh sounded natural and he flopped back in the chair that his weight and dug-in heels were keeping fairly steady. He had on a black cotton rollneck and the trousers he'd brought yesterday; his hair looked greyer, his face paler and a little drawn and he had twice nicked his chin when shaving this morning. He looked her over as if mildly pleased and this was not the first time he had seen in her in the jeans that made her look younger, smaller, more approachable and distractingly feminine.

'Will you just sit down and tell me why you look set for two years before the mast and aren't flat on your back puking your guts out.'

She laughed and flopped on to the foot of the spare bed, one hand gripping the footrail. 'Don't ask me why my stomach can take this sea but not even on dry land anyone else vomiting. Murder in the Bay – and worse than murder in Martha's till I learnt how to hold on to my own till I reached a sluice.'

'I never knew that!'

'Hell, man, who broadcasts their weaknesses?' She gave him a long, openly clinical appraisal. 'Off your bacon, I hear, but as you managed your scrambled eggs nicely and your skin and eyes are clear, you'll live.' She turned her attention to the cabin. His bed was unmade, the dressing-table top cleared and the only book visible the one he held. 'I've just had the impression Dixon is pining to get this cabin done.'

'He can do it round me.' Their eyes met. 'Some chances I'm not prepared to take, Ellie. No doubt that's middle-age. But thanks for looking in.'

'I wanted to thank you for the kind message.' He inclined his head. 'As Dixon said you weren't throwing up I thought I'd stop by on my way up to the lounge. My steward at breakfast insisted the best berth is the middle sofa against the forward bulkhead and nothing since the days of sail beats brandy-and-dry ginger in a sharp sea. You talk of me before the mast – he shot such a line I hadn't the heart to wreck it asking if Bligh allowed ginger ale on the *Bounty*. One of my new buddies'll tell me.' He smiled inquiringly. 'That's right – bosom buddies since breakfast. Only fifteen of us down, all the others either boarded yesterday or at Mombasa, and all of us oozing smugness and the Dunkirk spirit. Wow!' A sharper roll to port made her clutch the footrail with both hands and Paddy his chair arms. 'You're dead wise to stay put, Paddy. If you do a Father Gerachty and return in a double hip spica not just Hoadley but Chesty Alexander'll spring a coronary.' She saw his eyes quicken and stood up unsteadily, knowing what she had done and that she must leave the choice to him. 'I must get out of—'

'Hold it a moment. When did Joe Gerachty give you his war?'

She sat back on the spare bed. 'Last evening before he returned your stick. Smote me with guilt. I'd clean forgotten those ships came this way. Hadn't you? No,—' she answered herself before he slightly shook his head, 'of course not. Peter Elliot and Tony Barnes were in your year.' He nodded sombrely. 'My God, Paddy, can you imagine having to work with hundreds of D.I. or S.I.L. patients, in this?'

'I've been trying not to.'

'Yes,' she said and for a few moments their faces looked older. Then once again she stood up. 'I must get out. Poor Dixon's pining—'

'I've a better idea.' He reached for the bell. The door opened immediately. 'Dixon, can you spare a few minutes to give me a hand up to the lounge? Mrs Mackenzie has just reminded me that you'll need to get this cabin done.'

'Much obliged, madam. If that suits, whenever you're ready, sir,' said Dixon without a flicker of emotion, feeling as if he had been tipped a fiver.

They spent the rest of that day sitting on the middle sofa against the forward bulkhead and having their longest private conversation since their meeting in October, 1943. There were about a dozen other passengers either draped on, or sharing other sofas, but the screaming wind, roaring sea, and creaking and groaning of the ship reduced conversations across the lounge to occasional shouts, and made it only possible between those sitting close together. The violent motion made reading difficult as books kept being jerked from hands. None of them bothered to give more than cursory glances through the thick overseas editions of British national newspapers that had come aboard yesterday and were already up to one month old. The two lounge stewards, circulating with the technique of flies on a ceiling, offered beef-tea and dry biscuits, brandy-and-dry ginger ale, the latest weather, seasickness, sprains, cuts and bruises reports, and at lunch-time the special serving of sandwiches for those preferring not to go down to the dining saloon. And with every passing hour they found the strain of pretending their friendship was unaltered far more exhausting than the violence of the storm.

Elinor picked off the carpet an overseas *Daily Mirror* that had just slid off their coffee table. 'Want this?'

'No, thanks. I've checked up on 'Jane.' (A strip cartoon.) She's still losing her clothes so all must be well with the world. It can manage without me.'

'I've forgotten it exists.' She rested her head against the sofa and he removed his right arm that was draped along the back. 'It's frightening how egocentric I've become at sea.'

'It's certainly conducive to the study of one's navel, but one's self-absorption in a hospital bed beats all comers. One becomes so convinced it is not merely the centre, but the entire universe, that there's an overwhelming temptation to resent attempts to shift one out of it.'

This was the first open reference to his illness that he had made to her. She wanted to shout with joy. She said composedly, 'Which you successfully resisted – *vide*, your medical history.'

'Only as I was born bloody minded and with an insatiable appetite for trivia. In retrospect, that combination saved my sanity. When not in a blind fury, I dug the dirt with staff and patients.' He smiled mockingly. 'You've no conception what really goes on behind the scenes in a hospital ward.'

She had to force her eyelids to flutter. 'Sometime you must tell me about it.'

He nodded non-committally. 'Is it my imagination, or is the wind worse?'

She glanced away, perturbed by his taking refuge in the weather. 'I'm not sure. My ear-drums are too rattled to register properly.'

204

'Dixon says we should have cleared it by nightfall and once through, the temperature'll start dropping gently but steadily to the Cape.'

'Their winter's started. Polly says it roughly equates with a goodish English summer.'

'Should be pleasant. Incidentally, who did Polly Potter marry? Should I know?'

'Probably not. John Hargreaves. South African. A Benedict's man caught in England by the war. He joined the RAMC, and met Polly at a party in the winter of '45 when he was doing a post-grad at Benedict's. They married and went out to Cape Town – his home town – in '46. From Polly's letters, it's worked out very well, though he sounds as if he could be Mrs Van der Mann's son.'

'A lot of that about on this ship. How do you think you'll take it for – how long is it? Forgotten,' he lied.

'Roughly two months.' She smiled slightly. 'I'm glad one still can't fly direct to the Cape as this voyage gives one more than a vague idea of the kind of attitudes one has got to expect, if not accept and to keep the blood-pressure down by keeping the mouth shut. Not so easy if one suddenly flew into it. But, if necessary, I can keep up an act. It'll be lovely to see Polly again, and meet my godson and her two younger infants and see the country. Mr Carter said it's very beautiful.'

'So I've heard.' He had to look away. 'Think you may be tempted to stay on?'

'No idea yet.'

He had to persist. 'If you do, with your qualifications and record, you'd have no trouble getting a sister's job even were not all your ex-colonies shouting for British-trained nurses. So many going out, that at my last follow-up Hoadley told me that without the Irish and

West Indian nurses every hospital in the NHS would grind to a halt.'

'And without the doctors from the Commonwealth. You thinking of joining the brain-drain?'

His face tightened. Never yet on this ship had she asked about his professional future, nor – as still – been prepared to discuss her own. 'Why jump the gun? Hoadley hasn't yet signed me off.'

'He will at your next follow-up if you keep out of plaster.'

'I hope to spare his coronary.' He hesitated, then after nearly three hours, asked. 'Why should you think Chesty'll spring his if I show up in a double hip spica?'

She sat sideways to face him, steadying herself with one hand on the sofa back. 'He wants you back in the Thoracic Unit by early January.'

He had been braced against bad news for too long to believe this, even from her. 'Why? Evan Evans has had my job for the past two years, is a decent chap and good chest man. His job till Chesty retires and he takes over.'

'Yes. If he intended staying put.'

'Evan'll never chuck Martha's—'

'He is, Paddy. He's got three boys under seven, earns just over two thousand a year – no, not peanuts after the three hundred he – and you – got as SMO, but very much so against the one hundred thousand dollars he can earn annually in the States. He's been offered some very good jobs over there. Mrs Evans has finally persuaded him to accept one. Chesty's asked him to hang on to the end of the year to give him time to get you back.'

He flushed. 'How the devil do you know this?'

'Jean Driver.'

'Who—?'

'You must remember Jean! My set. The West and Angela Wade type who's been Sister Alex from '51 to this last January when she shifted up to Ass. Mat. She and Polly were my greatest chums in training. Hadn't you heard she's now Ass. Mat.?'

'Yes. Just forgotten her name.' And for years, he thought, incredulously, you. 'But when did she give you this gen?'

'The rough outline when she came up for Helen's funeral and stayed over the weekend. We talked Martha's non-stop.'

'A useful anodyne.' He looked and sounded dazed.

'Very.' She saw he needed the breathing space and that this was the moment for something else she needed to tell him. 'For more than the obvious reason. Jean's always been the only person in Martha's who knew about my ex – and though she never said it, passionately disapproved and loathed him for tying me down. She never realised – nor did I till this voyage – that I wanted the defence of that particular tie.' She read the expression that flickered through his eyes. 'You've diagnosed that?'

'Belatedly. When did she bring you up to date?'

'Yesterday. We've always kept in contact. I wrote her airmail from Aden telling her you were on board and how you helped me change classes. Yesterday's was her reply. She had already heard from Matron via Chesty that you were on the *Rose*. She suddenly smiled. 'No flies on Chesty and no finer prognostitian in Martha's. When did you last see him?'

'Oh – March or April. He was driving down to Surrey for the weekend and stopped for a chat.'

'Does Sir John still live in Esher?' He nodded slightly.

His defences were cracking and he didn't trust his voice. 'God bless crafty old Chesty! He won't have told Sir John more than that a bit of sun and sea air should do you good as he never, ever, raises hopes but always – always – bases his own on his clinical judgement. And he's always right, isn't he?' He gave another slight nod. 'So the fundamental reason why you're on this ship is that Chesty wants and knows he can have you back.'

He did not even nod in answer and suddenly he was so white that she urgently signalled a steward who raced up with a small glass of neat brandy and a sick-bag.

'Sign the chit later, madam.' He retreated as fast.

She held up the glass. 'Knock it back, Paddy.'

'Thanks.' He drained the glass and his colour returned. 'Your timing with lifelines, beats all-comers – Mother of God!' The empty glass was shot from his hand by a freak wave that lifted the bow of the ship so high that it seemed airborne for the second or so before it crashed down into a trough and the stern rose as sharply. He had flung his arms round Elinor – his arm muscles had been greatly strengthened by his illness – and he needed all their strength and those of his weaker leg muscles and stamped-in heels to keep them from pitching off the sofa. On the other sofas the couples clung together; the single occupants lay spread-eagled on their backs; even the stewards were rocked off their feet; and every item on coffee-tables and service counter, catapulted on to the carpet. Then the freak wave had rolled northwards and the old ship, creaked, groaned and comparatively steadily, pitched and rolled on southwards.

They fell breathlessly against the back of the sofa.

Elinor's hands still clutched his that were locked at her waist, when she gasped, 'Miller was not kidding this morning when he told me they knew how to build ships when they built the old lady.'

'Nor was I when the elements got into the act.' His breathless voice was one he had never used before. His chin brushed her hair as he turned his head to look down into her now whitened face. 'Whenever I've most needed a lifeline, you've thrown me one.' He slackened his hold and unlocked his hands, but could not yet bear to remove his encircling arms. 'So it's no wonder at all that I should feel about you as I do – or that more than one psychiatrist would say I'd to pick up polio to prevent my marrying the wrong woman and wrecking both lives. And that, as much else, is something I've only recognised since you came so quietly back into my life in the bright moonlight of that night in the Canal. My subconscious had known I was about to make an irrevocable mistake, my conscious refused to accept it, and as I'd been working all out, my resistance was down, so I picked up the nastiest bug around. Not the first nor last time the subconscious has filled a hospital bed. For all the new research into and talk of prophylactic medicine, there's still more than a grain of truth in the old maxim the old men dinned into us when I was a student, "The happy man doesn't get cancer." Or polio. Like you – like all of us – I must have met it countless times previously and had the natural immunity to resist it. Not then.'

'No.' Her eyes were bright but troubled. She had to be honest. 'You're a good physician, so you are probably right about this, but—'

'Wait, Ellie. Please. I've not finished—' But he had to stop and grip her more tightly as the suddenly increased roll slid them from one end of the sofa to the other. 'Moot point—' he gasped, 'whether the elements are for me or against me, so I'll deal with the rest briefly.' The whole truth was in his eyes. 'Ellie, I can neither explain nor understand how I feel about you. Sex can be defined and understood. Not love. It can only be felt. And I know it,' he breathed, 'for you.' He gently touched her wedding ring with his left fore-finger. 'And I know that as long as you wear this, you'll never replace it. I know you wore it with great joy for just the one week – and then for years, round your throat. And then for more years – and still – as the reminder of what it has really cost you. Aren't I right?' Her expression answered him. 'Yes. I know it, my love. So I'll say no more, though there is so much more I want to say. But not until – or if – you want to hear it. But there's a lot I still don't know that you can tell me—' he removed his left arm to signal an order to one of the stewards picking up scattered objects. 'What else has Jean told you? Give, woman, give and don't spare the dirt. We've only another thirteen days together and I want to hear all!'

He was wrong in one respect. Four days later Elinor had a cable from Polly Hargreaves and on the following morning her voyage ended at Durban.

ELEVEN
London
November 1955

He had just returned with the Sunday papers and was
fitting the key into the front door when he remembered
he was out of milk. He opened the door, dropped the
papers on one of the four unpacked tea-chests of books
that half-blocked the hall of the ground-floor flat he had
rented since the previous Wednesday and reached for
the stick he had not used earlier. But last night's heavy
rain had left the leaves lying around slippery as oil.

It was a cold, damp, grey November morning and
when he closed behind him the glass-panelled main
door of the one-time Edwardian private house in a side
street off the King's Road, Chelsea, he stopped to do
up two of the wooden toggles of the old duffle coat he
had bought when a house-physician. A taxi drew up
in front of the house as he was about to go down
the three steps from the porch. Having only told Dr
Alexander his new address and not yet met any of the

211

occupants of the two upper and basement flats, he glanced at it incuriously. And then felt as if kicked hard in the chest.

The driver jumped out, opened the nearside back door as the sole passenger emerged, Paddy recovered his breath and called, 'I'm glad you remembered the milk, Ellie. I was just going out for some.'

Elinor tightened her grasp on the pint bottle she held in both gloved hands and called back, 'One always runs out on Sundays.' She handed the bottle to the driver to unzip her sling handbag.

'I'll settle this.' Paddy was beside her. 'How much, driver?'

'Five-and-tanner on the clock, guv.' (Five shillings and sixpence.)

Paddy offered a ten-shilling note. 'That's all right, thanks.'

'Much obliged, guv! Just fetch your good lady's bag and the milk in for you, shall I?'

'Please. First right, ground floor.' He turned to Elinor and hooking the stick on to one pocket of his coat, took her shoulders in his hands. 'One should never disappoint one's public,' he said before kissing her lips lightly.

The driver had returned. 'You'll be glad to be home and put your feet up after the night sleeper, lady. Never known the one get the wink of sleep on any. Morning, all!'

They waved him off. Elinor had adjusted the stylish set of her small, black suede 'Robin Hood' hat, Paddy brushed the lipstick from his lips with the back of one hand, and then went indoors in silence. He removed her suitcase and the milk from the doorway to one of the tea-chests and said nothing until he had taken her into the living room, switched on the light and lit the large, unguarded, circa 1938 gas fire.

'Don't take off your coat till this room's thawed out. Facing north it's the coldest in this ice-chest of a joint.'

She looked vaguely around the large, impersonally furnished, book-strewn room. 'One day England will hear about central heating.'

'I wouldn't bet on it. Hence—' he held open his coat to show the heavy fisherman's knit sweater that hung like a tent over his navy woollen rollneck and navy cords 'Nanouk of the North.'

She smiled composedly and removed her black, kid gloves. She wore a tailored black and white dog-toothed tweed overcoat and skirt, a scarlet, cashmere twin-set and no jewellery aside from her wedding ring. And she looked to him as lovely and unreal as a model in a winter travel advertisement in a glossy magazine.

'Do sit down.' He pushed nearer to the fire a deep, faded, grey velvet armchair, then lifted from behind the book-littered sofa, the red leather-cushioned solid wooden camel-stool he had bought in Port Said. It was the only of his many purchases on the voyage that he had kept. All but one of the others had gone to his married siblings in Ireland, Sir John Foster-Green, the Hoadley-Easts, and the three senior staff nurses who had been his day, night and relief 'specials' when he was on the D.I.L. The exception that he had bought in Las Palmas, was in its original packing in a drawer in his bedroom.

He put the camel-stool to face her across the hearth and sat on it slowly. 'If you don't mind I'll take five before making us a hot cuppa. My incipient coronary needs more immediate prophylactic therapy.' He offered cigarettes and reached out to light hers. 'What would you have done with the milk if I'd been out?'

'Left it on your doorstep on this.' She took from her handbag a single, folded sheet of writing-paper and handed it to him. Her note was dated, timed 8.30 a.m., and ran, 'Sorry to miss you. Will call back this afternoon. If no luck, due home tomorrow evening. Riding Hill 247. What's your phone number? Love. Ellie.'

'Sound notion.' He pushed the note in one duffle pocket. 'It would have been taken for a bill and left till I found it. But how did you know where to find me?'

'Jean Driver via Evan Evans via Chesty. I rang Jean from home, Wednesday night. She rang me back with your address the next night and said you'd moved in the day before.'

He nodded. They were watching each other like chess-players and listening far more intently to the unspoken than spoken words. 'From the stickers on your case you flew back from Johannesburg on Tuesday. But in your last letter that I got in Dublin via Martha's last month, you said Polly wanted you to stay on at least until the New Year.'

'She did. Did you answer that letter, as if you did I haven't had it?' He shook his head without even the pretence of apology and for a few seconds she looked down at her left hand. Then, 'When I wrote that letter Polly's parents had not yet decided to stay on for at least another six months and probably permanently. I now think – and hope – they will stay for good. The novelty of meeting their adoring English grandparents has tremendously helped the children. Mr Potter's the stolid, kind, substitute father-figure they desperately need. Mrs Potter's an older Polly, and being an only, she and her parents have always been close.' She hesitated. 'But though Polly kept on insisting I stay, neither she nor the children now really need me and as there's a lot I need – want – to do back here, I decided to fly back.' She paused, but he stayed silent and the only sounds were the hissing of the gas fire and ringing of the church bells. 'Do you want to go to mass or have you been?'

He listened to the bells and smiled faintly. 'No, to both. Joe Gerachty'll be praying for my redemption and there's no doubt at all his prayers are worth more than mine – or that he shares La West's passion for a cream cake.'

A small smile touched her eyes. 'Yes. The church bells were ringing all that day,' she said and for a few moments both were back to the Sunday in July when the ship was anchored at the dockside of Lourenco Marques.

The cluster of wrecked ships lying about a mile from the rotting wooden breakwater at the southern entrance underlined the deceptive serenity of the pale grey sea, when the ship slowed to a crawl before entering the long, fairly wide harbour that was renowned for its treacherous sandbanks. The sky was grey as the sea on that Saturday afternoon, but when the passengers were woken by the church bells on Sunday morning, the clear sky was powder-blue, and the bright sun warmed, but no longer scorched. The sunshine accentuated the whiteness of the Spanish-styled public buildings, and the houses with red tiled roofs, and the wide squares and long wide boulevards. The sandy beaches were pale brown and the grass crowning the now ubiquitous long northern headland was a soft and not tropical green. And in the near-empty and unusually tidy docks, the African workers sat huddled under blankets and shawls and the Portuguese overseers wore thick sweaters.

The bells were still ringing from the cathedral and many churches when Mrs Mellor, in a dashing grey straw pillbox and grey silk coat, buttoned her gloves and cast over Elinor and Sister West the kind of glance that transported Elinor back to Sundays in her childhood whilst waiting to be taken to church. She had on her boater, a black linen duster coat, gloves, silk stockings and court shoes and Sister West in white straw halo hat, trim blue linen coat and skirt, carried a prayer book in her gloved hands.

'You both look charmingly and suitably dressed, my dears,' said Mrs Mellor. 'The Portuguese are a Catholic people with strict attitudes where young women are concerned. One must observe their customs. It would be quite correct for you two to attend Matins at the English church on your own, but not to visit this café Sister so recommends, unchaperoned. Where is that boy? Ah! My taxi here, Mr Yates?'

'Waiting at the foot of the gangplank, Mrs Mellor.' Mr Yates sighed piteously. 'How I wish I was off watch and could join you for church!'

'You're off watch this evening, Mr Yates. We don't sail until early tomorrow. You'll have plenty of time to attend Evensong tonight. Come along, girls!'

Mrs Mellor swept ahead regally and was nearing the foot of the gangplank when Father Gerachty and Paddy got out of a second taxi. They had been to high mass in the cathedral and stopped and raised their hats. Mrs Mellor waved them aside.

'You must forgive us, gentlemen! You have attended your immortal souls and we must attend ours! Can't stop! Be late for church – but if you both care to join us for coffee and cakes at noon at – what's the name again, Sister? – you'll be most welcome. Come along, girls!'

Paddy caught Elinor's eye and as she went by, whispered, 'Have you got your collection money in your glove and a clean white handkerchief?'

She answered with a smile that seemed to turn his bones to water. She had kept having that effect upon him during the last three days that the serendipity of their physiological ability to withstand the storm had transformed into a timeless era of quiet, unclouded enjoyment. He had never seen her look so happy as she had since the monsoon. He sensed that she, too, had gained a heightened recognition of their individual luck in surviving so much whilst still young enough to enjoy the challenge of the future, but old enough to savour present happiness as it could only be savoured by those who have learnt that happiness is no birthright, but a loan that, whether temporary or long-lasting, should be accepted with gratitude and wonder. He had just seen both qualities in Elinor's smile and he waited until his pulse-rate returned to normal to answer his very observant companion's, 'Why don't we take another taxi for a wider look round before we join the ladies, Pat?'

Next morning at first light the ship sailed on southwards. The Indian Ocean was calm and green and for the first-timers the weather was arguably the most perfect they had yet had at sea. It was the kind of northern, high summer day that in England filled cricket grounds, beaches and roads to the coast. It filled the swimming pool to the derision of the old-Africa-hands. 'Oh, well, if you want to get pneumonia – plenty of room in the ship's hospital again . . .'

After dinner there was another dance on the open deck in front of the veranda café. The fairy lights swung in the soft breeze blowing from the north and with extra clarity carrying the music up to the boat-deck where Paddy's chair was empty. He and Elinor had been amongst the guests at the Captain's cocktail party and once the dance started, for the first time he watched from the café with a few other non-dancers from the earlier party. The Latin-American session had the full attention of the sitters-out and Elinor was dancing her second rumba with the Captain when he made the excuse of wanting something from his cabin and left quietly. He left through the smoking room then went out on the starboard side of the deck and sat on a wooden settle bolted to the bulkhead just beyond the most forward lounge window.

It was after eleven and the lighted lounge was empty. The elderly had retired for the night and the other passengers were at the bar, the bridge tables, or dance. He sat back, lit a cigarette, and looked up at the brilliance of the Southern Cross that dominated the starry sky and rivalled the near three-quarter moon. The Latin-American spell was ending with 'Begin The Beguine' and his legs twitched involuntarily. He had been a good dancer and he so longed to dance again and with Elinor, that when the tune ended he had to brush a finger across his upper lip. The applause had barely faded when the musicians launched into 'Top Hat', a fast foxtrot, immediately followed by 'Cheek To Cheek', played, unusually, as a slow foxtrot. These were the folk tunes of his young manhood and even his slower left foot had begun to tap, haltingly, when Elinor swept

218

up the deck and stopped to face him. She wore her black silk taffeta and small diamond ear-rings and in the deck and moonlight her faintly flushed face was bright with hope.

'Please dance with me, Paddy.'

He dropped and ground the cigarette under one heel but did not rise. 'Want us both to fall over?'

'Like to bet?' She held out her arms. 'Don't waste this. I love it as a slow.' (As she had privately requested of the Captain.)

His resistance collapsed. He stood up and took her in his arms without saying more. And at first with difficulty, then helped by his former expertise and natural sense of rhythm and her expertise at following his stumbling lead, they danced slowly in a private circle at the fore end of the deck. There were no other dancers on that side as only the official floor was sanded. The passengers leaning their backs against the rail at the aft end watching the main dance discreetly glanced sideways and agreed it was rather good show, what? When the tune ended and the faster 'Isn't It A Lovely Day To Be Caught In The Rain' began, Paddy stood still, holding her closely. He said almost conversationally, 'Sure as hell is a long way from that ambulance, Ellie' and then, for the first time in nearly twelve years, he kissed her lips. Her arms slid round his neck as she kissed him and his hold tightened. He was still kissing her when there was an artificial, apologetic cough from behind his back. He raised his face reluctantly and still holding her, looked round in an enchanted daze.

'Terribly sorry to intrude, sir – Mrs Mackenzie—' the most junior Wireless Officer was puce with more than embarrassment. He offered Elinor a sealed cable envelope. 'This cable just come for you, Mrs Mackenzie. My Chief sent me straight down and – er – I'll wait as you may wish to reply.'

Paddy released her and she took the envelope. 'Thank you, Mr Jenkins. Won't keep you a minute,' she said quietly.

They read the cable together under the nearest deck light. It had been sent two hours ago by Polly Hargreaves from John Hargreaves' sister and brother-in-law's home in Pietermaritzburg, Natal, Union of South Africa and gave the full private address for the reply.

It read: 'Deeply distressed to give tragic news stop John killed car accident today stop children self staying relations at above stop brother-in-law Pieter de Bruyn will meet *Rose of Africa* Durban tomorrow stop Ellie please come need you love Polly.'

'More tea, Ellie?'

'Thanks.' She had taken off her hat and her coat was only over her shoulders when she held out her cup and her wedding ring sparkled in the firelight. The clean ashtray he had put on the hearth between them was filled with stubs, the church bells had stopped ringing, the rain had returned and was lashing the outside of the bay window. They had been talking of Polly and her children, and she went on, 'Once they got home they stopped looking like shattered little ghosts. Personally, I would have taken them straight home after the funeral. It was in Pietermaritzburg as John's mother and her parents are buried there. That was where she met John's father.' He nodded, watching her as if still unsure she was not an illusion. 'I thought the children needed the security of their own rooms, toys, friends, but as I've none and Polly and Jill – John's sister – have seven between them, I don't feel justified in giving my views. Not that the de Bruyns, all their family and friends in Pietermaritzburg, and John's and Polly's in Cape Town haven't been enormously kind and helpful. They were sweet to me, whether of Afrikaner or Dutch or British provenance.'

'I'm glad.'

'Yes.' She looked at him thoughtfully. 'But I was sorry to miss you in Cape Town. And Mrs Mellor. She had sailed the day before we finally got there.'

'So she told me when we met a couple of times when she stopped off in London before returning to the States.'

She nodded dismissively. She had more to tell him about Mrs Mellor, but not yet. The room had thawed; he had not. 'Did you get my letter to Cape Town when you docked?'

'Before. It came in the mail-bag the pilot brought aboard. Didn't I tell you?'

'No.' She smiled slightly. 'Like all your letters, brief, and off the point.'

His eyes were mocking. 'Did you expect reams of purple passion?'

'Not from you Paddy,' she retorted. 'What did you think of Cape Town?'

'As little as possible, though maybe Table Mountain has its points – when one can see it. It was a grey cloud in the background the night we sailed in. The only good look I had of it was next morning before breakfast. It was smaller than I had imagined and so exactly like the travel posters that it gave me no more joy than a picture postcard. After that I was quite glad the mist – the Tablecloth, as they call it – came down and stayed down whilst we were there. All that day people kept expecting me to enthuse over the damned mountain and I was in no mood for enthusiasm over any aspect of South Africa. Fag?' She shook her head and he lit another. 'In contrast, Ireland was an oasis of sanity. We may cherish our hatred of the bloody English but we don't plaster the place with notices warning the English to keep out. Nor do we risk immediate arrest if we take an Englishman into a pub, or so much as hold hands with an English woman in public. And we've no objection at all to sitting next to either in a tram, train or bus.'

'No.' The undercurrent of anger in his voice was echoed in her eyes. 'All these months—' she spread her hands, 'God knows how I've kept my mouth shut about apartheid. I had to. I was a guest in their country and everyone I met – including Polly – was passionately for it. And it is such a beautiful country, and, for the whites, superficially a paradise, if you enjoy a non-stop diet of lotus. And if you don't or won't notice the strain under the surface that to me was as omnipresent as those hideous notices. BLANKES – NIE BLANKES; EUROPEANS – NON-EUROPEANS; WHITES – NON-WHITES, on every public bench, beach, bus, shop, even post office counters. Horrified me from Durban – though roughly all I remember of Durban was Pieter de Bruyn trying to make small-talk about the splendid new skyscrapers and magnificent waterfront and me recalling Mr Carter saying when his father was there at the turn of the century Durban was a collection of mud huts. I do remember looking at those notices and thinking it a pity it was not still a collection of mud huts.' She hesitated. 'You go ashore there?'

'No.' He turned his head towards the window and did not see the fleeting expression that erased the anger from her eyes. 'But those notices had me wanting to puke in East London, Port Elizabeth and Cape Town. And at the last were no help at all to my end-of-voyage parties' hangover. Nor was your letter and having to say goodbye to Joe Gerachty and Mrs Mellor.' He turned back to her, smiling self-derisively. 'So lamentable was my condition I even pined at parting from Mrs Van der Mann and the beauteous dumb Belinda.'

She forced that smile. 'Paddy, you suffered.'

'You've no conception of the extent of my sufferings, woman! So many goodbyes, that day. So many surprisingly painful little wrenches. So many empty places in the dining saloon – but the lot had filled when we sailed. And then the elements got back into the act.'

'The Cape Rollers?'

'Yep. Before we left harbour in a tropical deluge, the crew had lashed everything moveable on the decks, cleared the lot from cabins, strung around ropes and shoved up the fiddles in the saloon. Before we were one mile out into the South Atlantic we knew why. The Rollers were waiting to hit us and hit nearly as hard as the monsoon.'

Her heart gave an odd lurch. 'Had you off your bacon?'

'Yep. And in no mood for scrambled eggs or anything else that would remind me of you.' He looked into the fire and his quiet voice had a new edge. 'I was desolate and sick of an old passion, so I used what I thought the right therapy. I stayed in my cabin re-reading *Crime and Punishment* and taking swigs from the last of the two bottles of brandy old John F.-G. gave me as a *bon voyage* present. But the strong dose of literary gloom, alcoholic depressant, and groaning, pitching, rolling old *Rose* proved my therapy incorrect.' He shrugged at the fire. 'Even Homer sometimes nods.'

She breathed carefully as she watched his averted face that, although as thin as when they first met, was infinitely stronger and still had a fading tan, but none of the frailty that had so shocked her in Genoa.

She said, 'But not Chesty Alexander. Jean told me you're due back in the T.U. in the first week in January and are doing a short refresher in the Brompton. She couldn't tell me – she said no one knows – how you managed to get this flat, as getting anywhere to live in Chelsea is just about impossible.'

He had faced her quickly, curiously, for once unable to fathom why she had taken this tangent. 'It is. Just luck – and a bit of help from the OPA (Old Pals Act). This belongs to one of the senior registrars in the Brompton who was a houseman when I did my special-ising stint there '49 to '51. He got married last week. Up to two weeks ago he had expected to bring his wife here, then suddenly, through an ex-patient, got the immediate offer of a larger flat in the Fulham Road. It suited him to shove this on to someone he knew. He offered me it furnished for one year with first refusal if he decides to sell. I snapped it up. I hope he will sell. This is reasonably handy for Martha's and I like it.' He gestured around. 'This is the biggest room but the two bedrooms aren't boxes – I'll turn one into a study – and though the kitchen and bathroom are antiquated, they've possibilities. I should have apologised for the chaos. Sorry. Forgot.'

She said truthfully, 'I hadn't noticed it. Waiting for bookcases?'

'Yes. They tell me for up to three months. Austerity may officially be over but that's not how it still looks in London. But I've no objection to living out of tea-chests. Well worth it for my own roof over my head even if rented. And the solicitor I got to draw up my tenancy agreement says the rent's very fair.' He smiled quickly. 'As well, as I'm still not earning, but mercifully the banks have a strange trust in medical qualifications. My overdraft can stand the eight quid a week plus one for the cleaning lady who comes in three mornings weekly.'

Her pulse-rate had shot up, but she said calmly, 'That's a very fair rent for Chelsea. How about key-money?'

'He hasn't demanded any. OPA.'

'Thank God for it. I heard yesterday people are having to pay up to one thousand in key-money round here. Any tea left?'

He looked into the chipped brown china teapot. 'Dregs for two. Do you?'

'Fine.' She waited until he had dealt with their cups. 'If you can buy you should be on to a good thing. Yesterday my ex said property in Chelsea is soaring and he thinks will go through the ceiling in a few years.'

His face tightened and eyes brightened with anger. 'Back to square one, Ellie?' he drawled.

'No.' She looked him straight in the face. 'I have not come to you from another man's bed, Paddy.' He coloured darkly. 'He had to go north yesterday and I asked him to break the journey in Newcastle as I wanted his advice. We had lunch in Newcastle then he went on to Edinburgh to see a client.'

He could believe her, but not control his jealousy. 'Bloody convenient turn-up.'

She hit back. 'Very. Like catching you on your door-step this morning. What are the odds against that?'

He ignored the question. 'How did you find him?'

'Unchanged. Like you.' She hesitated. 'But, I have. And as Richard – his name – saw yesterday. When I saw him on to the Edinburgh train I saw at the back of his eyes the expression I had seen in George's when we said goodbye at Beira.' There was a small, ironic smile in her eyes. 'Seeing that kind of relief in men who once fell for me, or kidded themselves they had fallen for me, is becoming a habit with me.'

He was unsympathetic. 'You'll survive it. You're a tough customer. Why did you want his advice?'

'He's got a good brain, loathes golf, so he sits on a lot of voluntary committees. Where's one that won't grab a lawyer who'll give them free legal advice? His special interest is education. I wanted to know precisely what academic qualifications I'll need and what I should do to get into some university for the next academic year.'

His expression had quickened and anger evaporated. 'To read medicine?' She nodded and watched the vitality return to his face and the quick brain behind his eyes. 'It'll help if you've a firm offer of a place in Martha's medical school.'

'Richard said that. What are my chances?'

He thought for a moment. 'I would say pretty good with your record. Martha's is still only admitting the five per cent of female students forced upon them from '47 by Nye Bevan, but still, as in all aspects, Martha's looks after its own.' His enthusiasm was soaring. 'I've always thought you should do medicine! You're a damned fine diagnostician and have already had infinitely more clinical experience at the bedside than any houseman and most registrars. You may have a bit of trouble with your first dogfish and you'll not enjoy carving up the cadavers but you'll have no trouble at all with the exams that matter. In fact, the only snag I can foresee is that you may have some problems getting a grant as – er—'

'I'm thirty-four next year. Yes, of course I will. Richard pussy-footed round that one till I shut him up with what I'm about to tell you.' She sipped the cold tea and grimaced. 'Foul! Couldn't we have fresh?'

'Not bloody likely till you give me the punchline! What was it?'

'That I don't need one.'

He breathed in sharply. 'Helen Mackenzie?'

'Yes.' She gave a sigh that mingled her relief at his reaction and sadness at her own former mental blindness. 'Though I know poor, dear, generous Helen would have been as shocked by my using her money in this fashion as Richard yesterday, Helen approved of my nursing as she considered nursing and teaching the only two respectable professions for women – and were the only two open to women up to these last few years. She would have been appalled by the prospect of any woman doctor. "A man's job, my dear!" ' She shrugged helplessly. 'Richard didn't actually say that yesterday, but it was written all over him. He couldn't understand why, if I insist on working, I don't go back to nursing. I tried to explain that I've got as high in nursing as I want to go, the next step up is away from the patients and I'm not an admin. type. And nor do I want to spend the next thirty years of my life running a ward to the exclusion of all else. And despite all the promises of shorter hours, that's still what a ward sister's job involves.' Again she looked him straight in the face. 'Yes. One can fit in an illicit love-life on one's alternate free weekends off – and deal with the sulks when one has to cancel at the last minute – but not have a real outside life. I know. I've done it. But I couldn't get that through to Richard.' She paused. 'I thought you'd understand.'

'You thought damned right! That why you're here?'

'One reason.'

His eyes narrowed. 'Spit it out. Ellie. What are you worth? At least give me the consolation of knowing what I'll be saving if I'm not to be responsible for paying your income tax.'

She coloured faintly. 'You've had that in mind?'

He looked straight into her face. 'Yes. It had taken root in my subconscious before I earned enough to pay the damned tax. It surfaced with the sharks in the Red Sea.' He stopped, then went on in another voice, 'And many's the time, my love, that I've tried to drown it. Specifically after getting your last letter. I thought you were softening me up for the news that you intended settling out there.'

'Paddy. When have I ever softened you up?'

He met her eyes. 'Maybe never, intentionally. You've just to look at me to turn me to jelly.'

She blushed. 'That's why you didn't answer it.'

'Uh-huh.' Their eyes met and neither could yet look away. 'You going to answer my last question?' He glimpsed and misread her flicker of anxiety. 'Scrub it. None of my business.'

She smiled very sweetly. 'When's that ever stopped you or I asking what we want to know? Of course, I'll tell you. I saw our family solicitor on Friday and he told me now all duties, fees and whatever have been settled, and the house, contents and garden have been valued, that lot's worth seven thousand, and my capital's just under sixty which should bring me a pre-tax income of around one thousand a year at present financial values.' His face had tensed. 'Yes. Still shatters me. I was in Mombasa before I even began to take in the idea of being financially independent. As Sister Luke I got two hundred a year, all found, and with that added to my one hundred and ten pounds a year Army pension, I felt rich.' She paused, but he said nothing. 'It could be said I'll never need another job.'

'Like hell it could by anyone who knows you, Ellie!' He grabbed the teapot and stood up quickly. 'We need that tea.' He went out quickly slamming the door behind him.

She looked at the door and then down at her left hand and thought of her last morning on the *Rose of Africa*.

The ship had picked up the pilot and the yellow scrub of the South African coastline was broken by the towering white skyscrapers of Durban when Elinor finished her early breakfast. She was leaving the saloon when Paddy stepped out of the lift in his white duck suit. He leant on his stick as if once more he needed it. He looked older and his deeply-shadowed eyes were very kind. 'I've just been to your cabin to ask if there's anything I can do for you.'

'Thanks.' She looked up at him numbly. She had been numbed since reading Polly's cable and this morning put on, without thought, the tan cotton dress she had worn at Genoa. The softly upstanding shawl-collar framed a wide V neckline and the tan enhanced the soft whiteness of her skin and shine of her black hair. 'Mr Weaver's fixed everything. Miller's standing by to get my luggage first in the queue directly customs and immigration come aboard and I've finished packing.

I'm just going back to make a final check in my cabin. Will you be on the boat-deck?'

'Where else?'

'I'll join you up there.' She walked on and up the main stairs.

He glanced at her swaying back then went on to the doctor's table, limping more markedly than had become usual. But he had his usual breakfast, took his usual part in the conversation, and, as usual when the ship was about to enter port, did not linger over the meal.

Miller waited outside Elinor's cabin, his face more mournful than ever and he spoke in the hushed tones the English, irrespective of social backgrounds, use to the newly-bereaved. 'Mrs Mellor called and is waiting to see you, madam. I showed the old lady to your armchair seeing as it's early like for her.'

'Thank you, Miller.' She braced herself before going through the door he held open. By midnight last night Sister West, Dr Morgan, Father Gerachty, Belinda and a stream of her new shipboard friends, had called severally to express their regrets and she had had a courteous note of sympathy from the Captain. She had then to spend so long with the purser that she had barely had time to say more than a public goodnight to Paddy. Perhaps it's as well, she thought, as when one has to leave, the quicker the kinder. And then as that thought had pierced her numbness, she thought – and it still hurts like hell.

Mrs Mellor sat straight-backed, a large diamond brooch at the high frilled throat of her grey muslin dress, more diamonds in her ears and on her fingers. She gave the expected explanation for her presence and with an imperious hand waved Elinor to sit on the spare bed. 'I will not delay you for more than a few minutes, but I want to talk to you.'

Elinor sat down obediently, her back straight and hands folded in her lap. Mrs Mellor's manner so recalled that of a matron about to deliver a reprimand that she was unsurprised at Mrs Mellor's checking the door was closed before continuing. 'I'm afraid you are in for a distressing period, but one of the few advantages of having known grief at first-hand is that one knows that second-hand grief, like second-hand clothes, wears out quickly. Of course you are right to go to your bereaved friend and her children! My generation would term it your duty to do so. And from all I have heard of you from Dr Brown, I would say that never have you failed to do what you regard as your duty. But I wonder if you have ever remembered the duty you owe yourself?'

Elinor said quietly. 'Thank you, Mrs Mellor, but I'm afraid you are too generous. I have a very selfish streak.'

'My dear girl, who but a saint, hasn't?' Mrs Mellor was briskly severe. 'Self-preservation demands it. What are you going to do about Dr Brown?'

Elinor blinked. 'Say goodbye to him on the boat-deck shortly. Have I any alternative?'

'Certainly where your phraseology is concerned. *Au'voir* would be kinder.' Elinor stayed silent. 'Or have you in the past found him too unkind to allow you to accept the love you must know he has for you?'

Elinor was too astounded for pretence. 'No. Never from our first meeting has he ever been unkind to me – the reverse – and I'm very fond of him. But after six weeks at sea – don't such delusions come easy?'

Mrs Mellor raised her formidable jaw. 'Remarkably

so, when that's all they are. And, of course, love has been called the greatest of all the illusions – and there is some truth in that. But not the whole truth when the love is genuine. I know.' She was adamant. 'My first and third husbands were good men who loved me nearly as much as they loved themselves. My second husband loved me more than himself – and that kind of love, child, is very rare! But that, I believe, is how Dr Brown loves you. Not that that will make him an easy husband – my second husband whom he greatly resembles in looks and temperament, was far the most difficult to live with.' Her old eyes lost their severity and shone with the memory of an old love. 'But I learnt how to handle him and he how to handle me, so our marriage became the nearest approximation to happiness anyone can expect on this earth.' Then she sighed gently and the severity returned. 'I have frequently observed how well you and Dr Brown already handle each other. How you complement each other. Since you cannot observe yourself, you can have no idea how you have already altered from the tense, rather cold, young woman who joined us in the Red Sea. Bluntly, my dear,' she said sternly, 'you have blossomed! And being a nurse you do not need me to tell you how Dr Brown has altered since then. At Gib. – even Port Said – he was still a sadly crippled young man. Belinda told her grandmother this morning that last night he was dancing with you. Is that so?' Elinor nodded. 'Remember that,' insisted Mrs Mellor, 'and this.' She raised a finger. 'He won't be an easy husband – but you won't be an easy wife. You are far too strong-minded and like independence too much to be content to be the docile heart of the household. But if you can love him – as you have long liked him – for his weaknesses as well as his strengths, since I believe that is how he loves you, I think you two could have an unusually successful marriage. Of course the final decision there – will be yours. As you very well know.' Mrs Mellor rose slowly and Elinor jumped to her feet. 'One thing more. Always remember the greatest sacrifice anyone can make in life is the sacrifice of time. I would say you have already sacrificed enough to others. Possibly, as now, you had no alternative. But before you do so again, stop and ask yourself – not, can I afford this time? But, is this the way I wish to spend it, as once spent, it is gone forever.' She held out her hand. 'I have enjoyed meeting you. I hope we may meet in Cape Town. *Au'voir*, my dear.'

The smallish sofa was less deep than her armchair and when Paddy returned with the tea she had cleared the books and duffle from the sofa and pushed it near enough to the fire for him to use the camel-stool as a footstool. She had shed her coat and pushed the sleeves of her twin-set to just below her elbows, and stood at the bay window looking out at the side-street. She looked to him so natural in that setting that he dreaded the thought of the room without her. Then he noticed what she had done to the sofa and even forgot his legs were aching badly. They always did – and would – in cold, damp, weather.

'You're stuck with the bloody aches for life,' said Hoadley-East, at his final follow-up. 'When you can, forget 'em; when you can't, sweat it out and rest up when you can.'

Elinor said, without turning, 'I remember this street well.'

'How come?' He put down the teapot and the flat packet in his other hand.

'The cousins who were my joint-guardians whilst my parents were in India and after they died, had a house at the river end, two streets on. I spent most of my school hols with them and married from their house. They were killed outright when Jerry got a direct hit on their house in May '41.'

He grimaced painfully, 'Mother of God, but I'm sorry! I never knew any of this.'

She spun round. 'My dear man, how could you? This was long before we met and by then had all learnt neither to talk nor think of yesterday or tomorrow.' She was concerned for his concern and that the deepening lines under his eyes showed his legs were hurting. She sat on the near end of the sofa to get him off his feet. 'And habits engrained in one's formative youth take a long time to shrug off. Much longer than pain, even although new pain invariably arouses the old. But for me, this particular pain is long spent. I've never forgotten those cousins as they were so good to me and I loved them. So I've always, and still, love Chelsea.' There was a loving smile in her eyes as she looked up at him. 'Had you not been in I would have taken the taxi to the hotel in Sloane Street Helen always used, booked in for tonight, then walked back for a better look around, then had lunch somewhere in the King's Road before coming back here.'

There was so much he wanted to say and ask, he needed the refuge of common courtesy. 'I'm very glad I was in.' He handed her the packet he had left by the tea tray on the side table he used as a desk. 'And for the chance to give you this. I got it for you in Las Palmas. A pleasant place. Pity you missed it.'

'Paddy, thank you.' She smiled up at him as she took it with her right hand. 'A very sweet thought.'

'Open it whilst I pour our tea.' He turned to do so feeling so weakened by her smile that he was unsure his legs would support him.

'You angel man!' Elinor was so delighted with the exquisitely handmade, fine, black lace mantilla, that momentarily she forgot she had taken off her wedding ring whilst he was out of the room. She held up the mantilla with both hands. 'This is glorious! Thank you very, very much!'

He smiled over his shoulder. 'Not at all. Great pleasure. Let's see how it looks on. I'm sure—' he caught his breath, then went on in nearly the same voice, 'it'll suit you. You look perfect in lace and – and they make very good lace in Las Palmas. A very Spanish place.' He had to drag his gaze from her left hand to take over their tea. A little spilled over into Elinor's saucer and his own was awash when he set it down on the tiled hearth, then sat by her, leant back and unconsciously propped his legs on the camel-stool. 'As I've just said, it's a pity you missed it. Columbus didn't. He called there on his way to discover America in 1492.'

She said, as if it were vitally important, 'I didn't know that.' She put her cup and saucer on the floor and sat sideways to face him as she carefully draped the mantilla over her head and shoulders. She had to do this carefully as her hands were shaking. But her grave eyes were steady. 'Have the Canaries always belonged to Spain?'

'No.' He pushed the forelock back from his passionately-questioning eyes. 'I'm hazy when Spain got the lot but it only took Gran Canaria – Las Palmas is its port – a few years before Columbus got there. At later times the French, Dutch and British tried to grab it. Nelson made the last failed try. It's easy to understand why they all wanted it and not only as the soil's embedded with a type of volcanic ash that makes it very fertile. The flowers were nearly as lovely as you look now,' he said, as softly as if singing a love song, 'red hibiscus, pure orange geraniums and jacaranda more purple than blue. And there's an avenue of eucalyptus trees that made the very decent Australian couple that had your cabin from the Cape, downright homesick.'

'I'm glad they were so decent.'

'So was I.' The ghost of a self-derisive grin brushed his taut face like a butterfly's wing. 'I consoled them and myself with the remains of old John's brandy. Every sea-mile was taking me farther from you and we had just come one hell of a lot of sea-miles up the South Atlantic. After twelve days of seeing nothing but that damned ocean – and that in a motorised vessel – Las Palmas was literally an oasis in the sea. After weeks under sail it must have seemed a haven dropped on to the sea from heaven.' He stopped a moment. 'Like you, for me, Ellie. Like you, for me.'

She inclined her head and the delicate lace fluttered as she said gravely, 'I know how that feels, Paddy – as Mrs Mellor knew before I did. And I can't explain it, either. But you said you had more to say. Give. Please.'

He gave a long sigh and instinctively crossed himself. 'Mother of God, my love,' he said unsteadily, 'there's no doubt at all – it's time I did.'